Marguerite Kaye has written almost sixty historical romances featuring feisty heroines and a strong sense of place and time. She is also the co-author with Sarah Ferguson, Duchess of York, of two *Sunday Times* bestsellers, *Her Heart for a Compass* and *A Most Intriguing Lady*. Marguerite lives in Argyll on the west coast of Scotland. When not writing, she loves to read, cook, garden, drink martinis, and sew, though rarely at the same time.

CW01499418

FORBIDDEN TO THE BANISHED LAIRD

Marguerite Kaye

MILLS & BOON

First published in Great Britain 2026
by Mills & Boon, an imprint of HarperCollins*Publishers* Ltd,
1 London Bridge Street, London, SE1 9GF

www.harpercollins.co.uk

HarperCollins*Publishers*, Macken House, 39/40 Mayor Street Upper,
Dublin 1, D01 C9W8, Ireland

ISBN: 978-0-263-41865-1

01/26

This book is for the two amazing Joans (or Seonags)
who inspired this story: my fabulous mum,
and her cousin, Joan Urban, who lives in Ness.

Cast of Characters

Jessica Smith, Landscape Gardener
Joan and John Smith, Jessica's parents
Neil and Bella Scott, Jessica's grandparents

Murdo Angus Macleod, owner of Taravay
Laird Angus Murdo Macleod, Murdo's father
Henrietta Macleod, first wife of Laird Angus Macleod
Margaret Macleod, second wife of Laird Angus Macleod and Murdo's mother

Norman Mackinnon—last crofter on Taravay
Mairi—correspondent with Bella Scott, Jessica's grandmother
Donald Macneil—resident of Isle of Harris
Catriona (The Foghorn) Macfarlane—resident of Port of Ness, Isle of Lewis
Grahame Macfarlane—Glaswegian, Catriona's husband

Finlay Murray—resident of Port of Ness, Murdo's childhood friend

Reverend Roderick Muirhead—minister of the Free Church of Scotland, Port of Ness

Prologue

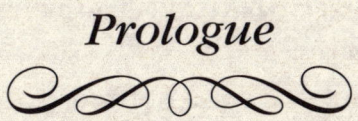

*Isle of Taravay, Off Lewis, Outer Hebrides,
October 1825*

In the distance, a storm was brewing. Despite the apparently innocuous blue autumn sky, spoilt only by a small trail of puffy clouds on the Atlantic horizon, Mairi Mackinnon, like everyone else born and bred here, could smell it in the air.

'Nothing to worry about for a couple of hours at least,' her brother Norman said, seeming to read her mind as he made final preparations to set sail. 'We'll be in Port of Ness long before the bad weather reaches landfall.'

'Aye, maybe so, but I don't want to have to spend the night in Stornoway with our precious cargo,' she answered, thinking of the long drive that awaited them, all the way from the northern tip of Lewis to the main port, from where she would board the ferry to the mainland.

'So long as you get to Stornoway in time, you'll be fine. Dodds is captaining the ferry. I can't recall a single occasion when he's refused a sailing, no matter what the sea conditions. He'll get you safely across the Minch. But first we have to get away from here without arousing suspicion.'

'I don't think we were noticed. Any road, we're doing what the Laird expressly bid, aren't we? It will be he who has to answer for this if the truth is uncovered, not us.' Settling herself beside the child, who was already huddled under a blanket in the stern, Mairi softened her tone. 'Are you warm enough there, wee one?'

'Are we going to find *Mamaidh*?'

Oh, but that plaintive question fair squeezed at her heart. At three years old, the poor wee mite was far too young to understand. Mairi looked down into the face staring up at her so trustingly, the skin drawn tight and pale from the scarlatina that had so nearly claimed the child as well as the mother. 'We're taking you to your new *Mamaidh*,' she said, struggling to smile. 'Though you must call her Mama, in the English manner.'

'I can speak English,' the little mite said proudly.

'Indeed and you can,' Mairi answered, switching to that language herself. One of the few things that *he* had been right about, insisting that both Gaelic and English would be spoken at the Castle. 'You speak very good English, wee one. You'll be quite at home with your new family.'

The child frowned. 'New family?'

'You will have a new Papa *and* a new Mama.'

She held her breath, waiting for the question about *Aither*, as he had always insisted on being addressed by the bairn. Father, never Papa. But the question never came, swallowed up by a huge yawn. 'I'm tired.'

'Coorie in then,' Mairi said, reverting to Gaelic. 'Sleep, wee one. We've a long journey ahead.'

Her words were barely out when the child's body became heavy with slumber, already lost to the world. The little boat turned out of the cove and into the strait, scudding over the waves as Norman expertly steered them towards the Butt of Lewis, and Mairi gazed back at Taravay, taking a final look on the sleeping child's behalf. The autumn light glittered on the sea, which this far out was a deep turquoise blue. The seals that crowded the rocks were getting ready to dive into the incoming tide, and there too, just above the harbour, safe in a natural dip of the land was the roof of her brother's croft.

It was the only croft within sight of Taravay Castle, where Mairi lived and worked, and which stood on the higher ground looking out towards Lewis. Even in to-day's bright light, the huge four-story building looked dark, brooding and forbidding, the windows gazing blankly back at her, the huge entranceway which nestled in the corner between the two wings firmly closed, and looking for all the world as if it would never open again. The Laird hadn't deigned to bid them good-bye. Was he watching from the turret, making sure that his command was obeyed? Or was he regretting his words, wishing them unsaid? Was he straining for a last look at the scrap of life nestled by her side? Or had he already consigned the child and this momentous day to history?

'No point in upsetting yourself,' Norman said, once again showing himself capable of sensing her thoughts. 'You know what Himself is like. Once his mind is made up, he won't change it, even if he wants to. And I heard what he said with my own ears, remember.'

As if she would ever forget! It gave her shivers even to recall the words. *Were it not for that child, my beloved wife would be with me still. Now both of them are dead to me. Take it away. Take it out of my sight and never let me set eyes on it again.*

'The Laird's decision has been made, Mairi. There won't be any changing it.'

'And he'll make sure his lie becomes the truth when he buries the Mistress today.'

As if on cue, the sonorous toll of the funeral bell carried across the water from the small kirk. Any minute now, the slow procession of the coffin from the Castle would set off for the church.

'It's for the best,' Norman said, 'a fresh start for that poor wee bairn there.'

'I know, I know. You're right enough.'

'I wish I wasn't. We'll need to make sure and pay our respects when you get back.'

'I know, Norman, I know.' Mairi sighed wearily. 'We need to stick to the story Himself will tell, and put the whole sorry episode behind us.'

'You can't afford to be judging the man too harshly. For better or worse, that island is our livelihood.'

'I can judge him all right, and I will too, but you needn't worry, I won't let him know it,' she retorted, her voice hardening. 'It will be an easy enough thing to keep my thoughts to myself, for he never looks beyond the end of his nose. So long as his tenants keep his lands in good heart, and I keep his Castle in good order, the Laird doesn't give a penny coin what we or any of the islanders think.'

Norman nodded towards the sleeping child. 'He trusted us with that one, all the same. That means something.'

'Aye, he trusted us to get rid of his baggage, and to keep our deed a secret! An honour and a privilege indeed.'

'Our family have served the Laird of Taravay…'

'Since the mists of time! I know that, brother. Loyalty and servitude, the values our father instilled in us from when we were no more than this wee one's age.'

Their father, who had lived and died in that croft, was buried, like their mother, in the graveyard on the other side of Taravay. Mairi herself had escaped, married to a Harris man, but when he died five years later she had come back here, done what was expected of her, what had always been expected of her, taking over the running of the Castle from her mother. And her brother—ach, but Norman was a bit fey, and had never been the marrying kind. Loyalty and servitude, that was the purpose of their life, though what did it benefit them? Not riches, that was for sure. For her brother, knowing that he was doing what he'd been reared to do was enough, but for her? Perhaps, like the child in her care, she was done with this life?

Norman's focus was on the sea, which was, as ever, choppier than it looked from the shore as they headed across the strait towards Lewis. 'I know as well as Himself that you won't talk,' he said to her. He hadn't turned around, but still he sensed her mood. 'Best for that bairn too, if you ask me. You mind your promise now, Mairi. Once the child is settled, there will be no more contact.'

'I mind fine well what I said.' And she remembered too that she'd crossed her fingers behind her back when she said it, but there was no point in telling Norman that. Whatever the future had in store for this wee one, she, Mairi, was responsible for laying the foundations of a fresh and happier start. She owed it to the bairn, and to the mother who would be laid fresh in her grave today, to make sure that they were solid foundations.

The deed was done now, Norman was in the right of

it—there was no point in looking back. Mairi tucked the blanket around the sleeping child and turned her gaze firmly towards Lewis. This was the first step on a long journey with no way back for the child. And for herself? Perhaps it was time for her to cut her ties with the island too.

But first things first. She had to deliver the bairn to a new family, and the pair of them had a long journey ahead of them.

Chapter One

Stornoway, Isle of Lewis, March 1879

She had never sailed on a steamship before. For that matter she had never been on an island before. Neither had she ever accepted a commission without first making sure she understood exactly what was required of her. Now here she was on the Isle of Lewis on a blustery spring day, having completed the first of two crossings, standing on the first of two islands, without a clue as to how she would traverse the one to reach the other unless someone—anyone!—turned up to meet her. And as to the nature of her commission? That was almost as vague as her scant understanding of the island landscape that she had now been employed to tame, information which had been garnered solely from reading the box of letters written to her grandmother.

Were it not for those letters, the island of Taravay would mean nothing to her, and the advertisement which she had replied to might have gone unnoticed. Were it not for those letters, she would most likely still be hiding away in the cottage at Thornhill, too frightened to test whether her rash actions had fatally blackened her reputation, still castigating herself for her massive error of judgement, fretting at her lack of gainful employment, licking her wounds and nursing her broken heart. In that order. Which was all well and good, but watching the throng of other passengers greeting relatives and the cargo being lowered from the deck in nets, Jessica Smith wondered if the leap of faith that had brought her here had in actual fact been too much of a leap in the dark.

The quay on which she stood seemed to be new, but the steamer which had brought her across the stormy waters of the Minch was the only modern ship in sight. The other boats she could see in the shelter of the bay were considerably smaller, mostly single-masted without decking or cover. Fishing boats, she assumed, and judging from the volume of masts she spied over on the over side of the shore, most had already brought in their catch for the day. The town of Stornoway, huddled around the seafront and the harbour, seemed to be in the midst of major change, ancient cottages, which had clearly been the centre of the original village, giving way to more modern stone-built houses and what looked like another jetty under construction. Across the bay, perched on a small hill in splendid isolation, stood a Castle complete with fanciful turrets, the stone-work clearly new despite its pretensions to antiquity. There were trees in the grounds, the landscaper in Jessica noted, then realised the reason that they stood out was because she couldn't see a single tree anywhere else on the almost flat, dun-coloured landscape un-folding behind the port.

All of the other steamer passengers had dispersed. Aside from the men unloading the cargo and stacking it onto drays, Jessica stood alone with her luggage. Her new employer had promised she would be met off the boat. His island lay about five miles off the coast of the far north of Lewis. She knew this much from his letter of appointment, and she knew from her grand-mother's letters that there was a Castle there, as well as a small community of crofters and their families. At least there had been back in 1839 when the last letter was written. It was safe to presume a great deal had changed over the following forty years, else her talents would not be required.

Jessica checked her watch once more, trying not to panic. Perhaps he had changed his mind at the last minute, leaving her abandoned in this remote corner of Scotland. No, no, she would not allow herself to despair. Her driver was simply late, that was all. She should find a porter to help her with her luggage and wait for him in a hotel, if Stornoway possessed such an amenity. A cup of coffee wouldn't go amiss either.

And perhaps some bread and butter, for she hadn't eaten since they sailed from the mainland.

Her stomach rumbled with embarrassing enthusiasm just at the exact moment that she spotted him talking to one of the ship's crew. Tall, dressed in a long black woollen coat, with a pair of scuffed stout boots on his feet and no hat. His hair was long and black and blew wildly about his face, and his beard, though short, was unkempt. She had the impression of strong features, skin made swarthy by the weather, a fierce stare. He was dishevelled and not in the least bit conventionally handsome, yet something about him appealed to her. She barely had time to acknowledge this unsettling fact, when he came striding towards her.

'Please tell me you are not J Smith,' were his opening words.

She had signed her name in such a manner quite deliberately, but his tone set her hackles up all the same. 'I cannot oblige, since that is who I am,' Jessica retorted. 'I assume you have come at Mr Macleod's behest? I've been waiting on this jetty for nigh on half an hour.'

'I'm Murdo Macleod, and I'm here now.'

'*You* are Murdo Macleod?' The words were out before she could stop them, her astonishment doubtless writ large on her face, surprise changing to embarrassment as she realised how rude she sounded, and too late, how much his cultivated voice contrasted with his appearance, which was more like a Highland savage than the genteel laird she had envisioned. 'I beg your pardon,' Jessica mumbled.

'What, were you expecting me to send one of my lackeys for you?' he asked, seeming not at all offended. 'Sorry to disappoint, but I'm afraid I don't have any. Why didn't you wait in the hotel?'

'Because I was concerned that you would think I'd missed the steamer or changed my mind.'

To her annoyance, his mouth quirked into a smile, and to her further annoyance, her insides gave an appreciative lurch. His eyes were hazel, thickly lashed under fierce brows, and closer up she could see that his hair was not wholly black but tinged with auburn and grey. He had a strong nose, decided cheek bones and chin that the beard did not disguise.

'Did it not occur to you, J Smith,' he said, 'that you stand out like a sore thumb? I'd have found you, even though I was under the impression it was a man I was looking for, and not a woman. What's more, it would seem by that look you're giving me, that I'm not the only one whose expectations have been confounded.'

'No, no, not at all,' Jessica said, flustered both by his perception and his bluntness. 'It's only that I was expecting someone—someone older.'

'I'm forty-one, not that that is any of your business.'

What she'd actually meant was that she hadn't been

expecting to find him attractive. The truth was, she hadn't been expecting to find any man attractive ever again, after her humbling experience. *Never!* 'It is neither of interest nor relevance to me,' Jessica said, for her own benefit more than his. 'I simply meant that I had imagined—that my expectations of you were— different.'

'As were mine of you. Was that deliberate on your part?'

'Was *what* deliberate?'

'You know fine and well what I mean.'

His tone was even enough, but there was a look in his eyes that told her he was not the kind of man who would take kindly to prevarication. 'Yes,' Jessica said, meeting and holding his gaze. 'I deliberately refrained from signing my full name in our correspondence.'

'Assuming I would not have employed you if you did? Do you find that deception is conducive to securing you work, Mrs Smith?'

'It is *Miss* Smith, and I did not deceive you, you deceived yourself by making assumptions. I would happily have supplied you with references which would have clarified both my sex and my reputation, had you requested them.' Provided, that is, he did not wish to consult the opinion of Lady Orton, her last employer. 'I assure you, Mr Macleod, that everything I wrote to you detailing my skills and experience was true.'

'And I'll tell you frankly, Miss Smith, that when

I read your letter, I thought *you* were too good to be true.'

'I assure you…'

'Only you omitted one vital fact,' he interrupted her ruthlessly. 'I don't take kindly to being deceived.'

His expression had hardened to the point where she wanted to take a step back from him. Jessica forced herself to stand her ground. 'I'm sorry you see it like that. The fact is that I have in the past, before my reputation was established I mean, been overlooked because of my sex. I wanted you to employ me on the basis of merit, without prejudice.'

He studied her for a long moment, then shrugged, pushing his long hair back from his face. 'Call it what you like, but if I'd known you were a woman, I wouldn't have considered you for the post. Not because I think your sex makes any difference to your ability to do the job. I've no opinion one way or another on female landscapers, never having met one, but at present I'm living quite alone on Taravay.'

'Alone! But surely—are there not small holdings—crofts, crofters?'

'Not any more,' he said, his expression darkening.

'What on earth happened?'

'That's not your concern. What matters is Taravay's future, not the past.'

'Yes, but…' His expression made her bite back her question. He was right too. What mattered was making sure *she* had a future. Which meant making certain that he did not renege on her appointment. 'The work you require to be carried out,' Jessica said, rallying, 'you can't imagine that I will complete it single-handedly?'

'Initially, that's precisely what I imagine. I know what I want done, the overall scheme, what I want to achieve. What I need from you—or rather, from whoever I choose to employ—is detailed plans, and what they will cost me to implement.'

'Naturally, I will provide you with estimates, it's integral to what I do. And you needn't worry if your funds are limited, I'm quite accustomed to adjusting my designs to suit the size of my employer's purse.'

'You misunderstand me, Miss Smith. Money is not an issue.'

'Money is *always* an issue, in my experience, Mr Macleod. It is very easy to allow oneself to get carried away with creating one's own Garden of Eden, but rest assured…'

'I'm not in the least bit interested in creating a Garden of Eden, and I told you, money isn't an issue.'

'You are very fortunate to be in a position to say so with such certainty.'

'I'm not fortunate, I've earned every penny.'

It was the way he spoke matter-of-factly, with not a trace of pride or boastfulness, that made her believe him. Obviously, he was not a man who wasted his fortune on clothes, but what it was he wished to spend it on perplexed her. 'What is it that you wish to create, then, if not a garden for yourself?' Jessica asked. 'You said there's no one else living on the island.'

'My plan is to remedy that.'

She stared at him, now completely at a loss. 'I'm sorry, but I don't understand. What exactly am I to contribute?'

'There's no *exactly*.' He gave an exasperated sigh. 'The Laird died eighteen months ago, which is when I came back, and...'

'Came back?' Jessica repeated, cursing her ignorance and the fact that she must sound like a complete dolt. 'So you were an islander once, yourself?'

'Taravay belongs to me. I inherited it eighteen months ago.'

'When the Laird died.' She repeated his words once more, feeling extremely foolish. 'So he was a relative?'

'My father,' he replied, as if it was obvious, in a tone that made it clear he was reaching the end of his patience. 'It seems I'm not the only one who failed to do their research into this appointment.'

'You were in a great hurry to appoint me,' Jessica said, defensively.

'And you were in a great hurry to be appointed.'

He had hit the nail on the head. Mortified, Jessica struggled to recover her composure. 'I was looking for a new challenge. I've never worked on an island, nor on land this far north.'

He gave a short laugh. 'If you came to Taravay, it would be a challenge all right. I'm looking for someone to do more than design a few parterres. I've a whole island in need of a fresh purpose.'

It took her a moment for the full import of what he had said to sink in. 'How big is it?' Jessica asked faintly.

'About four miles square.'

A whole island! This was the sort of commission that, if she was successful, would eradicate all other question marks over her reputation. It was the sort of commission that might never come her way again. The sort of commission that would allow her the scope to…

Mr Macleod cut into her thoughts. 'Having second thoughts, Miss Smith?'

'No! A thousand times no. Quite the contrary. I'm having so many thoughts, I can hardly keep track of them. Who do you anticipate living on your island, Mr Macleod? Who would I be designing for? What would be the purpose of the work I am to do? I presume you mean the land to be functional as well as appealing? My goodness, I had no idea that this commission would provide such an opportunity and a challenge.'

'Aye, well you'd best curb your enthusiasm.' He ran his fingers through his hair again, shaking his head. 'No matter how excited you are, and no matter how well-suited you might be, and no matter that it pains me to say this, for to be perfectly honest I don't give a damn about what people think, but I'm not so far gone as to wish to damage your reputation. You can't come to Taravay with me. It would be viewed as quite improper.'

Chapter Two

It would be viewed as quite improper. The words echoed horribly. *She said it would be utterly inappropriate*, Edward had said, meaning, you are a lowly landscaper, Jessica had surmised. Meaning, you are not good enough, she had assumed. And so it had proved when Lady Orton, Edward's sister and her employer, severed Jessica's contract with neither payment nor references, making it very clear just how easily she could destroy the reputation that Jessica had worked so hard to establish, should she choose to do so. After six months tending to her many wounds, like a sickly plant being nursed back to health, Jessica's overriding desire was to salvage her career. Now she was being presented with the opportunity to do this and so much more, she was most certainly not going to relinquish it without a fight.

'I'm thirty-five years old, Mr Macleod, not some simpering girl, and you have just told me that you're over forty.'

'Thirty-five! I wouldn't have placed you a day over thirty. I wish for both our sakes that you were a *Cailleach*.'

'I've no idea what that is, but if it meant you taking me to Taravay then I would happily turn myself into one.'

'It means an old woman, and unfortunately for both of us, you're about as far from that as it's possible to be.'

According to Edward, or rather, according to Edward's sister, one of Jessica's many sins was her age, well past prime breeding years, but she doubted that Mr Macleod would be swayed by this argument. Ought she be attempting to sway him at all? He was younger than she'd expected, he was bewilderingly attractive, he was short of temper, lacking patience, and as to his appearance—yes, she could quite easily believe, looking at him, that he had been living alone on an island for the last year and a half without access to human interaction, or even a mirror, come to that! Even if Lady Orton did decide to cast a slur on her, there would be other commissions, safer commissions, more familiar commissions.

But nothing on this scale. A whole island for her to work her magic on. Not a garden, but an entire landscape. No, she would not fall at the first hurdle. 'How long do you imagine it will take for us to reach a stage where work can begin?'

'There is no *us*, Miss Smith. I don't know. A few weeks. A month or so? There are all sorts of problems with getting supplies to Taravay that I haven't yet looked into.'

'I can help you with that. Supplies—' Jessica enlightened him '—labour, that kind of thing is part of my job. What about the accommodation on the island?'

'I've made over the most habitable croft cottage for you—for the man I thought you were. It's about as distant from my own accommodation as it is possible to be on Taravay. But it's basic, to say the least.'

'My needs are very simple.'

'They'd have to be. We're only a few miles off Lewis, but even in the height of summer there are times when Taravay is cut off.'

'All part of the challenge. I'm very resourceful.'

'Again, you'd have to be, but…'

'So we would be working together,' Jessica interrupted, determined not to allow him to protest. 'But other than that, living quite separately.'

'Yes, but…'

'And you'd make sure that anyone who has any interest in the matter knew that to be the case.'

'Do you mean the Niseachs? The people of Ness,' he clarified in response to her blank look. 'Are you suggesting I make some sort of proclamation? Here be J Smith, a landscape gardener of thirty-five, a *Cailleach* in spirit if not in appearance, and quite beyond her prayers, so you needn't be worrying about my taking advantage of her? Which, for the record,' he added, 'despite the fact that you're a surprisingly attractive female, I would not dream of doing.'

She struggled with a completely inappropriate desire to laugh. 'Are you always so forthright?'

'I've no idea. I've not had much need to make polite conversation this last while.'

Clearly not, but it did beg the question as to what need there had been before. Jessica decided, however, not to ask it. 'I'm afraid I've lost track of our conversation entirely.'

He sighed heavily. 'You want me to assure you there will be no gossip, should you persuade me to take you to Taravay, and what I'm trying to say is that I can't do that. Can I put it about that you're the landscaper? I *could* do that, but I doubt it would make much difference. People will talk.'

Exactly what she was worried about. But there was an enormous difference between Lady Orton's orbit and that of the people on an island in the Outer Hebrides, wasn't there? What were the chances of a Gaelic-speaking Hebridean discussing her with any future employer? 'If you genuinely don't care what is said, Mr Macleod...'

'I don't.'

'Then I am willing to take the risk,' Jessica said

firmly. 'Ultimately, it will be my work that speaks for me.'

'You seem very confident of that.'

'If you will only give me an opportunity, you'll see that I have every reason to be.'

To her disappointment, he seemed rather more sceptical than swayed by this. 'I don't think you realise what you're letting yourself in for. Life on an island as remote and neglected as Taravay, can be tough.'

'You have survived there for eighteen months.'

'My needs are few, and I'm more than happy in my own company. There might be times when you'd be trapped there with me, at the mercy of the weather, unable to leave, even if you wished to.'

'I won't dissolve in the rain, Mr Macleod. I am a woman at the top of a profession almost entirely given over to men. I am extremely self-sufficient, I'm as hardy as a thistle…'

'Ha! And every bit as prickly.'

'Oh! Talk about pot calling the kettle black.'

'You think *I* am prickly?'

'I think you are…' Belatedly, she bit back her words. She was supposed to be placating him. She was supposed to be endearing herself to him. She was supposed to be persuading him to take her to Taravay.

'Go on, speak your mind,' Mr Macleod said, infuriatingly.

Was there a smile lurking behind that fierce expression? No, surely she must be mistaken. 'I think you are in need of a landscaper,' Jessica said, meeting his gaze. 'I am a very good landscaper. One of the best, in fact. I think you would be very foolish indeed not to employ me, and I don't *think* you are a foolish man.'

'I never thought so myself, before…' He broke off, wincing, then resumed his glare. 'What makes you so certain?'

Before what? Resolutely refusing to be distracted, Jessica chose her words carefully. 'The fact that you do *not* question my abilities, even though I am a woman, for a start. Then, there is the question of delay, should you decide to appoint someone else in my place. Why do that, when I am here, ready and willing, right now? It is already March too. You might miss all of spring, even part of summer, and given what you've told me about the weather, once you are into autumn and winter…'

'Yes, yes, you've made your point.' He gazed over her head, deep in thought for a few tense moments before he spoke again. 'If I did take you to Taravay, you'd have my word that any time you want to leave, and I can get you safely off the island, I'd make it happen. You can have my word too, that I would not abuse the situation. But why should you accept my word, Miss Smith? We've only just met.'

Why? She wanted desperately to trust him, but could she really do so? His behaviour was unpredictable, to say the least. She wanted this commission. She *needed* it. And Murdo Macleod, it seemed, was beginning to accept that he needed her. 'To put it bluntly,' Jessica said, 'it's in your interests not to offend me.'

His bark of laughter had a harsh edge.

'Mr Macleod! The fact that you find me *surprisingly attractive* leaves me quite cold. You could be an Adonis, and I would not be in the least bit interested. And though, as you pointed out, we have only just met, and despite your somewhat fierce and unconventional appearance, I am as certain as I can be that you are a decent and honourable man who would never force himself on a woman, particularly not one who has made it very clear she would rebuff him.'

He stared at her for a moment, long enough for her to worry that she had gone too far, before a smile lit up his face. 'I'm not sure whether to be flattered or insulted.'

'I would rather you were reassured,' Jessica replied, trying to ignore the way his smile made her insides flutter, for it quite transformed him. 'Forget that I am a female, remember only that I am a...'

'Landscaper,' he finished for her. 'You're quite set on coming to landscape Taravay, aren't you? I'm beginning to wonder why. I mean, a landscaper of such renown must have her choice of commissions. Why have you come to the back of beyond to take up mine?'

Her stomach fluttered in a very different way at the

hardening of his tone. One wrong word now, and he'd be loading her luggage back onto the steamer, and she *needed* this opportunity to redeem herself, not only in the eyes of the world, but in her own eyes. 'I am here because your advertisement spoke to me. The name of your island, Taravay, resonated with me. When I read it, it seemed like fate. You'll no doubt laugh at me...' Jessica broke off, swallowing hard, for the truth of what she was saying had brought a lump to her throat.

'Go on, I'm listening.'

Reassured, she drew a steadying breath. 'My mother died last year. I was working, but when my employer discovered how ill she was, she—we agreed to terminate my contract.' True, though not the truth. 'I went back to the Borders, where I was born and raised, to the cottage my mother had left me—my grandparents' home, actually. Being there, without my work to distract me, it confirmed how much I love what I do—that what I do is everything to me, in fact—but I realised I needed something quite new, a fresh challenge. When I saw your advertisement in the *Glasgow Herald*, it seemed to me that fate was taking a hand in directing me.'

'What did you mean when you said that Taravay resonated with you?'

'It's a very odd coincidence. I found a box of letters in the cottage written to my grandmother by a woman called Mairi, who was a housekeeper in what she referred to as a "big house" in Glasgow. She mentioned Taravay in a few of them.'

His eyebrows shot up. 'How extraordinary.'

'Not really. Many of the domestic staff in places like Glasgow are from the Highlands and Islands.'

'What did she say about Taravay?'

'Nothing of particular interest. That she'd "heard from Taravay", which I took to mean she had a relative or a friend there. She never signed her second name, and the last letter was written in June 1839, nearly forty years ago. I don't remember my grandmother ever mentioning her, so I've no idea what her connection might have been, either to the island or to my grandparents, but the name Taravay somehow stuck in my head after I'd read the letters. Then when I saw your advertisement it seemed to me that fate had intervened.'

He raised an eyebrow. 'And sent you to me?'

Jessica nodded, hoping that it was enough, for it was a great deal more than she had intended to say. She could not tell him that a remote island had seemed the perfect retreat she needed to lick her wounds and more importantly give Lady Orton time to forget all about her. And as for Edward—but she wouldn't think of Edward. 'Please, at least give me a chance to prove myself.'

A deep frown drew his brows together once again. 'I can't argue with your enthusiasm, and I can't lie. I don't want to waste any more time now that I've made my mind up. I'm anxious to get started. But it would be a leap of faith for both of us.'

A leap of faith. Exactly how she'd phrased it herself. Jessica held out her hand. 'I'm willing to risk it, if you are.'

His gloveless hand dwarfed hers. His skin was deeply tanned, and through her own gloves, felt warm on her cold fingers. 'On your head be it then, Miss J Smith.'

'Jessica.'

'Jessica.' He laughed softly. 'Not James, or John, as I had imagined.'

'My father was John. I was named for his mother.'

'I was named Angus, but I've always been known as Murdo.' His smile faded as he looked down at her. 'Are you sure about this?'

'Yes.'

'I hope neither of us regrets it.' His fingers tightened around hers, then he let her go. 'Are these all your bags? I'll get them loaded on the cart. We've just time for some coffee and something to eat. It's a long drive and I don't want to sail to Taravay in the dark if I can avoid it.'

Chapter Three

Murdo checked that the luggage was securely fastened before hoisting himself up onto the seat beside Jessica Smith, picking up the reins and urging the sturdy pony forward. What he'd hoped would be the first step towards realising his dream for Taravay had turned into, if not exactly a nightmare, a far more complicated situation than he wanted or needed. Damn the woman, but he was stuck with her now.

He'd left the object of his ire to finish her coffee in the hotel while he had the cart loaded and had taken the opportunity to pick up his mail from the steamer office. There were the usual reassuring updates from his London financial agent, who, over the last eighteen months, had proved himself extremely adept at acting on intermittent strings of telegraphed instructions which had kept his financial interests ticking over nicely. One other letter, from his lawyer, confirmed that the implications of what Murdo thought of as the Emily situation, were now fully, legally resolved. All that remained to be done was to announce the fact, were he so inclined. Murdo was not so inclined, at least not yet. The scar had taken a long, painful time to heal, and he didn't want to risk ripping it open again. The lawyer did not say what Emily herself wanted. If it mattered, she'd have asked him, wouldn't she, and she'd asked him for nothing. Not a word, in fact, in eighteen months. Had she forgotten him, or was she being kind? Either way, it was for the best. He could draw a veil over the past. The problem was solved. It was over between them, and the pair of them had their lives to be getting on with.

His own life had taken an unexpected turn today, right enough, in the form of the woman sitting by his side, and he had no idea if it would turn out to be for the better. Jessica Smith had turned her gaze to the road ahead, so he took the opportunity to study her profile. Short, neat nose, a high forehead, full mouth, a chin that was neither square nor pointed. It ought to amount to something nondescript, but was actually rather striking. Maybe it was her eyes, which were almond-shaped and dark brown, wide-spaced and straight-gazing? And her colouring—her skin the same pale cream complexion of a Highlander, her hair, what he could see of it under that bonnet, a midnight black that was also common up here. Fact was, her features didn't look out of place, yet she was far from common-place. If only she was a *Cailleach*! Then he wouldn't be noticing the press of her skirts and her coat against his thigh. He wouldn't be noticing the silkiness of that long strand of hair whipping across her cheek, or the soft, creaminess of her skin either.

Murdo cursed himself under his breath. This woman could play a vital part in the future of Taravay. He'd spent too much time on his own, starved of human company, that was all. What he should be worrying about was not the effect she had on him, but the effect she'd have on Taravay. He'd nurtured his dream for the island for so many years, he could see it so perfectly in his mind, and now he was finally going to make it happen. If she really was the best, he was fortunate to have her, but her tendency to voice opinions worried him. He didn't want her to challenge him or question his decisions, he wanted her to realise his dream.

'I will do my very best to make sure you don't regret employing me, Mr Macleod.'

Jessica Smith's voice interrupted his thoughts, something else he wasn't used to, after so long alone. He'd lost the habit of keeping a guard on his expression. Murdo shook his head, forcing his frown away. 'You're not what I was expecting, that's all.'

'You have said so already. I'm not a—a kay...'

'*Cailleach*,' he repeated for her, slowly.

'Kay-ach? Is that the Gaelic language? You speak it?'

'Of course I do, it's what everyone speaks here. I was

rusty after so long away, but it's been coming back to me since I returned.'

'And others on the island—others who once lived on your island, I should say—would it be unusual then, for them to speak or even to write in English?'

'Gaelic would be their first language, but on Taravay the Laird insisted on speaking English, so yes, some of them had a good command of the language, especially those who worked in the Castle.'

'If the Laird was your father, doesn't that make you the Laird now?'

'It's an honorary title. I don't use it.'

'But you live in the Castle, I assume?'

'It was more or less closed up by the time the Laird died. My croft suits my needs well enough.'

She was frowning. He could see the wheels turning in her mind. 'You said you returned to Taravay when the Laird died, so I presume that means you were raised there? Wouldn't that make the Castle your childhood home?'

'Yes, but I can't see what relevance that has. As I said, it is not habitable.'

She opened her mouth to pursue the matter, but whatever she saw in his expression made her change her mind. 'And you've been alone on Taravay for the last eighteen months?'

'I have.'

He meant to close the subject down, but Jessica

Smith had other ideas. 'The loss of a parent forces one to look at one's own life anew. Having lost my mother recently, I do understand.'

'I doubt it.' She flinched, and Murdo immediately regretted his tone. The Laird's death had been a convenient excuse made to all his London friends and acquaintances for wanting to flee the capital, while she had clearly been genuinely grieving. 'I'm sorry for your loss. What I meant was, I doubt the circumstances were the same,' he amended. 'The Laird and I were estranged.'

'Oh.' She looked stricken. 'I'm so sorry. That must have been—no, I cannot imagine how that must have felt.'

No, you bloody can't, he wanted to say, but he bit his tongue. It was hardly her fault, and just as importantly, he didn't wish her to think he cared. Which he didn't. 'At least I can now finally breathe some life into Taravay,' Murdo said.

'Eighteen months is not so very long in the grand scheme of things. I will still be able to see the bones of the gardens and farmland, and I assume there will also be records in the Castle that we can use.'

'I want fresh ideas, uncontaminated by the past. And I want Taravay to be useful.'

'I'm delighted to hear that. Too often, I find, landowners take no account of the people who live and work the land. But I also think that whether it is a formal garden, a kitchen garden, or a broader landscape, then it is important to take account of what nature has put there in the first place. I confess I'm not an admirer of the revered landscaper Capability Brown, with his rolling hills, his pretty dells, his lakes and his follies.'

'We already have two lochs, and trees don't grow on Taravay.'

This, as he had hoped, left her with nothing more to say for now. He hadn't deliberately misled her, she had assumed she would be dealing with eighteen months of neglect rather than seven years' worth. But she'd see for herself soon enough, and for now—no, that was a tale he'd have to gird his loins to tell her later.

The pony, well-fed and rested, had made short work of the cobbled main street of the growing town of Stornoway, her newly shod feet making a pleasant clip-clop sound, and now they were headed out towards the moors. 'I hope you're comfortable,' Murdo said, resolving not to be quite so tetchy, for he'd have to get accustomed to her questions. 'It will take us about six hours to reach Port of Ness. It's about twenty-five miles, much of it over the moor that's ahead, and there's not much of a road. Fortunately at this time of year we've plenty daylight. We should be on Taravay before nightfall, the tide will be with us.'

'That is good news,' she replied, sounding uncertain. 'I'd never been to an island until today.'

'You'll have been on two before the day is out.'

'I was thinking precisely that, while I was waiting for you on the pier.'

Her smile took him aback, for it completely changed her stern countenance. 'Taravay is a tiny wee place compared to Lewis,' Murdo said.

'I know, I looked it up on a map.'

'I had no idea we were on any map.'

'It was in the library at Drumlanrig Castle. The Duke of Buccleuch has a significant collection of maps there, and his archivist helped me to find what I needed.'

'You are very well-connected.'

'My father was the head gardener at Drumlanrig for many years, and I was apprenticed there myself,' she informed him. 'I have worked in the gardens of many great houses, but that doesn't mean I get invited to the garden parties. I am the daughter of a gardener and a housekeeper. I'm green-fingered, not blue-blooded.'

'It's your pedigree as a gardener that interests me,' Murdo said, taken aback by the bitterness in her tone.

'Then you won't be disappointed. I started trailing after my father in Drumlanrig almost as soon as I could walk and Drumlanrig, if you're not aware, is famous not only for its formal gardens but for the large market gardens too. People—men and boys, to be more accurate—travel from across the world to train there.'

'So as a female, you're a pioneer in your profession, then?'

She smiled again at that, though faintly. 'Often in country houses, as with Drumlanrig, it is the lady of the house who takes an interest in the design of the gardens, but there are very few paid female landscapers. I know of one other woman, Gertrude Jekyll. She is slightly younger than me, but she is fast gaining a reputation for her more natural designs.'

'Your father must be proud of what you have achieved.'

'He died some years ago, before I became established, but he was my greatest supporter, and continues to inspire me. I never travel without the book he wrote. It is quite famous, and has gone to six editions.'

She spoke with pride, and Murdo felt a pang of envy. 'You were obviously close,' he said.

'I was an only child.'

'It was fortunate that you shared his passion for gardening.'

'I take it,' she said diffidently, 'that you and your father did not see eye to eye?'

'We shared a love of Taravay, but I reckon that's where it began and ended.'

'Do you have any brothers and sisters?'

'No, I do not. I was the sole, disappointing son and heir.'

He regretted the words as soon as they were out. There was a charged silence, when he fervently hoped that Jessica Smith would refrain from telling him that he wasn't a disappointment. When she did speak, she surprised him.

'My father was delighted that I wished to follow in his footsteps, but had I chosen another path, though he would have been disappointed and we'd have seen a great deal less of each other, it would not have come between us. I've seen it though, on the estates where I have worked, a son forced to walk in the father's footsteps. The relationship is never a happy one, with two generations, each having their own strong views.'

He met her gaze at that, startled by the sympathy and the understanding. 'As you'll see for yourself soon enough, it is the island and its islanders who paid the price for our respective *strong opinions*. It's in a pitiful state.'

'Well, that is something I hope to help remedy. When I was a child,' she continued, 'I used to dream of finding a neglected walled garden that no one knew about and making it my own.'

Her smile warmed him. He began to think that maybe, just maybe, he had been fortunate that she had deceived him into bringing her here. 'There is a walled garden, actually, and a large glasshouse, though some of the panes have been broken.'

'Oh how wonderful! Please, tell me more.'

'Well, there are a number of abandoned crofts— that's small farms. An old school. A mill that may be worth saving. A bakery. As to livestock, I have a pony, a cow and some hens but the sheep live wild now, though at least they keep the grass short in the old gardens.'

'Do you wish to rebuild the village, have people farming—crofting—again?'

'There's no future in crofting alone,' Murdo replied, once again eschewing the opportunity to explain. 'It's too hard a life, it has been for decades. I want to make Taravay fit for the future, bring it into the Nineteenth Century. I want others to appreciate it, and to have a taste of island life for themselves.'

'Others? Are you thinking of it as a destination for holidaymakers?'

'Maybe that. Maybe it will be a respite from the city air for some, or a place where they can get the benefit of the sea air.'

'As they do on the Continent?'

Miss Smith's voice, he was delighted to hear, reflected some of his own excitement. 'Why not? One thing I'll say about our weather in the Hebrides, it never fails to be bracing.'

He waited for her to sneer at this, or for her excitement to fade as the reality of the island's location set in, or for her simply to pour scorn on what he was saying. But her eyes were sparkling. 'I think it's a wonderful idea. I haven't even seen Taravay yet, so I won't make any suggestions until I know the island better, but I wonder if a palm house would be a draw?'

He couldn't help it, the relief of hearing someone, for the first time, endorse his idea, made him laugh. 'Why don't you plan in a pinery too, so that the visitors can have pineapples for dinner.'

'Oh no, the cost of heating such a construction would be formidable.'

'Aye, I'm aware of that. I was teasing.'

'So was I, and about the palm house too. The expense would be enormous.'

'I'm not bothered about the expense. Money isn't the problem, I told you that. I made my fortune in banking, on the Square Mile, and thanks to the wonders of the telegraph office in Port of Ness, and the man who acts for me in the City, my fortune continues to increase. I'm not short of cash, Miss Smith.'

'It's Jessica,' she reminded him. 'Attractive as the idea of a palm house and a pinery may be, I think we must use the glasshouses for a more practical purpose, Mr Macleod.'

'It's Murdo, and I leave that up to you to decide. It's why you're here.'

They had completed the shallow climb from the sea onto the moor, and she was surveying the landscape with interest. 'What are those mud blocks that have been dug from those ditches?'

'Peat. It's just been cut, and it's stacked here to dry out. It's used for fuel. We use stone to build with, we're not that primitive.'

'And does Taravay have peat? Is it as flat as this? Tell me more of what to expect.'

'It's not flat, the land is more rolling with dips and hollows which protect the crofts from the worst of the weather—though they are all abandoned, as I mentioned. The island is about four miles square, and it's divided into two parts, which are connected by a narrow spine. You can see Lewis from the eastern side, but to the west there's nothing but ocean. There's a sheltered bay on the eastern side, mostly pebbles and stones, a jetty in sore need of repair where we land the boat and supplies, and the coastline there has some cliffs. On the Atlantic side the machair—that's what was once good grazing—it goes right down to the dunes, and there are some beaches, the sand silver and the sea, as a result, the most startling colour of turquoise. The waters are clear, full of fish, and teeming with dolphins, seals, whales.'

'You are making it sound like paradise.'

Her eyes glittered, her cheeks were rosy with the drive in the cold air, and her smile was infectious. 'You won't say that when the wind howls across the landscape—for we've no trees to shield us—and the rain comes down in buckets,' Murdo told her, though he too was smiling now. 'Though there are times—I remember when I was a boy, fishing, swimming, with the sun blazing down, the sand hot on your feet and the machair in full flower. Back then, on days like those, Taravay was a fine enough place to be.'

'The sand hot on your feet, and the sea icy cold. I would love that.'

Walk barefoot in the sand? Are you mad, Murdo?

Emily had stared at him, aghast at the suggestion, putting an end to one of his stupid romantic fantasies. He'd never had the opportunity to change her mind either, for the Laird would not even acknowledge her existence. Now he had the letter in his pocket that confirmed he no longer existed for her. He hoped she was happy. He hoped his suffering and sacrifice had been worthwhile.

'Mr Macleod?'

He started. 'There won't be time for paddling.'

'No, of course not, I didn't mean…'

'I've wasted enough time already.'

'I see.'

She didn't, but he wasn't about to enlighten her.

Another mile passed before she spoke again, her voice tight. 'Do you by any chance have a camera?'

'A camera, on Taravay! There's as much chance of that as finding a steam engine.'

'Both would be of use. It would be wonderful to re-cord the transformation of the island. It would be a re-cord for your family to look back on.'

Her words were like a kick in the gut. 'There won't be any family. I'm the last of the line. I'm not married, and I am not interested in being married. I'm perfectly happy being alone.'

She flinched at his tone, the colour fading from her face. 'I'm sorry. Your personal circumstances are none of my business.'

'Well, now you have made them your business,' he said unfairly, 'you know more than sufficient.'

'I do beg your pardon, I didn't mean to intrude.'

She was biting her lip, her hands clasped tightly together. She knew nothing of his history, he reminded himself. She could have no idea that she had poked at a still-raw wound. 'It's Murdo,' he said gruffly by way of an apology.

'Murdo.' Jessica gave him a very small, forced smile and turned her attention back to the moorland.

Chapter Four

Jessica, who had already been travelling for three days, found the final stage of the journey from Stornoway to Taravay a test of endurance, though her gardener's eyes automatically recorded the scenery around her. The long, straight track over the moorland was pitted with pools of stagnant water. For mile upon mile, there was nothing to see but the brown marshy land studded with heather, the deep trenches dug into it, the sods of peat stacked alongside, and the vast sky, pale blue streaked with crisp white and silver-grey. On and on they drove, she silent as the sick feeling that she had inadvertently caused so much offence combined with carriage sickness—though you couldn't call the rough-hewn cart a carriage—took over from the seasick-ness she'd fought on the steamer. Beside her, Murdo Macleod, checking his pocket watch and muttering about tides, concentrated on getting them to their des-tination as quickly as the terrain and the sweating pony would allow. When they at last turned off the moor to drive parallel with the coast, there was little of the sea to be seen, though it could be smelled and tasted—a strong, salty tang carried on the breeze.

Her new employer seemed relieved by her silence and, happily oblivious to her suffering, his mood once again settled and focused. He was a strange mixture: on the one hand a successful City businessman who must be logical, level-headed, cold-blooded even, in stark contrast to the moody Highlander, who referred to his deceased father distantly as the Laird, and who flew into a temper at the hint of any remotely personal subject. Such as the possibility of his marrying and having a family.

She shuddered inwardly, recalling the blaze of anger in his eyes when all she'd done was suggest in a perfectly natural way that his island would be passed on to his descendants. He loved Taravay, by his own admission it was the one passion he shared with his father, but the fact that he was willing to spend an unimaginable fortune on it spoke of something that went deeper. The rift between father and son must also have run deep, to keep him away from the place for—goodness, she had no idea how long he'd been away. Long enough for his command of Gaelic to become rusty. Had the island's desolation come as a shock when he had returned after the Laird's death? Had he regretted the rift? The one positive thing that Jessica had held on to after Lady Orton had dismissed her, was that she had been in the cottage at Thornhill for her mother's last days. Six months had given her time to come to adjust to her loss, though there were still times when she forgot, and the grief washed over her like a crashing wave. Mama had been too ill to burden with her own heartbreak, and Jessica was thankful for that small mercy too. Mama had died with the pride she took in her daughter's achievements untarnished.

Murdo Macleod had made it clear that grief was another topic he didn't wish to discuss. He was a highly emotional man, who seemed intent on denying that he had any emotions, Jessica decided, eyeing him covertly. Was she being unfair? Eighteen months alone on an island would be bound to affect one's temperament. Which brought her back around to the question of why? Had he run away from something—or someone? His vehemence on the subject of marriage had chimed with her. If she was the type of female to be intrigued, then Murdo Macleod was the type of man to intrigue her. But she was not. And she would never, ever again make the mistake of letting her heart interfere with her head.

She had persuaded him, against his better judgement, to take her on. What she needed to do now was prove that he had made the right decision. She would devote herself to the work she had been brought here to do, Jessica resolved, as her employer intoned the names of the little hamlets they passed through, and though the words, in his increasingly Scots accent, had a lilting beauty, they sounded very strange to her. Shadier? Shadow? No, that couldn't be right. Something like Borve? Dell, that was easier, and Cross, that one she understood. Each hamlet was similar, a huddle of small farms or crofts, each a long, squat stone-built cottage with tiny windows facing inland and roofs thatched with heather and bracken with a central chimney. Blackhouses, he told her they were known as. There were no trees or shrubs, no windbreaks for whatever crops grew in the poor soil. She could see sheep in the fields they passed, hens scratching, but very few cattle, and there seemed too, scant evidence of cultivation, though it was probably too early in the year, this far north.

Finally, when she thought she'd faint from a combination of nausea and hunger, Murdo announced their arrival at Port of Ness, which was not a port so much as a fishing village, the houses clinging to the top of a sheer cliff, with a steep cobbled incline down to a wharf, where a very small boat was tied up.

'It will take me fifteen minutes or so to load up. Do you want to stretch your legs?' Murdo asked.

Jessica nodded, happy to be spared the sight of that alarmingly tiny craft if only for a few moments, jumping out of the cart before he could help her down. The breeze whipped at her cloak, and tugged at her hair. She had walked only a few steps when the door of one of the cottages opened and a woman about her own age, dressed in a dark skirt and draped in a shawl, beckoned her over.

'Catriona Macfarlane,' she said, smiling and frowning at the same time, speaking in a soft, lilting English that was almost musical. 'Surely you are not the J Smith that Himself, Murdo Macleod went to collect?'

'I am indeed Jessica Smith. How did you know I was coming?'

The woman gave a snort of laughter. 'Nothing happens around here that we don't know about. Murdo Macleod sent a telegram to you with the Stornoway ferry times from the telegram office here. Will you come in for a moment, Mrs Smith, and have a cup of tea?'

'Thank you. I feel as if I've been travelling for days—which I suppose I have. You're very kind.'

'The truth is I'm very curious. We all are. We get very few new faces around here, so when an intriguing stranger turns up, well, you can imagine.' Mrs Macfarlane ushered her into a cosy room where a peat fire burned in the open grate, tipping a fat black cat from a chair as she did so. 'Don't worry about Himself, that's my husband down on the quay with him. He'll not be setting off for another half hour. Have you eaten? I've crowdie—that's a cheese I make fresh— and some bread? Now sit down and tell me what brings you here?'

What would *Himself* think of her taking tea with one of the locals? She was fairly certain that he would not approve, but the opportunity to satisfy her own curiosity, if she could, was irresistible. 'I am a gardener—a landscaper,' Jessica said.

'Well! I would not have guessed that in a month of Sundays.' Catriona filled a brown teapot with water from the kettle which hung on a hook over the fire and took two chunky mugs from a dresser. 'So he's about to do something about the Castle gardens then, is he?'

'I believe that may be part of his plan,' Jessica said warily.

'So he does *have* a plan.' Mrs Macfarlane poured the tea and sat down on the other side of the table. 'Does he mean to share it with us any time soon, do you know? Or is he his father's son, after all, and likely to get on with whatever it is without a word? Ach no, what a question to ask when you've only just arrived. Drink your tea while it's hot and eat your crowdie, you're looking a bit green about the gills.'

Mrs Macfarlane produced a set of knitting needles from somewhere about her person and set about what looked like a very complicated pattern without giving it so much as a glance. Jessica took a sip of her tea, took a bite of the bread spread with delicious soft white cheese curds, and decided that it would be foolish not to do some digging about Murdo, considering she was about to sail off to spend an unspecified time quite alone with him. 'I understand that Mr Macleod has been alone on Taravay for some time now?' she said.

'He came here for his father's funeral and did not leave. The Laird's death must have sore afflicted him, for he has barely a civil word to say to anyone here in Ness.'

'Yet I understand that he and his father were not close?'

'No, indeed they were not.' The clacking of the needles stopped for a few seconds, as Mrs Macfarlane took a sip of her own tea and resumed her work. 'Murdo Macleod left Taravay for London when I was a girl, and to the best of my knowledge has not been back since. He kept in touch with no one, and only the old Laird's lawyer in Glasgow knew how to find him. It is a mystery to us Niseachs why he has decided to remain on Taravay now, when he spent his whole adult life avoiding the place like the plague.'

This last was spoken with an air of enquiry, but Jessica shook her head, every bit as baffled as to Murdo's motives. 'Yet it seems to me,' she said, 'that he does genuinely love the island. He spoke very affectionately of his childhood.'

'Did he now? Yet he chose my husband, who is from Glasgow and had never met him until he returned for the funeral, over Finlay Murray, who was his closest friend when they were boys, to provide him with supplies, and to bring him his telegrams and his news-papers.' Mrs Macfarlane got up to top up their cups.

This was very odd, given that Murdo wanted to re-populate Taravay. Where was he expecting the people to come from, Jessica wondered uneasily, and where did he think the people who would be required to do the renovations would be recruited from?

'And now he's going to make himself a pretty gar-den, is he?' Mrs Macfarlane said, needles clacking once more in time to the ticking of the large clock on the mantel. 'Well that, as my own husband would say, takes the biscuit when you think of all those crofts abandoned to the wilderness. There were a few in Ness who hoped that he would remedy that when he returned, but they were proved sadly wrong. It will not go down well here, Mrs Smith, when it becomes known what he is about, I should warn you. For all he has been gone a long time, he is still the Laird. If he has no notion of doing his duty by Taravay, there are many here who think he should take himself back to where he came from.'

Conscious of the time, and of a growing panic at her situation, Jessica set down her empty cup. 'Will you tell me please, why the crofts were abandoned?'

Mrs Macfarlane gave a deep sigh and shook her head forcefully. 'I'd rather not,' she said, holding up her knitting. 'Stockings, for one of my nieces. She puts her toes through a new pair every other week, her mother cannot keep up.'

'You are very skilled, I've never seen anyone knit so fast.'

'My mother taught me, when I was a bairn. This is nothing compared to what some of the other Ness women can do, with some of the finer yarns they spin. Morag McGregor claims she can knit a jumper while making the dinner.' She tucked her knitting back into the folds of her skirt and rose to look out of the window. 'The boat looks set to sail, you'd better get down to the harbour now.'

'Please,' Jessica said desperately. 'Won't you…'

'I'm sorry, but it's not my story to tell.' Mrs Macfarlane folded her arms, but her expression was concerned. 'What does your husband think of you spending time alone on an island with another man?'

'I'm not married, but I assure you,' Jessica added hurriedly, 'I am going to Taravay as Mr Macleod's landscaper and nothing else. There is no question of any—of anything improper between us.'

'No question of…' Mrs Macfarlane said something soft in Gaelic under her breath. 'You know that there are some here who think the man is mad, as well as a heathen—for he does not come to church? Are you sure this is a wise decision?'

'Do you think he's likely to murder me in my bed?'

She meant it as a joke, but Mrs Macfarlane's face

told her it was a poor one. 'I think he is a deeply troubled man, though what ails him, I have no idea. He is a Macleod of Taravay, and though they have many faults, to my knowledge neither murder nor ravishment are among them.' She cast an anxious glance out of the window. 'He's putting the sail up. If you are intent on going, then you had better get yourself down to the harbour, but if you have changed your mind, you can spend the night here, and we'll find a way to get you back to Stornoway.'

'I've come this far,' Jessica said with far more confidence than she felt. 'And Mr Macleod promised that if I changed my mind, he'd sail me back himself.'

'My husband brings supplies most mornings. I'll ask him to look out for you. His name is Grahame.'

'Thank you.' Jessica gave the other woman a shy hug. 'I'm sure I'll be fine, but I am very grateful nonetheless.'

Mrs Macfarlane ushered her out to the door. 'I hope the Mackinnon croft is to your liking. Norman Mackinnon was the last crofter on Taravay, until his death. My husband was asked to take over fresh blankets and what not, but it will be far from homely. He lived alone there many a year. Would you like some oatcakes to take with you for the journey? There are more in the supplies that my husband has been loading, mind.'

'You're so kind, but my stomach is already protesting, looking at that sea.'

'Och, away with you. That's as calm a sea as I've seen in weeks. Good luck to you, Miss Smith, I'm afraid you're going to need it. Now hurry, or you'll miss the tide.'

Jessica had no idea whether the tide was going in or out, but she did know that Murdo wanted to catch it, whatever that meant. It was late afternoon and the sun had given way to clouds, and to a freshening breeze. Afraid that if she looked around to wave, her courage would fail her, she clutched her cloak around her and picked her way down the steep incline to the wharf, where the frighteningly small boat was tied up, the pony and cart standing empty now, with Catriona's husband holding the reins. One question answered, she told herself, at least she wasn't going to be sharing a deck with a horse. Then she recalled that Murdo had mentioned a pony on Taravay. Where was Taravay? All she could see was sea. Sea the colour of turquoise, crested by bright white waves. And spray. And further out, an ominous swell which made her newly filled stomach give an ominous lurch, the contents curdling. She really shouldn't have eaten the crowdie.

'Where the devil have you been? Are you ready to go?' Murdo Macleod asked her impatiently. 'Unless you've changed your mind?'

It was very strange, but standing beside him, her doubts began to recede. As Mrs Macfarlane said, Murdo was deeply troubled. If he'd ever been polished, then he was tarnished from living alone, and he may well be a heathen—not that she cared about that—but a lunatic? No, absolutely not, any more than he was a murderer or a seducer. There was bound to be wild speculation about his presence on Taravay, but hadn't he already told her more than anyone here knew? Why he had come back after such a long absence—now that was a different matter, but none of her business.

'I'm ready,' Jessica said, then dropped her gaze to the boat. 'I think I'm ready.' When it strained at its rope, there was a gap between the jetty and the open deck, just wide enough for a person to fall into. 'Is it safe?'

'I wouldn't sail if it wasn't,' was his answer. 'And if you need further reassurance, the Ness fishing fleet is out.'

'There's a fleet here?'

'Six of seven boats, any road.'

'I can't see them. Or the island.'

'We'll pass the fleet, and the island will come into view just as soon as we've sailed around the Butt of Lewis—that's the point over there, to the north west. Do you see the lighthouse there?' Oblivious of the seething sea between the jetty and the boat, Murdo held out his hand. 'It's less than an hour in this weather, and I learned to sail these waters as a bairn.'

His focus on reaching Taravay had dispelled his lowering mood, and her own spirits lifted. 'I'm afraid of losing my stomach, not my heart.'

'Don't look down. Just one step, and I'll catch you.'

She took the hand extended to her. The boat bumped against the jetty. Spray misted her cheeks. She closed her eyes and stepped away from solid ground. Her cloak caught around her ankles as her foot touched the heaving wood of the boat, and she stumbled, but Murdo was as true as his word. Strong arms around her waist held her firmly.

'You can open your eyes now.'

She did, to find him gazing down, a breath's distance away. His quizzical smile faded as their eyes locked. The boat rocked, but he steadied her.

'Don't fight it,' he said, tightening his hold on her, and for a tiny, tiny moment, she thought, no, I don't want to fight it. Then he shook his head, broke eye contact, let her go. 'Here, sit down. You've a bit of shelter from the stores and your luggage. I'll get you a blanket.'

Huddled under the plaid, Jessica told herself she had imagined it. That flicker of attraction. The double entendre. It had all been in her head, not his. She watched him prepare to set sail, steady, lithe, sure, reassuring. He cast off, waving a brief farewell to Grahame Macfarlane, then set about steering them away from the harbour and out to the darker blue swell. The sun glinted through a gap in the clouds, making her eyes wince. Gulls and seabirds she didn't recognise circled the mast, screaming at them, sleek black ones plummeting into the water, dropping like stones only to emerge further on, soaring up, then diving again. There were more birds on the rocks, different ones. She felt her ignorance weighing her down. She knew nothing of this terrain, nothing of what grew in this wild, exposed landscape, and next to nothing of this man who was her companion, and the only thing between her and shipwreck.

He seemed at peace at present, content to be in charge of the boat, his eyes fixed firmly ahead, but his mood could turn faster than the Hebridean weather. As did the tone of his voice, one minute harsh, clipped, the accent of a Scot who had spent most of his life in London, switching to the softer, lilting accent of a Highlander and drifting into Gaelic. What was he thinking? What was he hiding from? Why did he seem intent on isolating himself from everyone here, even his childhood friend? Was he grieving for his father, or was he glad the Laird was dead? And perhaps the most baffling question of all, why, when she was so wary of him, when he was the key to the re-establishment of her precious career, did she find him so unsettlingly attractive?

She would not be such a fool as to act on that. That moment when he helped her on board, when their eyes met, when she had convinced herself that Murdo felt what she was feeling, was all in her head. Even if he did find her '*surprisingly attractive*'. Jessica smiled to herself at that, and recalled *his* smile, when she'd informed him that, even if he was an Adonis, she'd be immune to his charm. True, but he was not an Adonis, and she was not immune, though Murdo's very raw appeal was a long way away from what she'd felt for Edward. Love! That boat, like the one she was seated in, had sailed.

They bounced off a wave, spraying her face with icy seawater. She would do well to take her new employer's advice and think about the future, which was hers to make, and not the past, which she heartily wished she could unmake. There was a wild beauty to this place, the sheer rocks on one side spattered with the guano of the gulls who nested there; the glitter of golden and silver sand in narrow coves streaked with black seaweed; the seething sea on the other, so dark it was almost navy in colour; and above her the huge expanse of sky. A silver-grey blob transformed into a seal, with big brown eyes and whiskers that gave it a human look as it stared at her, sizing her up for an entrancing moment before diving again. The wind whipped at her hair and her cheeks stung with salt. It was frightening, but even more exhilarating.

Her broken heart was on the way to mending, and she wouldn't be so careless with it again. One thing, then, that she had in common with Murdo—she was single, would remain single, and would be perfectly happy being so. With every bounce of the boat on the swell, she was leaving her past behind her. She would redeem her reputation here. No, better. A whole island, and the chance to put some of her most precious ideals into practice, she would do a great deal more than redeem herself. This was her second chance, and she would seize it with both hands. A new test, a new venture, a new landscape. An island, where she would be cut off from the world, with time to heal, and only this man for company.

Murdo was pointing out the lighthouse now, his words lost on the breeze, his hair whipped around his face, relaxed, at ease with himself and with the sea, looking exactly what he was, in essence, despite his long absence, a Highlander born and bred here. A very attractive Highlander. Irrelevant, Jessica reminded herself. He might not lay claim to his honorary title, but Murdo was the Laird, and she was a hired hand.

As they rounded the tip—no, the *Butt* of Lewis, he called over to her, pointing to a dark shape in the distance. Taravay. His island. Her home, for the next few weeks at least. It was spring. A time for new shoots, new growth. Jessica pulled the blanket around her, the warmth of anticipation enveloping her. New beginnings. Who'd have thought she'd find them here, in this wild and remote corner of Scotland. It was exciting, and more than a little scary. What on earth had she let herself in for? She was about to find out.

Chapter Five

The weather had turned ugly almost from the moment Murdo landed on Taravay with his unexpected cargo. In the week Jessica Smith had been here, the rain had been relentless, the wind blowing a hoolie, sending the clouds scudding across the sky from the Atlantic, over Taravay and on to Lewis in a relentless procession of grey. No sooner had one squall passed than another began, with the full repertoire of Hebridean rain playing out over the course of every day, from mizzle to stair-rods, from smir to sleet with the occasional flurry of hail thrown in for good measure. Rain dripped through gaps in the thatch roof of his croft. It found its way through the rotted window frame, under the door, and it ran in a small stream down the walls in at least two places. His clothes were permanently damp, and he himself was permanently cold and miserable.

His dreams were haunted by the faces of the islanders he once knew. In the grey and windswept daylight hours, he tormented himself with memories of the place when he was a boy, the crofts bursting with life, the school full of children, and the weather—ach, he knew that not every day was wall-to-wall sunshine, but it seemed as if it was. Once upon a time. In the story he told himself of those days.

At night, unable or more often afraid to sleep, Murdo took to wandering the island as he had when he'd first come back here eighteen months ago, when the sod lay fresh on the Laird's grave, and the wound that Emily had cut into his heart was raw and bleeding. All his carefully nurtured confidence in his future plans for Taravay had evaporated. Doubts picked and pecked at his ideas like the crows on the carcass of a newborn lamb. Drookit, night after night, despite his resolution to stay away, he found himself at the door of the Castle. Night after night, he haunted the halls and rooms carrying a lantern, feeling like an intruder with no right to be here, wandering stealthily about as if at any point the Laird would discover him and cast him out. Again.

The ghost of his younger self peered down resentfully from the window of his childhood bedchamber, where he had been locked in for whatever his latest misdemeanour was. There, at that side door, his ghostly self slipped out, running down the path to the harbour, where his boat lay, desperate to join his friends fishing, and just behind him came the Laird's roar, summoning him back, to stay away from the riff-raff. That door opened into the Laird's study. On that carpet, just inside the door, stood so many ghosts of his former self: aged five, sobbing at the death of his mother and cowering at the Laird's anger for displaying such weakness; aged ten, trembling in anticipation of a caning; aged fifteen, begging for permission to spend the week with his friends in their sheilings on the Skigersta moor over on Lewis, bringing in the peat. Whatever he wanted, it seemed the Laird wanted something else of him.

You're a Macleod of Taravay, and ye must act like one. Don't ever forget that. Don't ever let anyone tell you otherwise. Over and over, it seemed to Murdo, those words had been hurled at him through the years, until he would happily have claimed any other name but the one the Laird was so proud of. He was a Macleod of Taravay, but the Laird would not let him have any say in the future or the island, nor any say in his own future. Eventually, inevitably, Murdo had been forced to choose for himself.

The Laird had been dead a year and a half, yet here in the dead of night, in his inner sanctum, facing that desk, Murdo could all too easily imagine what he would have said about his rebellious only child's current situation: *You're a Macleod of Taravay. I tell't you to stay put here. If you'd done as I bid ye, this wouldn't have happened.*

It wasn't his fault. He couldn't have tried any harder

to mend the breach. *Compromise* was not a word that had been in the Laird's vocabulary, and there came a point when bending ever more backwards to appease him, as Murdo had tried to do, was simply not possible. If the Laird had shown any affection for his only son, then perhaps they could have found a way, but he never had. The final tipping point had come that last time he'd seen the Laird alive. Murdo had arrived, determined for once to make the Laird listen to his side of the story, in the hope that his new circumstances would pave the way for a reconciliation, but history had simply repeated itself.

He had been met with the same old script. *You're a Macleod of Taravay, and ye must act like one, which means you'll do as you're tell't. I know what's best for ye, and what's best is that you stay here and we'll forget all about what you've told me.*

Against his better judgement, Murdo had argued, his words becoming more heated as the Laird's face became stonier, leaving him no choice but to issue that ill-fated ultimatum. *I'm leaving, and I won't be back. You won't see me again, unless you change your mind.* But the Laird had not changed his mind. And Murdo had kept true to his word.

Taravay was his now. The Castle was his. The Laird was dead and buried. Every morning, Murdo resolved to get on with his plans, scraping about in the residue of his exhausted brain for the willpower to do just that.

But the rain and the wind continued relentlessly, and the memories wouldn't leave him alone, and his doubts kept him from doing anything but listening to them, over and over. What if the Laird was in the right of it, and Murdo really wasn't good enough for Taravay? An experimental night on the whisky kept him sleepless and left him wasted, head thumping, stomach protesting. He resolved not to touch the stuff again.

It was Jessica Smith's fault. Or rather, it was his own for bringing her here against his better judgement. Seeing the place as if through her eyes, the scale of what had happened overwhelmed him, the suffering that had been caused, the souls who had been cast out, was too much to bear. He couldn't help thinking that his landscape gardener's presence had put a curse on the island, though he knew he was being ridiculous. She assured him, when he dropped off her supplies each morning, that her own croft was warm and dry, but there were dark shadows under her eyes he didn't care to ask about.

She had taken up residence in the one sheltered spot of the island during the day, in the potting shed inside the old walled garden. He watched her from the doorway of the garden, pacing up and down the narrow space, stopping to think, to scribble something in a notebook. He watched her, careful to keep himself hidden. He tortured himself by watching her, so tantalisingly close, so temptingly near, yet he dared not join her. He feared he would contaminate her mood with his own. He didn't trust himself not to frighten her, to hurl accusations at her that would make him sound like a lunatic, blaming her for his mood, for the weather, for persuading him to employ her against his better judgement. He stayed away from her because he knew, deep inside, that at some point his own mood would lift, and he'd be glad, once more, that she was here. He didn't want to be the object of his own downfall, for his foul mood to result in her begging him to sail her back to Ness. He wished he had not brought her here. He wished he'd let his own instincts triumph and left her in Stornoway. But now she was here, he didn't want her to leave.

Some nights, to add to his torment, she ousted the islanders from his dreams. Then, she was not a landscaper but a temptress, and on those occasions he woke aroused. Appalled at his own imagination, appalled by the extent of his desire, he lay awake, refusing to give in to the need to relieve himself, for to do so was to be weak. To do so, would be to submit to that side of him he considered dead—which had been more or less dead, these last eighteen months. He would never again be in thrall to another woman. He would master his base needs. When he failed, the guilt slayed him. It was perverse of him to so fervently desire what was forbidden to him. He could not want her. Yet he did.

This alluring, attractive, nocturnal version of Jessica made it even more difficult for him to face her in the day. His mood, dark and lowering like the weather, was proving difficult to shift. What must she think of him, keeping his distance, leaving her almost entirely to her own devices? Most likely, his behaviour was confirming whatever Catriona Macfarlane would have told her. Jessica had said nothing about the encounter, but it was a safe bet that the Ness woman would have said nothing positive. It was his own fault, he'd made no effort to explain himself to any of the Niseachs, not even Finlay. Whether they blamed him for having done nothing or believed he was complicit made no difference. The deed was done. His duty now was to accept that and build the foundations of a new future. That's what he'd done for Emily. That's what he would do for Taravay.

Yet back and forward his resolve swayed all the same. Would he ever manage to make all good? He'd been away too long. How could he dare to imagine that he knew best for the island? What if the Laird had been right after all, all those years ago, when he'd laughed in derision at Murdo's cherished ideas for change. Jessica Smith had had a wasted journey. He'd take her back to Lewis on the morrow.

But on the morrow, every morrow, seeing her blurred figure through the rain-drenched panes of the potting shed, Murdo changed his mind. God love her, she was clearly trying to marshal her thoughts, do something positive even though he hadn't given her a scrap of direction. He blamed her for the state he'd got himself into, but she was also the one ray of hope that kept him going, that kept him trying to dig himself out of the mire. He'd not been good enough for the Laird and it turned out had been second choice for Emily, but he would prove himself good enough for Taravay.

Then, as night fell, the doubts would fly back in.

Chapter Six

Jessica awoke with a start, completely disoriented. The blanket she had wrapped around herself had slipped to the floor. The peat fire was nothing but embers. She picked up her father's watch from the little table where it lay beside the half-drunk mug of milk she had heated for her supper, disheartened to discover it was only just past midnight. The wind was howling through the rafters of the cottage, as it had every night for the week she had been on Taravay, although tonight it sounded like a full-blown thunderstorm was underway.

She had got into the habit of falling asleep by the fire. Somehow the rustling of creatures in the thatch made of bracken and heather and the relentless pounding of the rain outside were less frightening here, snuggled into her fireside chair, than they were when she lay under the rough blankets of the bed that she was pretty certain the last tenant must have died in—hadn't Catriona Macfarlane said he'd died in this croft?

Though thankfully the blankets and sheets themselves were new.

Norman Mackinnon, she knew his name was, from the rent book she'd found in the dresser drawer. She was cooking on his fire with his pots, making her tea with his kettle, eating and drinking using his scant crockery, but there was little in the house to tell her anything more about the man who had lived and worked here. He'd kept hens, their descendants still roosted in the old henhouse, and he'd grown potatoes on a strip of land on his croft. There were no books here, no photographs, and only what looked like a religious tract in Gaelic on the walls. What would he make of her, sitting alone here at his fireside, a complete stranger, brought here to make radical changes to the island that had been his home, most likely for his whole life?

She shivered, telling herself once again that the rustling above her head was only mice, nothing bigger, nothing more sinister. It was not the ghost of Norman Mackinnon, nor the ghost of any of the islanders looking down at her, trying to frighten her away, grudging her taking up one of their abodes when they no longer lived here. Had they left or perished? Catriona Macfarlane's hints and cryptic words gave her no inkling, allowing her imagination to run wild as she sat here, waiting for the dawn to break on another windy, wet, cold day.

She could leave. It had been too stormy for Grahame Macfarlane to sail these last few days, but Murdo had promised he'd take her, if he could. Standing at the jetty yesterday, looking out at the white-topped waves, listening to the roar as they crested onto the beach, the idea of going to sea had even less appeal than the idea of staying here. Besides, she wanted to stay here. She had a point to prove, and this would be a wonderful project—if only the weather would abate. And if only Murdo would come out of whatever vile mood had seized him and talk to her about his plans.

He was a distant presence. Were it not for his appearance each morning with supplies, she may as well be alone on the island. Occasionally, the hairs on the back of her neck prickled, and she glimpsed him lurking in the doorway to the walled garden, but he never approached her. Why not? It could not only be the weather, though the sudden and dramatic change in the skies could easily be seen as an ill omen, if she let it. Over and over, she replayed her conversations with him on that first day. Had she really convinced him that she could fulfil the commission, or had he simply been buying time, letting her do the spadework—ugh, terrible pun!—while he offered the full commission to another, male candidate? Did he think her too forward? Had he simply decided that they wouldn't get on? Or had he noticed that she found him attractive? When he had reassured her that he would not abuse the situation, had she been too vehement in her response? Would he think she *wanted* him to make advances, or did he think her constitutionally indifferent?

Would that were true, but she seemed quite unable to stick to her resolve to think of him only as her employer. Too many times, she found herself wondering where he was, what he was doing. Her body would conjure up the memory of his brief touches, of the way their eyes had locked, of the frisson that rippled through her when he'd put his arms around her to help her into the boat, and her imagination would leap at the opportunity to paint the most vivid pictures of what might happen next. Images that shocked her, roused her, made her hot, made her shiver.

It was Murdo's fault. If only he would stop avoiding her, if only he'd start barking orders, acting like a bear with a sore head, then the reality of him would wipe away all these distracting thoughts. It was his fault for leaving her alone, for not forcing her to focus on the work that he still had not explained. She had to confront him. She resolved to do so every day. But he didn't give her the opportunity.

Why was he avoiding her? Had he telegraphed Lady Orton for a reference, or had a rumour of her doomed, foolish engagement somehow reached him? She knew neither were likely, since he had no idea that she'd worked for Lady Orton, but the fear gnawed at her nonetheless, helping to keep her awake into the small hours, no matter how exhausted she was by her day's endeavours. Every morning she started afresh, telling herself that all she could do was what Murdo had bid her, do it to the best of her ability, and hold her nerve. This was the biggest, most important assignment of her life. She must not fail. She must not let him down, or just as importantly, let herself down. But she had so little clue as to what he wanted from her. Then she'd find herself staring into space, falling into a dwam, thinking of the man, not his island.

The wind gusted under the door of the Blackhouse, making the fire flare and then smoke. Jessica got up to gaze out the small window at the night and the dark hulk of Taravay Castle. Two nights ago, she had convinced herself that she'd seen a light flickering in one of the windows. Though the front facade faced east towards Lewis, she had a clear view of it from here, a substantial but plain building, a practical edifice built to withstand the weather with none of the fanciful turrets and parapets of the Castle she'd seen in Stornoway. The next morning, she had taken advantage of a brief spell when the rain had eased from bucketloads to a soft mist and went to look at it. All of the windows were shuttered. What she could see of the roof seemed sound, and there were no obvious signs of damp on the grey walls. The kitchen door was padlocked. The outbuildings yielded up gardening tools, a cart, a small pony trap, but very little else. She had gone so far as to rattle the iron handle of the front door, to peer through the keyhole into the darkness beyond, heart thudding, but to no avail. She must have imagined the light.

But it was there again last night, a flickering light emanating from a different room. Murdo? But why would he go there at night rather than during the day? Was he looking for a more comfortable bed than he had in his own croft? If he'd moved back to the Castle, she'd have seen him come and go during the day, wouldn't she? Was it a ghost, then? Did ghosts carry candles?

The fire was almost out, and she had forgotten to bring in more peat from the stack. Did she want to get soaked or get cold? The door to the Blackhouse crashed open, making her jump to her feet in fright. The storm, it was the storm, that's all. She rushed to push it closed just as a jagged fork of lightning illuminated the Castle and the silhouette of a figure standing on top of the turret. Then the night was plunged into darkness again. A second flash of lightning a few seconds later lit up the Castle again but the figure had gone. Her heart was pounding. Had she imagined it? Was it a ghost? She did not believe in ghosts she told herself sternly. Either there was a stranger hiding there, or it was Murdo. Either way, she was not going to stay here trying to persuade herself she was seeing things, she was going to find out.

Grabbing her cloak, Jessica fastened it over her

nightgown, stuffing her feet into her boots. The wind was much stronger than she expected as she left the shelter of the cottage, all but blowing her off her feet. Head down, she battled on, hugging the wall of the garden, making for the forbidding front door. Thunder rumbled ominously. The rain had already soaked through her cloak, her hair was sodden, and her face was icy.

Furious with whoever it was that had forced her out in this foul weather, she battled on. She had her hand stretched out to try the handle of the front door when it was suddenly and violently thrown open. She screamed, cowering back as a hulking figure loomed in front of her, and she would have fallen down the stairs had a strong hand not grabbed her by the arm and pulled her inside the door.

'You! What the hell are you doing here?'

'Murdo!'

'Who did you expect? A ghost?'

'I thought I saw someone standing at the top of the turret.'

'I've every right to be here!'

His grip on her was painful. His hair and his beard were damp, tousled, his expression wild. He looked, in fact, as if it was he and not she who had seen a ghost. 'But it's the middle of the night,' Jessica protested.

'So why aren't you tucked up asleep in your bed?'

'The storm woke me. Then you scared the life out

of me when I saw you up on the turret. What on earth are you doing here in the dead of night.'

'I can't sleep,' he said. 'They won't leave me alone.'

His eyes were dark pools, deeply shadowed. A troubled man, Catriona Macfarlane had called him, and Jessica could see why. 'Who won't leave you alone?'

He stared at her silently for a long moment, then he blinked. 'You're soaking wet.'

He was wearing a shirt, half buttoned, and a coat, not buttoned at all. The shirt was damp, clinging to his body, emphasising the muscles of his chest, the dip of his belly. 'So are you.' The air between them changed in an instant as she met his gaze. She felt it, the crackle of attraction, unmistakable and most definitely not one-sided. Now was the time to disengage herself. Now was the time to demand more information from him. To ask him if he had changed his mind about employing her, to ask him why he was avoiding her. But it was there in his face, why he had been avoiding her. There in hers too, judging from the way he was looking at her.

'Are you sorry you came here, Jessica Smith?' he asked, his voice now soft, lilting, hypnotising.

She shook her head. His grip on her wrist loosened. She told herself to step away, but she stood rooted to the spot. 'Are you sorry you brought me?'

'Sorry?' He reached with his other hand to touch her cheek. A flutter, just a flutter, before he yanked his hand back, but it knocked the breath from her, made her heart race.

'You've been avoiding me,' she said, inching towards him, telling herself it was wrong, terribly wrong.

'Waiting for the storm to pass,' he said, reaching for her once again, stroking back a long strand of her damp hair. 'You should have stayed in the croft.'

She wanted to agree. She knew she ought to agree. She lifted her hand, echoing his own movement, to push his hair back from his brow. He shivered at her touch. 'Shall I go?' she asked.

'Yes.' His fingers were warm on the nape of her neck. 'This is wrong. I can't—I don't…'

'Nor I.' She closed the gap between them. 'It's the storm.'

'Yes, it's the storm.' He leaned in to her, his lips on her brow. 'And the dreams.'

The storm. The dreams. 'It will pass,' Jessica said, for herself as much as for him. She could feel his breath on her face. She placed her palm flat on his damp shirt, feeling his heart thudding wildly, every bit as wildly as hers. 'Tomorrow.'

He gave a strangled laugh, lifting his lips from her face to gaze deep into her eyes. 'Tomorrow, it will pass. And tomorrow will be a new day.'

'Yes.' Her hopes. Her thoughts. 'Tomorrow will be a new day.'

'Will it?'

He spoke with such a desperate look that she ached to comfort him, and that's all it was, she told herself, comfort, as she slid her arm around his waist, as their bodies touched, and as their lips met.

His mouth was warm. He smelled of rain and of troubled nights. She closed her eyes, her mouth softening to his, his fingers tangling in her hair, pulling her closer, and in that second she was lost, wanting nothing more than the kiss she had dreamed of almost from the moment she met him.

But a gust of wind whistled like a banshee through the portico, and they sprang apart. Wide-eyed, they stared at each other, teetering between horror and desire.

It was Murdo who spoke first, cursing in Gaelic under his breath. 'That should not have happened.'

'No.' Mortified, suddenly acutely aware of her state of undress, Jessica clutched at her cloak.

'I didn't mean…'

'No, nor I.'

'I gave you a fright.'

'And I gave you a fright.' They both knew they were lying. 'The storm,' Jessica said.

Murdo opened his mouth to say something, then changed his mind, shaking his head. 'Let's get you back to your croft.'

'I can go myself, it's only a few steps.'

'No, I insist.'

He pulled the door wide for her to pass out into the weather, then shut and locked it behind him. They walked the short distance to her Blackhouse in silence.

'I'm sorry,' he said gruffly. 'I shouldn't have given in to—I'm sorry.'

'It wasn't—I shouldn't have either.'

He winced. 'I wish you hadn't said that.'

As did she. She wished she had not given in. She wished she had given in further. Jessica opened the door of the Blackhouse and stepped inside, away from temptation and madness. 'Goodnight, Murdo.'

'The weather's on the turn,' he said, staring out at the sea. 'If you want to leave…'

'I don't want to leave.'

He studied her for a long moment, then nodded. 'Then it's time we talked properly. I'll see you in the morning.'

Chapter Seven

Jessica awoke heavy-headed. Touching her fingers to her mouth, she wondered if she had dreamt that kiss? The hem of her nightgown, splashed with mud, confirmed that she had not, and the flutter in her belly at the memory of Murdo's touch, the softness of his lips, the tickle of his beard, the unmistakable blaze of desire in his eyes, made it impossible for her to deny that she had wanted it every bit as much as he had. Oh, how much she had wanted it, and how much more she had longed for. But oh, how very wrong it was! Her toes curled in mortification as she recalled how forward she had been, how much encouragement she had given him. If only it had been a dream.

It should not have happened, she told herself firmly, leaping out of bed. That was the first and only time, and it was done and dusted. Time for her to concentrate on what she was here for, and not go dreaming about something that could lose her the work, her reputation, her career. For heaven's sake, had she not learned her lesson?

The water in the kettle, which hung permanently over the fire from a hook, was hot enough for her to make a pot of tea. While she waited on it brewing, Jessica opened the door to see what form of rain was currently falling. The Hebridean spring rain took many forms, she had discovered over the last week. There was the driving rain that raced in on a squall from the Atlantic, a drenching from a hitherto blue sky, huge droplets from a small cloud that settled directly overhead and disgorged its contents especially and entirely on Taravay. Then there was the mist, a soft, grey wispiness that crept stealthily in, wrapping the landscape in a cloak. It made her feel as if she was on an island floating in the clouds, but the rain which accompanied it soaked through her clothes and into her bones by subterfuge. Then again there was the rain that fell like it was falling from a multitude of taps, drip, drip, dripping, with the constant promise of being just about to turn itself off, but never actually doing so. This morning, astonishingly, though the ground was saturated, there was no rain actually falling. A silvery light turned the sea to pewter, and the sun, shining in a watery, diluted way, was making steam rise from the ground.

It was still early. Jessica dressed quickly and took her tea with her to the walled garden. She had established a base in the potting area of the glasshouse, which was constructed against the northern wall, and therefore faced directly south. It was in surprisingly good condition, the wrought-iron framework in need of a lick of paint but barely corroded, and though a number of glass panes were cracked, only a few were entirely broken. Inside, the beds were a tangle of dead plants and voracious weeds, and most of the large pots contained only dust and mould, but Jessica had uncovered a small, resilient collection of succulents protected from the weather by dead foliage.

She sat down at her make-do desk and sipped her tea, gazing up at the Castle, which lowered over the walled garden. What on earth had Murdo been doing, wandering about in there at night? Ghost-hunting, by the look of him, and from the look on his face, he'd been successful. He had tacitly admitted that he'd been avoiding her, but he had not really said why. Waiting for the storm to pass, was his explanation. Did he mean the weather, or was it the turmoil inside him? Yes, if those dark shadows under his eyes were anything to go by. What was it that kept him awake? If those on Ness, who already thought him strange, knew just how oddly he behaved…

But then, what would they say about her own behaviour? She had known perfectly well, when she saw the lights in the Castle that it could only be Murdo, though she'd told herself it might be a ghost or a stranger.

She'd known it was him, and she'd sought him out in the middle of the night in a storm. It was the fright, they'd both had, they'd agreed, that had made them kiss, but she hadn't been frightened—or at least not of him. She'd been drawn to him. She'd thrown herself at him. God help her, she'd throw herself at him again, given the opportunity.

No! A thousand times no! This was not like her at all. Had Murdo's tortured soul somehow infected her, made her act completely out of character? She'd never been so forward. She'd never had such vivid, lurid daydreams about Edward, and she'd certainly never felt that torrent of passion when they made love. It had been very enjoyable, like a warm summer's day, like a bowl of sweet strawberries, but she had never lost control, any more than he had. In comparison, she wanted to bury herself in Murdo's skin, to lose herself in him, to…

Her cheeks burning, she set down her empty mug. This was all a product of her imagination, with no grounding in reality whatsoever. They hadn't even kissed properly. Perhaps it was the oppressive weather. Or the fact that she had been almost completely alone here for a week. Or it could be that the blatant blaze of desire that she'd seen in Murdo's eyes had lit a fire inside her? No, she couldn't blame him. The fire had been smouldering since she'd first set eyes on him. She had to find a way to extinguish it. Such as remembering what it was she was here to do.

Today the weather had changed. The storm had finally passed. It was a new day. Time for a fresh start. Time to have a proper conversation with Murdo about what he wanted to do with Taravay. Time to remember that he was her employer and nothing more.

Murdo had made no attempt to sleep when he returned to his leaky croft. Last night had been the kick in the guts he'd needed, even if it had also been a taste of what he knew was forbidden. Jessica. It was the thought of what might have been that had kept him wide awake, the memory of the taste of her which had been too fleeting, of the way she responded to him, the passion in her eyes that he was sure he'd not mistaken. Jessica's eyes were not blue, they were dark brown, set in a very different face from Emily's heart-shaped countenance. Jessica could never be described as beautiful, as Emily invariably was, but he desired her in a way that he could not recall wanting Emily. He had cherished Emily, tended to her needs, taken gentle care of her. His desire for Jessica was raw, urgent, flaming. And Jessica wanted him the same way. That was what made it so difficult for him to put all thoughts of her from his mind. She had wanted him, in that moment in the portico of the Castle, as much as he wanted her. If only she didn't want him. If only she'd rejected him. If only she'd been a bloody *Cailleach*. Why the devil, after all this time, did the one person he needed to help him realise his dream, have to be the one person he wanted to—no, he would not start again with imagining what it was he wanted to do with her.

It wasn't real. It was an aberration. It was the storm. It was the shock they'd both got when she appeared at the door. That's what they'd agreed, so that was the story he'd stick to. It didn't matter, in the end, what the hell it had been, what mattered was that it must not, could not, would not happen again. A curse on Jessica Smith for being desirable. A curse on her for stirring him up, for heating his blood, for making it so difficult to think of her as his landscaper. Because that's what she was. That was why he'd brought her here, and it was time he got his head out of his own backside and got on with it. Time he stopped indulging himself with his dreams and his doubts. Enough with the woe-is-me attitude that consumed him in the months after he left London. High time he was done with that, once and for all. There was important work to be done.

But first, there was a story that had to be told. As the dawn filtered in to banish the night, Murdo faced up to the task in hand. If Jessica was to understand his vision for Taravay, she must first understand the tragic history that lay behind it.

The weather, as he had predicted, was on the turn.

The rain had finally abated, and the sun was making a valiant appearance. Murdo took it as a sign. Sick with dread but resolute, he stared at his face in the small mirror over the washstand for the first time in many weeks. What he saw appalled him. His hair was too long, his beard was straggly, there was a fretwork of lines around his eyes, and he looked as if he had not slept for weeks—or if he had, it had been in a hedge. How on earth had Jessica brought herself to let him near her, never mind kiss him? It had been dark, mind, but all the same.

Murdo filled the bowl with hot water, dug out a pair of scissors, and set about trying to civilise his appearance. An hour later, wearing a damp but clean set of clothes, he made for the walled garden.

Jessica was in the potting shed, but when she saw him, she came out to greet him. She was dressed in a plain brown gown, bare-headed, her inky-black hair caught up on top of her head, from which the wind was already tugging tendrils loose. 'Oh,' she exclaimed, stopping in her tracks in front of him. 'You look very— very different.'

'Aye well, it was overdue. You needn't think I've ti-died myself up on your account.'

She coloured. 'I'm sorry, I didn't mean to be rude.'

Murdo sighed, irked at himself for his flash of temper. Not the best start. '*Madainn mhath* to you.'

'*Mateen va?* Good morning?' She smiled warily at

him. 'You were right about the weather. After all the rain we've had, it looks like it might just turn into a beautiful day.'

'At the moment, maybe, but you know what they say: if you don't like the weather in Scotland, just wait five minutes.'

'I've never heard that, but I know exactly what you mean,' Jessica said. 'Sometimes it seems there are four seasons in the space of four hours on Taravay.'

'*Latha na Seachd Sian—gaoth is uisge, cuir, is cathadh, tarnanaich is dealanaich is clachn meallain.* That means something like, a typical day has seven different storms—wind and rain, snowfall and blizzard, thunder, lightning and hailstorms.'

'We've certainly had all of that and more.'

'Jessica…'

'Murdo…'

'Go on,' he said.

'Last night, I don't know what came over me, I…'

'Ach, no.' He waved her words away. 'We agreed it was…' The excuse they had snatched at momentarily deserted him as he stood beside her now. Her cheeks were flushed. She was gazing down at her boots, digging at a loose bit of paving with her toe. 'It was my fault. I gave you a fright. I'd forgotten you had a view of the Castle from the Mackinnon place.'

She glanced up at that. 'I'll know now not to disturb you.'

And that was that, he told himself, done and dusted. It was contrary of him to want her instead to tell him it wasn't only down to him, but it didn't matter because it wouldn't happen again. 'Right then,' Murdo said.

'Good,' she agreed, though what to, he had no clue. Abandoning the stone, she looked up. 'Could you—do you think—Murdo, I really need to understand more of what it is you want from Taravay before I can make any real progress.'

'I know that, but before we talk about it, there's something else you need to know, to put it in context, so to speak.'

Her eyes widened. 'You mean, what happened here?'

'So Catriona Macfarlane didn't tell you?'

'I asked her, but she said it wasn't her story to tell.'

He eyed her in disbelief. 'I'm surprised, for they call her Catriona the Foghorn.'

'Oh no, that is unkind. I promise you, Murdo, she would not be drawn. I know nothing other than what you told me, that the island was abandoned eighteen months ago when your—when the Laird died.'

He'd forgotten he'd led her to believe that. He wished now, that he'd taken the opportunity to disabuse her of the assumption, but she'd been a stranger then. Now—though it had only been a week—but time passed on an island, he'd learned, in a very different way. 'You misunderstood me,' Murdo said, prevaricating. 'When

I came back for the funeral, Taravay was already abandoned.'

'I must admit I've been wondering about that,' she said warily. 'What little I've seen of the island—to be honest, not much more than the Castle gardens—it does seem to me that it's been left to be reclaimed by nature for more than a couple of years.'

A cloud scudded over the sun, casting a dark shadow over the garden and the pair of them. Murdo glanced up at the sky. The cloud had passed, but there were more on the horizon. 'Come on,' he said, 'before the weather catches up with us. I can show you what happened, then maybe you'll understand better what we're up against.'

Chapter Eight

Jessica expected him to lead the way to the Castle, but instead, Murdo took the path that led them towards the Atlantic coast. He had cut his hair and made a very poor job of it, for it sat jagged on his brow. His beard too was cut short but unevenly. Was it a coincidence that he'd made an effort after last night, or was it because, like her, he saw today as a fresh start?

'You can see the Butt of Lewis from here, and the lighthouse,' he said, stopping to point.

The sky was cloudless for the first time since she had arrived. The sea, rolling into a sandy bay below the cliffs, was an astonishingly clear turquoise close in to the shore with the darker patches of seaweed showing clearly, turning a deep blue and then almost black further out, with only a few white horses whipped up by the breeze. 'Look at this,' Jessica said, suddenly exhilarated, spreading her arms wide. 'I have never seen anything like this view, not ever. It's utterly enchanting. On the one hand, you feel a sort of superiority because here you are on Taravay, and there is the Isle of Lewis, so close yet so far. And on the other side is the Atlantic, and nothing of significance between us and America. My goodness, you feel as if you're on the edge of the world, so insignificant and yet so privileged. When you see it on the map, you simply can't imagine *this*.'

'It's the contrast you're enjoying,' Murdo replied dourly. 'The last week we've had, has made this one day—which might not last—seem perfect in comparison. Stay for a winter, and you might change your mind. Shall we get on?'

He strode off, his face set, forcing her to follow. She castigated herself once more for speaking without thinking. The weather had changed, but Murdo's mood seemed not to have lifted with it. Hurrying to catch up, she was grateful for her boots as the ground became boggy, with tussocks of grass and heather bordering a small lochan.

'This is where the water supply comes from,' Murdo said, allowing her to pause for breath. 'You will see the original pump when we get closer to the village. It's one of the few innovations the Laird allowed, having water piped to the Castle and to the pump at your croft. It doesn't extend to Taravay Beag, where I am living. That's one of the tasks on my list.'

'Taravay Big? isn't that the smaller part of the island?'

'*Beag*,' Murdo repeated, spelling it out for her. 'Pronounced *bick*. It means small, though now you say it, I suppose it could be confusing as it sounds a bit like big.'

His choice of abode struck her once again as odd. He was forswearing even the most basic of amenities to be as far away from the Castle as possible, and yet he was drawn there every night. As they passed the lochan, the main settlement came into view, making her stop in her tracks and forget all about Murdo's accommodation. It was a melancholy sight, a cluster of Blackhouses, some without roofs, the outlines of the cultivated land facing out to the Atlantic all but obscured.

'The machair here has the richest soil on Taravay,' Murdo said, 'thanks to decades of being fertilised with seaweed.'

'But it's so exposed. What did they grow?'

'Kale. Potatoes. Neeps. Oats. Barley.'

Jessica could see almost no signs of cultivation. The land had not been farmed in a long time. 'The people who lived in these crofts,' she asked, 'do you know who they were?'

'Nicolson,' Murdo replied, pointing to one croft. 'Morrison,' he said, pointing to the one beside it. 'Murray.'

Finlay Murray was his childhood friend, she knew. Had he lived on Taravay? One look at Murdo's face and Jessica decided to keep silent. Instead, she pushed open the door and stepped into the Blackhouse, which was the most intact in the village. The roof had held, though she could see daylight peeking in through the bracken. The layout was familiar, the same main room with a partition wall separating the animals' quarters from the crofters. There was a rusted bedstead in one corner of the main room, a rotting dresser set against a wall, two chairs facing each other, a large, rusting pot where the fire once was. In the Nicolson Blackhouse, she found similar remnants in a more advanced state of decay, with the addition of a spinning wheel at the window. In the next, beside the bedstead a child's cradle. There was a weaving shed, complete with a loom. There was a schoolhouse with a huddle of small desks. There was something that looked like a large garden shed, with a table and chairs, and what looked very like an old still. There were creels stacked against the wall of one Blackhouse. Against another, there was a rustic plough.

Deeply saddened by the scene, Jessica joined Murdo, who was standing by the millpond. 'It's as if they were spirited away,' she said, shuddering. 'Was there a plague?'

'Not a plague. A Clearance. Do you understand what that means?'

'I've heard—I remember my father telling of some labourers he employed, who had been forced off their land in Sutherland to make way for grazing for sheep.

The common land was fenced in, a factor installed to make sure they did not go back. I remember my father telling me that those who protested were thrown in jail.'

'And others burned out of their houses when they refused to leave.'

Horrified, Jessica gazed around her. 'Surely that didn't happen here? It doesn't make sense, there are hardly any sheep on the island. In fact there's no one, not even a factor. Why would the Laird Clear Taravay, and then simply let if fall into rack and ruin?'

'It's a question I'm sure that the islanders all asked themselves at the time, and doubtless to this day.'

'Is there an answer? Was your father—the Laird in sound mind?'

'As sound as he ever was, I reckon.'

'Then why...'

'It's *what* happened, not *why* that matters,' he snapped.

'Why don't we sit down and you can tell me,' Jessica said carefully, leading the way to an old stone bench that faced onto the millpond, before sitting down beside him. 'Take your time.'

Murdo laughed bitterly. 'I've had this—what happened here—I've had it constantly running through my head, for over a year. You'd think after all this time I'd have the words ready.'

'If you'd rather wait...'

'No!' His hands formed fists on his lap. 'You need to know what happened here. How can you do your job, if you don't know what it is you're trying to fix? What I'm trying to fix.'

His throat was working compulsively as he stared out at the millpond. Jessica waited, almost afraid to breathe, wondering if he would, despite what he said, simply get up and walk away. He did get up, pacing over to the pond, but he came straight back to sit heavily back down beside her. 'There's generations of memories tied up in this place. It's full of ghosts. I see them every time I come here. The people who lived and worked those crofts, when I was wee I knew them all. I was part of it all.'

He was staring around him, as if he could indeed see the ghosts of the past, his hands tightly clasped together on his lap. Jessica sat silent, terrified to say or do the wrong thing, trying to keep her feelings from showing on her face. He would not welcome pity. He would not want sympathy. What he needed was an impassive listener, as all that he had bottled up was bitterly disgorged for the first time.

'Sitting right here,' he continued, 'I can hear the steady thudding of the mill-wheel turning. I can see old Etta Morrison sitting at her spinning wheel outside the front door of her cottage. She had a huge black cat, a vicious thing, but that cat loved Etta. He used to sit at her feet while she worked, drawing everyone such a malevolent look as they passed, ready to dig his claws in if you came too near. Her daughter dyed the wool she spun. She used all sorts to make the dyes, moss I remember, and seaweed, which she had us gather for her.'

He paused, staring blankly ahead, and when he resumed, his voice was not much more than a whisper. 'I dream of them packing up. I can see it clear as day, as if I'd been here myself when it happened. The misery of trying to decide what little you could take from a lifetime of belongings. Walking around the island to favourite spots. Making their farewells to their kin in the kirkyard.

'I see them sobbing, the women, and the men hard-faced, trying to be practical, trying not to show what they were feeling. The bairns crying. The animals— they'd have swum the cows over to Ness, but the chickens and the sheep were left to roam wild. What about the dogs? Did Etta take her cat?

'And at night.' Murdo continued, shuddering, 'at night it's the worst. I can hear the curses they left behind, howling in the wind. I can hear the wailing as they set sail for the last time from here. Generations have lived and died on Taravay, and all of it is gone.'

He rubbed his eyes with his knuckles. 'When I came back, I couldn't believe my eyes. I'd had no word, nothing at all to warn me. The shock of it just about made me keel over.'

Jessica's heart ached at the tortured look on his face, at the pain in his eyes, the unshed tears on his lashes. She put her arms around him, meaning to draw him into a comforting embrace.

'No!' With a harsh cry, he pushed her roughly away, jumping to his feet.

Mortified, Jessica cowered back on the bench. 'I wanted to comfort you, that's all.'

'I don't need comforting. It's not me that bore the brunt of the Laird's cruel and heartless decision.'

'But you did suffer, when you saw the consequences. I cannot imagine how you felt.'

'I'm not asking you to. I don't know why I got so upset, I've had eighteen months to come to terms with it.' Murdo took several deep breaths. 'What happened cannot be laid at my door, no matter what people may think, but it's my responsibility now to find a way forward, to make recompense for the crime that was committed, and that's why you're here.'

Last night in the Castle, she had seen a man haunted by the past, and now she understood why. He was so obviously still fighting for control, Jessica forced herself to remain silent, having proved conclusively that sympathy of any sort would not be welcome.

'What I can't do,' Murdo continued, 'what I won't do—is try to turn the clock back, no matter how much people might want me to. That's something you need to understand. I can't un-Clear the island. I've wasted too much time, these last eighteen months, railing against things I can do nothing about. What's the point in beating yourself up, going over and over what might have been, when something is done and dusted? All that does is rub salt in the wound.'

Was he still talking about the village? She had the distinct impression he was referring to something else. 'Whatever happened here,' Jessica said tentatively, 'whatever the Laird's reason for forcing people to leave, it wasn't your fault. You said so yourself.'

He whirled around at that, his colour high. '*It's not your fault!*' he snarled. 'Have you any idea how sick I got of hearing those words? Aye, maybe it was not, but it was my heart that was broken all the same.'

'Murdo!' Jessica jumped up, but his glare halted her in her tracks. 'I don't know who you're referring to, but they were right, whoever they were. What happened here…'

'What happened *here*?' He blinked, gazing about him. 'Forget it. My head's all over the place. Maybe what happened here was not my fault either, but it's still my problem to solve.'

'I'm sorry, I have no idea…'

He held up his hand. 'It's simple enough. It happened, it's over, and it needs fixing, same as before. That's why I brought you here. To help, not to question. Do you understand?'

She didn't understand at all, but the warning was

clear enough. 'Completely.' Jessica's legs shook as she sank back down on the bench, her mind in a turmoil. What was going on in Murdo's head? Was he a little mad, after all? She resolved to say nothing more, terrified that his next act would be to bundle her onto the boat and sail her back to Lewis. Or perhaps he'd make her swim, like the cattle.

'What?' he snapped, as the silence stretched, catching her unawares.

A wave of frustrated anger saved Jessica from tears. She folded her arms and glared back at him. 'I want nothing more than to help you, but I'm at a loss as to how I may do so when you forbid me from asking questions.'

Murdo exhaled impatiently. 'You know fine I don't mean those sort of questions. Ask away.'

'Very well then. When did the Laird Clear the land? Where are the people who once lived here? Do you expect them to come back?'

'No, I don't expect that many of them will return.' He dug his hand into his coat pocket and handed her a piece of paper. 'This is where most of them are.'

'The Celt, *sailing from Stornoway August 1870, to join* The Hercules *in Campbeltown, for onward passage to Canada,*' Jessica read. '*Passenger Manifest for Taravay islanders on board.*'

Chapter Nine

Jessica's initial ideas, lists, and sketches were spread out before her, but after yesterday's revelations, despite the fact that Murdo had still not given her any more details on his plans for Taravay, she instinctively knew they were wrong. The rain had come hurtling in from the Atlantic as they sat by the millpond, and he had seemed relieved to have the excuse to cut short his confessions.

Gazing out at the walled garden, with the rain continuing to teem down the panes, the sky showing a blanket of grey, Jessica wondered where he was and what he was doing. It was not lights in the Castle that had kept her awake last night, it was her mind, churning over and over the story of Taravay that he had recounted, her heart aching for the suffering of the islanders which he had so vividly brought to life. Whole families forcibly banished to Canada to begin life anew, leaving behind everything they held dear. The Laird paid for their passage, Murdo had discovered from the Castle's account books and had given each family money to help them settle when they arrived. A small number too old or disinclined to face the journey had gone to live with relatives on Lewis or Harris, or perhaps made a new life in Glasgow. Only the Laird and Norman Mackinnon had remained on Taravay.

Despite his adamant assertion that he needed no sympathy, her heart ached for Murdo. Tears burned Jessica's eyes as she recalled his pain, his anger, his sorrow. A tormented soul, indeed. Why hadn't anyone warned him? He and his father were estranged, and Catriona Macfarlane had implied that no one in Port of Ness knew anything of his life away from Taravay, but someone must have got in touch with him when the Laird died.

It was infuriating to know so much and so little. Jessica picked up an old cracked pot and threw it onto the floor of the shed where, annoyingly, it refused to break and instead rolled under her chair. She knew she should be focusing on Taravay, but Taravay's owner refused to be ostracised from her mind. She was certain, when he'd been muttering about beating himself up and railing against what he couldn't change, that he was thinking of something very different from the village. And then when she'd pointed out that it wasn't his fault, he'd exploded.

It was my heart that was broken all the same, he'd said, and with such a look, her own heart had felt as if it was contracting. Such pain, such suffering etched on his face, and then wiped away with such force. *It happened, it's over, and it needs fixing, same as before.* What on earth was he referring to? Was he, like her, recovering from a doomed love affair?

Murdo's heart was none of her business. Burning with shame, Jessica recalled that moment yesterday when she had reached to comfort him, only to be flung away in horror. He was her employer, for goodness sake, and Taravay, the island which he owned, was her route to redemption. Had the debacle with Edward taught her nothing?

Murdo was nothing like Edward. Murdo was like a volcano, a bubbling pit of emotions that seethed under the surface until they erupted, only to be tamped down once more, allowing him to present his granite-like self to her. He suffered for others, but would not give credence to his own feelings. The Laird, his own father, had Cleared Murdo's much-loved Taravay of its heart and soul, and part of that heart and soul was Murdo. He too, for reasons that he had kept firmly to himself, had been Cleared. He fought a constant battle between excoriating himself and blazing a path towards retribution. It was compelling to witness in all its crude visceral energy. No wonder that being anywhere near him set her alight. Not the gentle love she had for Edward, but raw desire. Nothing to do with her heart, and everything to do with the needs of her body? She missed being held, she missed being touched, she would probably be feeling the same were she living alone on Taravay with any attractive man.

Unconvinced, but willing to persuade herself, Jessica tried once again to put Murdo from her mind. Outside the rain had gone off, and the sun's rays were warming the glasshouse. She breathed in the smell of damp soil, imagining the verdant growth which she would cultivate here. She pulled her drawings towards her, but was once again struck by how wrong, how small-minded in fact, they seemed. If she was to help Murdo put the heart back into Taravay, she needed to understand the island more completely.

As if she had conjured a guide, the man himself appeared at the entrance to the garden and came striding towards her. She had time to tell herself to ignore the flutter in her belly, to remind herself once again that he was her employer, before he reached the glasshouse.

'Grahame Macfarlane came over with supplies,' he said by way of greeting. 'I've left some provisions in your croft. Are these your initial ideas? Can I have a look?'

He picked up her notebook, and she tried to grab it from him. Their hands touched. He dropped the notebook back on the desk, as if he had been scalded, and took a step back from her. 'Why are they so secret?'

'They're not.' Hurt and embarrassed by his obvious terror that she might be planning another assault on him, she averted her gaze. 'It's only that after what you told me yesterday, I realise that I was thinking on far too small a scale, concentrating solely on the gardens. I need to understand more about the people who will live here in the future. I'm assuming that some of them will be crofters?'

'I've looked at the accounts for Taravay over the last few decades. Life was tough, and likely to get tougher for those living off their land. I won't say it again, whatever the future holds for Taravay, I won't be trying to turn the clock back. There will be some limited crofting, of course, but there will have to be other ways too, for people to make a living.'

'What people, Murdo? Are you thinking of the relatives of those who left?'

'If they'll come.'

'Have you asked anyone?'

'I want to have a lot more detail before I talk to anyone. I need to convince myself that what I'm proposing will work before I start trying to convince anyone else. I need to put meat on the bones of my idea, and that's where you come in. I don't want people to ask me questions I can't answer. How would that look?' Murdo picked up one of the succulents which she had repotted. 'Where did you find this?'

'In the glasshouse. There was a little cluster of them. Look, just in the last few days, there's a flower forming on the stem just there.' She looked up, took a step towards him to point, and Murdo jumped back. Flushing, she placed her desk between them. 'There's more over on the shelf there, if you're interested.'

He set the pot back down and retired to lean against the door-frame, and despite all her resolve, Jessica felt her temper flare. 'It is my experience,' she said, 'that radical change is more successful when those who are affected by it are involved from the start. If you consult the people you hope will live here, or indeed, the relatives of those who once did, then they will be much more positive about the whole endeavour, and you will also benefit from their experience.'

'Well it's my experience that the relatives of those who once lived here won't be at all inclined to discuss anything with me.'

'How can you say that, when you haven't even tried?'

'Said who? Ah wait, let me guess, Catriona the Foghorn. So I'm to be guided by her now, am I?'

'That's not what I meant. You've been away from Taravay for a long time, Murdo...'

'I was born and raised here.'

'Yes, and you love the place and you want the best for it, I know, but...' Jessica sighed in exasperation, sitting back down at her desk. 'At present no one even knows that you've got plans of any sort. You can't impose a new Taravay on them. Can't you see that doing so could make you seem exactly like the old-fashioned Laird you're determined not to be?'

'How dare you! I'm nothing like the Laird.'

'*I* know that, but they don't.' Jessica drew a few short breaths, striving for calm. 'Who do you think is going to carry out all the work that needs done? Don't you think they'll make a better fist of it if they agree with what you're trying to do?'

'And if they do not? What if they're as tied to the old ways as the Laird was? That way the island will fail, a second Clearance by stealth, if you like, and this time it would be my fault. I can't and won't let that happen.'

'I do understand that,' Jessica said, only half convinced, 'but you brought me here to help you, and I'm almost as much in the dark about your ambitions for this island than the knees—niss—neesas—people from Ness.'

'Niseachs.'

'Niseachs!'

'I brought you here to implement my ideas, not to question my methods.'

'I'm simply trying to give you the benefit of my experience, but if you don't want it, then fine! You tell me what it is you do want from me, and I'll do it.' Jessica made to push past him, and he leapt out of her way. 'And for your information, I am not contagious.'

'You've bloody well infected me.'

She stopped in her tracks, tears welling up and

spilling down her cheeks before she could stop them. 'Please don't say that. I don't mean to overstep the mark. Yesterday, I promise you I only meant to comfort you.'

'Overstep the mark! Ah no, Jessica, don't cry. It's not you, it's me. I tell myself every day to stop thinking about you in that way, and then I look at you…' Murdo shook his head, fumbling in his pocket and handing her a clean, if wrinkled handkerchief.

'Thank you.'

'I didn't mean to upset you.'

She dabbed frantically at her face. 'I am trying to do what you brought me here for, but when I ask you questions, you bite my head off. I've been on Taravay for over a week now, and I'm making next to no progress. I know, the weather hasn't helped, but…'

'Nor have I?'

'Frankly no. We have to find a way to work together.' She steeled herself to meet his gaze. 'If we can knuckle down and get on with the task in hand then this—this—then we won't have time for any other distractions.'

He nodded slowly. 'Two of us alone here. I knew it was a mistake.'

'No, Murdo! No, it's not a mistake. I promise you, I'll prove it to you. I won't—I'll keep my distance.'

'Ach, don't.' He caught her hands in his. 'I can't have you taking the blame. Yesterday, as you say, all you wanted to do was to comfort me. And as for that night in the Castle…'

His voice trailed off, for it was there again, a crackling tension that was almost tangible. She heard his sharp intake of breath. Her heart started hammering. Their fingers tightened together. Slowly, as if mesmerised, he bent his head towards hers. She lifted her face. Their lips hovered, then met. She couldn't breathe. Their hands remained locked together, their eyes locked together as they kissed. A soft, gentle kiss, so unexpected, so entirely at odds with the temperamental man, yet there was nothing soft or gentle about her response. Heat flared inside her. A cloud of butterflies took to flight in her belly. The distance between them closed, bodies pressed together, their hands between them.

Then something distracted them. They blinked. She stepped back. He shook his head, looking dazed.

'Work,' he said. 'You're right, that's what we need to focus on. Come on, we'll go to the Castle.'

Chapter Ten

Work, Jessica said to herself as Murdo turned a huge key in the lock of the Castle's front door and led the way into a large gloomy hall. Work, she reminded herself as she followed him, work was what she had to concentrate on. It smelled of damp and mouse droppings. Above the fireplace, a huge shield with a coat of arms was surrounded by some vicious-looking weapons.

'Legend has it that they were used in Culloden,' Murdo informed her. 'The Macleods of Taravay fought for the Stuart cause—that's Bonnie Prince Charlie, as history now knows him. The names of the men who died are written in the family bible.'

'The bible must be very old,' Jessica said, aware her voice sounded forced, for her body was still tingling from the surprisingly gentle kiss they had shared.

Murdo was either better at disguising his feelings or better at dismissing them. 'It is. Funny, I don't recall seeing it anywhere here, I'll need to look out for it. The Laird was laid out here.'

'What are these?'

'Trestles, for the coffin to rest on, before the walk to the kirk. The place hasn't been touched since that day.'

All of the furnishings were pushed against the walls, to make room for the mourners, Jessica surmised. On top of a carved chest, neatly folded, was a tartan blanket. She picked it up, and moths fluttered.

'The Macleod plaid,' Murdo said, eyeing it askance. 'It was draped over the coffin.'

Carefully, horrified, she set it down. There was rustling from behind the walls.

'Mice,' Murdo said. 'There's probably bats too, and birds nesting. Flesh and blood creatures, not ghosts, don't worry.'

The air was still, fusty, damp, lit only by the misty daylight creeping through the door. She could see the trail of Murdo's footsteps to the door on her right and up the central staircase. Despite his assurance, Jessica half expected the ghost of the old Laird to appear. 'Was he living quite alone here?'

'More or less. Norman Mackinnon died two or three years before he did. Kirsty Mhor, who is Catriona Macfarlane's aunt, kept house for the Laird until it was too much for her, and then between them, Catriona and her husband kept an eye on him. Catriona was with him when he died, and it was she who organised the wake.'

'Did you know, Murdo? That he was ill, I mean?'

'Why wasn't I here, is what you really mean, isn't it?' he responded harshly. 'Because he didn't want me, is the simple answer.'

'Oh no! I'm so sorry.'

He swore viciously. 'How many times do I have to tell you that I don't want your pity? My family were not like yours—from what you've told me, they couldn't be more different. My mother died when I was a child, and she was never much interested in me anyway. As to the Laird—ach, I was never the son he wanted. After I left, I wrote once a year every year, but he sent each letter back unopened. *Come back or stay away*, he wrote on them. Same words, every year. He knew where to find me, but he chose not to. I heard of his death from his lawyer. The telegram arrived the very same week that I…'

He bit back whatever he was about to say. Jessica waited on tenterhooks, but Murdo seemed lost in the past, and she knew better now than to interrupt his reverie. After a moment, he picked up the Macleod plaid. 'So to answer your question, no, I did not know he was dying. As it turns out, the timing could not have been better, though if he'd known that, he'd doubtless have held on another year or so just to spite me. As it was, they had to postpone the funeral until I arrived, which did me no favours in everyone's eyes. I don't know why we're talking about this, it's quite irrelevant.'

* * *

What was it about Jessica? Murdo asked himself. Why was it that he found himself blurting out things he'd not meant to say, things he didn't even know he was thinking? And why did her opinions matter so much? He glowered over at her, as she stood beneath the portrait of the Laird in his full Highland regalia. The future was what mattered, but every time he reminded her of that fact, she managed to drag him back to the past.

He remembered it as if it was yesterday, that telegram from the lawyer arriving to tell him that Laird Angus Murdo Macleod had breathed his last. That very same day, he'd spent the morning with his own lawyer, still reeling from Emily's news. It had almost knocked the stuffing out of him, the end of two eras in the space of a few days, but at least it had given him the impetus to get the first sorted, so he could deal with the second, a mad flurry of activity that took his mind off the pain, as he set about dismantling his life, acutely aware of the clock ticking towards the date of the funeral. In the end, they'd had to put it off for a day. Another black mark against him, as Finlay sailed him, silently condemning, across from Ness, and he without a clue why, unaware of what awaited him on Taravay.

'What?' he growled, suddenly realising that Jessica was looking at him enquiringly. How long had he been silent?

'Nothing,' she said, flinching at his tone.

He knew he was being unfair. He kept forgetting that she was an employee and worried about keeping her job, as if there was any chance of him dismissing her. He really should reassure her once and for all. Why was it such a struggle to resist her? If only it wasn't obvious that she too was struggling, then he'd easily put an end to wanting her.

'The Laird must have been about your age when this portrait was painted.' Jessica's voice once again roused him from his thoughts. 'Is it a good likeness?'

Murdo reluctantly joined her to look up at the painting. 'He had this done when he married my mother.'

'Is there a companion piece?'

'One of my mother, you mean? I've never seen it, if it exists.'

'He married late, then? Is that usual here in the Hebrides?'

'He was married before. His first wife died young, about ten years before he married my mother, I think. There was a child, but it died at birth, unfortunately. His marriage to my mother was almost certainly for the sole purpose of getting an heir.' Murdo gazed up at the stern face, the shaggy brows, the aquiline nose and thin lips of the Laird. 'It's a very good likeness.'

'You must take after your mother, then.'

'One of the many things the Laird held against me, if that's true.' Abruptly aware that once again Jessica had managed to direct the conversation to the past, Murdo turned on his heel. 'Come on, I'll show you the main rooms of the Castle. I've in mind to have it serve as a hotel.'

He led the way briskly, with Jessica trailing behind him. Through the doors to the parlour, across the room, dodging the tables and chairs strewn in his way, to the shutters that were locked over the long window. They opened, creaking and protesting as he folded them back, flooding the east-facing room with light, and showing it up in its shabby, perfectly preserved entirety. 'This was my mother's room,' he said. 'The Laird never used it after she died, but I liked to read here, over on that window seat.'

He hurried on, reminding himself that there was no need to share his memories. 'The dining room, obviously, though it hasn't been used in decades. The Laird ate in his study, I'm told.' Which he had no intentions of showing Jessica. Up the stairs he rushed. 'Principal bedrooms,' he said, without stopping, and up again, past the second floor, waving vaguely at the corridor. 'More bedrooms.' On the third floor he paused, straining to hear himself, peering into the gloom for a sense of that unhappy, rebellious child he had been. Nothing. 'Servant's quarters,' he said, which was mostly true.

At the end of this corridor was the door to the turret. Murdo opened it, bidding Jessica to wait until he climbed, finding his way easily despite the dark, up the worn, spiral staircase to push open the door at the top and let in the light, before calling her up. 'There,' he said, when she arrived, 'this is the best view of the island.'

The sun was filtering through the soft grey clouds. Murdo leaned on the parapet, drinking in the sheer wild beauty of it all: the Atlantic Ocean, navy blue and glittering in the sunlight that streamed through a gap in the clouds; the narrow causeway leading to Tara-vay Beag, the sands dazzling white and gold on either side. The ruined village, the old mill, the tumbledown Blackhouses, the runrigs clearer from here, where the crops had been tilled.

'It's utterly stunning.' Jessica, standing beside him, was gazing out, looking rapt. 'If this was mine, I'd never want to leave.'

'I thought the exact same thing as a bairn. Standing right here, I used to think I was at the centre of the universe. When I went off to school in Edinburgh, I learned different. I loved Edinburgh, it was a revelation to me. None of the other boys at school had even heard of Taravay. For the first time, I realised there was a whole world out there that I knew nothing about. I wanted to explore it, and so I did, though I had to brave the Laird's wrath for doing so.'

'Taravay is your home. You love the island, you would always have come back to it eventually,' Jessica said.

'You've known me less than two weeks, and you understand that about me. If he'd have given me free rein of course I'd have come back, but he didn't understand that, or any other aspect of me. I wanted to go to university after I finished school, I wanted to study mathematics, but he wouldn't fund me, and I had no money of my own. He thought that was an end of it, but at eighteen, I wanted to spread my wings. I told him, "I'm a Macleod of Taravay, we set our own path". I used his own words against him, thinking I was being smart, thinking he'd be persuaded. He told me not to come home until I was ready to follow *his* path.'

'He should have been proud of your wanting to make your own way in life,' Jessica said. 'He *must* surely have been proud of your success.'

'When I made my first fortune, I sent him a bank draft for five hundred pounds. He sent it back to me, that's how proud of me he was.'

'Perhaps, he was too proud to take it. You said yourself, people here found it difficult to make a living, which means the income from the island can't have been substantial.'

'For the good of the island, he should have—though maybe you're right,' Murdo said, struck. 'I should have thought of that.'

'You wanted to impress him. You did nothing wrong.'

'Well, he wasn't impressed.'

'He probably was, Murdo.'

She was standing right beside him. Somehow, without either of them meaning to, their arms were touching as they leaned on the parapet. Somehow, without either of them meaning to, her skirts were tangled against his leg. Somehow, without either of them meaning to, their eyes met and locked.

'Men like the Laird,' she said, 'they don't give out praise easily, they think it's a sign of weakness.'

He opened his mouth to tell her she was wrong, but said instead, 'Do you think so?'

'It's likely.'

She smelled of fresh air, fresh soil, and lavender. 'I'm not like him,' Murdo said.

'No, you're not. You loved him though, didn't you?'

She was biting her lip, already regretting the words, expecting him to bark at her. He caught her arm before she could turn away from him. 'He wouldn't let me.'

'Stupid man.'

The Laird? Or himself? Both, maybe. He wanted to cry for all that he'd lost. He wanted her to be right, he wanted it so much it took him aback. He wanted to thank her. He wanted to kiss her. 'Jessica?'

'Murdo?'

Reluctantly, he dropped his hand from her arm. 'I need you to believe me when I tell you that I want you to complete this commission. No matter how I might rail at you, or how ill-tempered I might be, or how resentful I might seem when you question me, your employment here is safe.'

Colour flamed her cheeks, then faded. She swallowed, a sheen of tears in her eyes. 'Thank you.'

'I should have said so before. I didn't realise how worried you were, or how—I don't want you thinking you can't share your opinions with me. I might bite your head off—I probably will—but I won't dismiss you for it.'

'I can't tell you how much that means to me.'

'I can see that,' Murdo said, touched, 'though I don't understand, to be honest, why you're so worried. You told me yourself that first day, that you're the best.'

'And I'll prove it to you, I promise. I won't let you down.'

'I don't think for a moment that you will, but I have to say, I wonder why you keep harping on about it.'

'Don't wonder. Just let me get my sleeves rolled up and get to work properly,' she said, turning back towards the view. 'Tell me your dream for Taravay.'

'My dream? It's not—well, in a way I suppose it is. It's been a long time coming.'

'But you can afford it. That's one very positive aspect of your success,' she said, turning back to him. 'I take it that the Laird would not approve?'

His smile faded momentarily. 'He'll be turning in his grave.'

'Stupid man,' she said again, making him absurdly

relieved that she had not been referring to himself after all. 'Tell me then, paint me a picture of your future Taravay, and let's start him spinning.'

Chapter Eleven

Jessica watched the sun make an appearance over Lewis, the larger island a dark flat hulk in the distance, with a slice of pale blue and lemon light suspended above it, the rest of the sky an eerie mixture of lilac, navy, and cerise and below a pewter sea with silver-crested waves. The sight filled her with such joy, she determined to ensure that her plans included several viewpoints to allow Taravay's visitors to share it.

With a happy sigh, she made for the walled garden. It had been a hectic but entirely satisfying week, even the weather cooperating obligingly with her furious drive to sketch out her thoughts for turning Murdo's dream into a reality. The scale of his plans took her breath away. There were huge projects such as upgrading the jetty to allow supplies to be landed, extending the water supply, and transforming the Castle into a hotel with an astonishing ten water closets. He wanted the village to provide crofts and homes, but also to bring traditional crafts back to the island, not only to provide more income, but to allow visitors to purchase the goods. Her own ideas included gardens for strolling in, promenades and beach huts, shelters with a view, to make the most of the island's changeable weather. To her delight, Murdo was happy to encourage her desire to use native plants to create different rooms in what had been the Castle's formal gardens, where people could be alone, have time to think, such as were once popular in monastery gardens. This morning, she was turning her focus to designing an apothecary garden.

There was so much to do, so few hours in the day, and even when she retired to her Blackhouse for the night, her mind was whirling with yet more ideas. Now that she and Murdo were both immersed in the work, they spent a great deal of time together, discussing his latest thoughts and Jessica's complementary ideas for the landscape, a task so wide-ranging she veered wildly between delight at the challenge and fear of abject failure.

They were both at pains to keep a physical distance from each other, yet there had been fleeting moments when their hands brushed, when their eyes locked. Moments of tense silences, when she was acutely aware of the space between them and was sure he felt the same. Then one or other of them broke the spell. She was safe now, from making a fool of herself. She had recovered her passion for her career, and that was all that mattered. Waking in the early hours, restless and stirred, she could easily banish her passionate dream of her employer by turning up the lamp and picking up her notebook. Well, fairly easily.

Outside, the sun was shining once again. Jessica decided to pace out the promenade she was proposing, and to take a closer look at the church, which she had as yet not found the time to visit. It was on Taravay Beag, Murdo's side of the island, and if she so happened to bump into him, then there were plenty of things she needed to discuss with him.

On the narrow strip of land that connected Taravay Beag to Taravay Mhor, with the slope down to the beach on the Lewis side, the drop more sheer, with dunes and some rocks on the Atlantic side, was one of her favourite views. The tide was well out, revealing the two beaches in all their glory—the silvery sand that, unless the tide was particularly high, remained sinkingly soft, scattered with shells, and on either side of it, the compacted, darker sand, the ebbing waves leaving ripples behind where the sand-worms left their trails. Her gaze on the white crested waves rolling onto the beach on the Atlantic side, she stopped.

The one question she longed to ask of Murdo, but which she dared not, was why. Why had the Laird Cleared the land? It was not why it happened, but what happened that mattered, according to Murdo, but if people understood, it would make them so much more amenable to a new Taravay and less likely to pine for the old one to be restored. Did Murdo know the answer? His vehemence in ignoring her question led her to believe that he did. It was not his fault, not even he said that, so why then wouldn't he talk about it? The longer his silence continued, the more hostile the Niseachs would be, and the more self-inflicted obstacles he'd have to overcome.

She sighed. He'd been so adamant though, and she suspected he was secretly afraid of the reception he would receive, hence his desire to make his plans as clear and watertight as possible. She did understand that, and she did understand why he was so reluctant to declare that his long absence wasn't his fault. The Laird was a despot, but he was Murdo's father. It made her furious, thinking of those wasted years when the Laird could have benefitted so much from his son's company, his son's intelligence, his son's wealth, and his son's love. She had been fortunate enough to have spent a great deal of time with her mother before she died, and she'd been holding Papa's hand when he passed away.

The telegram arrived the very same week that I... The very week that I, what? And what had Murdo meant, that the timing could not have been better? Why had Murdo chosen to abandon his life in London after all that time? Was it really so simple as a desire to claim Taravay for his own?

Jessica sighed, telling herself for the umpteenth time that it was none of her business, any more than her reasons for coming to Taravay were Murdo's business. She had to admit, just to herself, she was feeling guilty about not being completely honest with him, but why tell him about the debacle with Lady Orton and her sad, foolish love affair? What good would it do, save to make her look rather pathetic? None at all. What's more, she was an employee and entitled to her own private life, just as he as her employer was entitled to his.

Dragging her mind once again back to work, she continued with her walk. The church was a small squat building constructed from the same stone as the Castle. It looked more like an oversized cottage than a place of worship, and was bounded by a low stone wall. Her hair in disarray and out of breath after battling with the wind, Jessica was pondering the practicalities of transporting religiouslyinclined invalids from one side of Taravay to the other, when she spotted Murdo in the churchyard and stopped in her tracks. His coat was flapping in the breeze, his hair tousled, his gaze was fixed downwards on a tomb that was cordoned off by an iron railing, a large stone with a Celtic cross atop it. It could only be his family crypt.

Whether he sensed her presence, or whether he was done with his contemplation, he looked up and beckoned her over, pointing to the gate in the wall.

'I wanted to see the church,' Jessica said as she approached him, trying to gauge his mood, 'but I didn't mean to disturb you.'

'This is where they laid the Laird to rest,' he replied, by way of greeting. 'I know you were imagining the possibility of a deathbed reconciliation, but it was never going to happen. I was gutted, for I always thought that at some point—but it wasn't to be. He could have sent for me, Jessica, but he didn't. It was always his road or no road with him.'

She lifted her hand to touch his arm in sympathy, then changed her mind.

'I'm fine,' Murdo said, making no comment though he noticed her gesture. 'I'm of a mind to seek out Finlay though. Make my peace with him. And maybe make an ally of him too, though I'll take it one step at a time. You see, I do listen. Happy?'

Jessica returned his smile. 'For now.'

He laughed. 'No, nothing will content you but a pinery, I forgot.'

She hit her head with her hand. 'And I forgot to cost one. I shall remedy that straight away.'

He was still smiling at her. She almost wished he wouldn't, because now she wanted to step closer to him. She took a step back.

'Did you notice,' he said as she did so, 'that there's no women on this side of the graveyard? They're all over there, including my mother.' He pointed to the west-facing side of the graveyard. 'Come and take a look. I don't know why or how such a custom arose on Taravay. Over on Lewis they are buried together in their villages.'

'Together with their neighbours? That seems much more convivial, if that's the right word.'

Stumbling over ancient stones, fallen crosses, and trying to avoid standing on the odd mounds that contained multiple remains, she followed him to the other side of the churchyard.

'Here you are,' Murdo said, gesturing. 'The women of Taravay.'

Though the Atlantic, beyond the graveyard wall, heaved and sighed against the rocks, it seemed more peaceful here. The sun appeared suddenly, as it was wont to do, casting bright beams through the grey scudding clouds, sending the black birds she now knew were shags into a vortex of spinning circles. The church, windowless on this side, and sunk into the ground, looked even more like one of the abandoned crofts. She began to wander among the graves of the women, trying to read the inscriptions, but the names were incomprehensible, worn away by the wind and the salt, or written in a script she couldn't read, in a language she didn't understand. At a much larger stone with the Macleod name clearly etched at the top, she came to a halt. There was a long list of names and dates. She traced them with her finger, resting on the last one. 'Margaret,' she read, but could not understand the rest.

Murdo appeared beside her. 'It reads Margaret bhean Cairstiona Mhuraidh, Margaret, daughter of Christina daughter of Murdo. Then it also reads, roughly, wife of Angus Murdo, Laird Macleod.'

'So Murdo is your mother's grandfather's name?' Jessica said, frowning at the complexity. 'Your great-grandfather, have I that right?'

'Yes, though I was named for the Laird, Murdo Angus, known as Angus. There are very few given names used here, so on gravestones like these and in the baptism registers, they are clarified to make sure everyone knows what particular Margaret or Murdo is being referred to. In life, people are known by more descriptive names. Take Cairstiona, which is also Ca-triona, Christina or Kirsty. Where there's more than one Kirsty, then they might be known as Kirsty Mhor and Kirsty Beag—Big Kirsty and Little Kirsty—older and younger, not anything to do with their height.'

'What would my name be?'

'I've never come across another Jessica, but if you mean your formal name, it would come from your mother. What was her name?'

'Joan.'

'Johanna, or Seonag in Gaelic,' Murdo said. 'It's another very common name here. What was her father's name?'

'Neil Scott was my grandfather, and he was born and bred in the Borders, as was my mother.'

'Well then, it would be something like Jessica, daughter of Joan, daughter of Neil. Or more familiarly, Jessica *an gàirnealair*,' Murdo said.

'An garn yellert?'

'Close enough. Jessica the gardener, how do you like that?'

'It sounds much better than Jessica Smith.'

She turned back to the Macleod women's gravestone. 'Who is this Henrietta?'

'The Laird's first wife, buried with her infant.'

'Oh, I'd forgotten, you mentioned that he'd been married before. The dates are the same, so I presume she died in childbirth?'

'I presume so. I really must have a look for the Bible, though if the bairn died at birth it might not even be recorded. Odd to think that if it had survived, the Laird wouldn't have had to put himself to the bother of finding another wife, and I wouldn't be here.'

'Murdo! Don't unwish your own existence.'

'I don't, and I'm glad I'm here. I'll tell you something, Jessica, I'm very pleased indeed with all that you've achieved in the last week.'

'Why thank you, though there's so much more to be done.'

'I know the feeling,' he agreed with a rueful smile. 'All the same, I'm beginning to see just how fortunate I am that you came to Taravay.'

'You and this wonderful island have inspired me.'

'Well now, maybe, just maybe, between us we'll be able to inspire a few others, when the time is right.' Murdo took her hand, surprising her by bowing formally over it. 'Thank you for that, Miss J Smith,' he said.

She dropped a small curtsey. 'You're more than welcome, Mr Macleod.'

Still smiling, he lifted her hand to his lips, kissing her fingertips. Her heart fluttered in response, as he let her go, his smile now rueful. 'I'd better go.'

Chapter Twelve

Murdo had spent a very satisfactory morning going through the preliminary drawings and estimates for the new jetty that had been submitted by a Glasgow engineer, whom he had employed at Jessica's behest, after she pointed out that in her experience the secret to a successful project was to delegate key tasks to experts in their field. Detailed costings for this and the improvement of Taravay's water supply would require them to send a man to the island at a time convenient to both. After eighteen months stagnating here, things were moving apace. He had a purpose. He was back in control of his life. He was making a new life for himself. The old one…

Setting down his pen, he stretched his legs out under the table. The old one suddenly seemed very far away. Scrabbling amongst his correspondence, he pulled out the last letter from his lawyer and re-read it. Maybe it was time now, to do as the man suggested and announce the Emily situation to the world? Funny, but it was difficult to care too much, one way or another.

The change in his attitude took Murdo by surprise, for he'd felt very differently when he read it the first time around what—three weeks ago, slightly less? Three weeks, slightly less, since he'd first met Jessica. Time on Taravay had a different meaning, but for the first time since her arrival, he was aware of the clock ticking down on their time alone here together. They were making such excellent progress, but there would come a point soon when they needed external help.

He checked his watch, surprised to discover that it was midway through the afternoon. He'd barely spoken to Jessica for two days, not since she'd come across him in the churchyard making his peace with the Laird. She'd be pleased to hear about the jetty, he reckoned.

Outside, the sun was shining with a real warmth. The tide was low, and the wind no more than a gentle breeze. He caught sight of a pair of lambs as he headed towards the spine of the island, and was relieved to see their mother only a few yards away keeping a watch on them. He was halfway across when he spotted Jessica. She was on the Lewis-facing beach, standing in the shallows, her face tilted up to the late-afternoon sunshine, her eyes closed. Tendrils of her inky-black hair blew in the gentle breeze, giving her an ethereal look. The skirts of her brown dress were tucked up at the sides into her belt, showing her slim calves, her skin milky-white against the turquoise of the sea. She was quite still, lost in her thoughts.

Murdo stopped, knowing he was intruding but too entranced to move. He could imagine every sensation, the sun kissing her face, the icy water rippling against her ankles, her toes curling into the soft sand. He knew the temptation to step out just a little further, then stop, to feel the freezing cold creep of the sea on your shins, the way your skin tingled, numbed, became accustomed, tempting you to wade even further out. He watched her take a step, saw rather than heard her gasp of surprise as the cold water crept up, but then she stopped. Waited. And turned to come back to the shore. Which is when she saw him. And waved and smiled. And that smile went straight to all the parts of him it shouldn't.

'I was on my way to talk to you,' he said.

'And you've caught me playing truant, but the water is so lovely, I couldn't resist. I promise you though, I barely went in.'

Telling himself that he'd simply be making sure he kept her safe, Murdo jumped down onto the beach, crossing the sand towards her. 'You're fine, so long as you don't go too far out.'

'I thought I was, but I promised you I wouldn't do anything foolish. It's such a wonderful feeling though, the sand between your toes and that freezing cold water on your skin. Even though you know it's going to get colder and colder, it tempts you to go further. I found it difficult to resist.'

'I know exactly what you mean. It draws you in, deeper and deeper, and when you finally go under it knocks the breath out of you, but at the same time, you never want to get out.'

'I didn't want to get out. I wanted to go deeper.'

She had given him so much, her time and energy, her thoughts and ideas, her exuberance, her joy, and her commitment. As she looked so yearningly at the sea, he thought, why not indulge her? Murdo hauled off his boots and thick fisherman's stockings, and threw his coat onto the sand. 'Come on then, so long as you don't mind your skirts getting a bit wet.'

'Are we going to swim?'

'Don't be daft, in all those clothes you'd sink like a stone.' He held out his hand. 'But we can wade out a bit deeper, if you like.'

'Like! I would love to.'

The water lapped over their feet, then their ankles. A small flounder ruffled the sand in the shallows, flapping away from them in a panic. Murdo caught Jessica's hand as she stumbled on a hard ridge of sand. Her gaze was fixed ahead, intent on the sea, as they walked a little further, until the sea crept over her knees and soaked through her trailing skirts. 'Further,' she said, tugging at his hand, so they went further, until it was over his own knees and soaking into the legs of his breeches, and her skirts were billowing out on the water.

'That's enough, now.' The weight of the sea on her clothes could easily drag her down. She was in no danger by his side, but he didn't want her getting a soaking.

Jessica nodded, stopped, lifted her face up to the sun, and closed her eyes. Her lashes were long, dark as night. Despite her days spent outdoors in the Hebridean air, her complexion was still the same creamy-pale colour as when he had first met her. She trailed her free hand in the water, shivering with delight.

He knew he shouldn't touch her, even as he gave in to the temptation to touch her face, losing himself in the pleasure of soft, sun-kissed skin, the planes of her cheek, her jaw, the warmth of her nape, the silkiness of her hair. 'I remember, that first day we met, you told me you thought you were meant to be here.'

'It's Taravay,' she said, reaching for him, her hand wet from the sea, mirroring his actions. 'It's the island,' she said, as if she had no control over herself. 'It has magical powers.' Her thumb brushed his mouth, and his tongue brushed her skin. She exhaled, eyes wide, but made no move to free herself, holding his gaze as he dipped his head towards her.

'We shouldn't be doing this,' he said.

'No, we really shouldn't,' she agreed, tilting her head.

Their lips met, and he almost groaned aloud with

pleasure. A salt-tasting kiss. Not so much a kiss, as lips meeting and holding. A kiss that could be so easily broken. He wanted to pull her into his arms, but he made no move, waiting, until she turned towards him, and then he put his arm around her waist, and her mouth opened under his.

'Jessica,' he said, not knowing himself whether it was a protest or a plea.

'Murdo,' she said. Her hand crept up to his neck, her damp icy fingers curling into the nape of his neck. He felt her sigh against him.

His tongue touched hers, and he shuddered with long-suppressed desire. The waves lapped around them, the cold water making his skin tingle. Her skirts were sodden, moving and shifting with the waves.

The sun warmed the back of his head, and Jessica warmed him from the inside, and the kiss, such a gentle, careful kiss, went on and on, until they both drew breath and drew apart, gazing at each other incredulously. Then of one accord they turned, making their way slowly, hand in hand, to the shore, where they sat on the sand at the highest point of the beach, gazing out to sea.

'I don't want anything from you,' Jessica said. 'I don't expect anything. What happened there, it doesn't mean anything. I've worked so hard here, I don't want to ruin it.'

'No more do I!' Murdo cursed under his breath. 'Did I? Ruin it, I mean?'

'Did I?'

'No, of course you didn't. It was my fault. I started it.'

'I could have put an end to it, but I didn't.' The smile she gave him was twisted. 'If only I'd been a *Cailleach*.'

'What you are is perfect for this place, and I don't want to lose you.'

'That's what I meant, Murdo. It doesn't mean anything, I know that. You're my employer, and I won't forget that again.'

He frowned. 'Again?'

Flushed, Jessica picked up one of her stockings and peeled it on over her sandy foot. 'I should have told you before. The real reason I left my last employment.' She picked up the other stocking and forced it on. 'My mother's illness was an excuse.' She got up, shaking out her sand-encrusted, still-damp skirts. 'I was dismissed, for falling in love with my employer's brother.'

He was on his feet, catching her by the wrist before she'd gone more than a few steps. 'You can't tell me something like that and then walk away,' he said. 'Come back, sit down, and tell me properly.'

'There's nothing more you need to know. I lied to you about my last commission. If you'd asked me for references, or worse, written to Lady Orton…'

Her words brought his mind well and truly into focus. 'Good God, is that why you've been so eager to prove yourself, and so worried I'd dismiss you? You didn't lie about your talent or your experience, and as to your previous employer—do you think I care for the opinion of such a woman? I'll wager she didn't even pay you for the work you did before you left, did she?'

'No, she didn't. Please don't be angry with me, I can't bear it.'

'I'm not angry with you, I'm outraged by *her*. Come,' Murdo said. 'Sit down with me and tell me properly. Did I not tell you, only the other day, that nothing you could do or say would make me dismiss you?'

'Not even if I insisted on a pinery?' Her voice wobbled. 'Sorry, a poor joke.'

'Sit down.'

She did as he bid her, lacing her hands together, curling her stocking-clad toes into the sand. 'There's not much to tell. Edward, Lady Orton's brother, asked me to marry him. When she found out, she threatened to tell the world that I had abused her trust and ensnared him, seeking wealth and privilege. If she had done that, it would have destroyed my career. So I agreed to leave, and she agreed to let it be known that the reason I'd left was because my mother was ill. Which she was.'

'So you gave up the man you were in love with, because his sister didn't approve?'

Jessica winced. 'She was right. Our stations were

so far apart, neither of us had considered the implications. It would have been a huge mistake.'

'And what did her brother have to say for himself? Surely he stood up for you?'

'I don't know. I left him a note. I feel so guilty about that, but I hope he understands I truly believed it was best to make a clean break.'

To Murdo's horror, she was on the verge of tears. He wanted desperately to comfort her, but how? Could she still be in love with the feeble fool? Why hadn't this Edward sought her out? Why hadn't he stood up to his sister? It occurred to him that if either of those things had happened, Jessica wouldn't be here now, which was an even more appalling but entirely selfish thought, so he pushed it to the back of his mind. 'You know, the chances of that woman slandering your reputation are almost nil. Apart from anything else it would paint her and her precious brother in a very poor light.'

Jessica sniffed, winking the tears from her eyes. 'I couldn't take that chance. My career is everything to me.'

'But when you came here and discovered that you'd be quite alone on the island with me...'

'Of course I considered the risk of further damage to my reputation if that was discovered, but it is so very small as to be non-existent. I cannot imagine that anyone in Port of Ness is acquainted with Lady Orton, and more importantly, Taravay is a once-in-a-lifetime opportunity for me. If I am permitted to see it through, no one will be in the least bit interested in the fact that my early weeks were spent alone here with you. And that,' she added, blushing, 'is why I wish you to believe that when I kissed you it didn't mean I had any—any expectations.'

'It didn't even occur to me. I was so damned well obsessed with the fact that it was wrong of me to be kissing you...' Murdo broke off, shaking his head. 'I'm so sorry. Is there no chance of you and this—this Edward—being reconciled—though I have to be honest and say, I don't think he deserves you.'

'I hope he has realised, as I have, that we would not have made each other happy.' Jessica lifted a handful of soft sand and let it run through her fingers. 'I assumed that I would continue with my work once we were married, and I see now that was a very foolish assumption to make. A man may combine marriage and a career, but it is almost unheard of for a woman to do so. Looking back, I'm incredulous, but we simply never discussed it. Without my work I would be miserable, and as for Edward—though he never thought the difference in our stations mattered, I think now that a woman from the same background, with the same ideals, would suit him much better.'

'Do you still love him?' Murdo asked, unable to resist the question.

Jessica bit her lip, picking up several more handfuls of soft sand as she considered this. Eventually, to his extreme relief, she shook her head. 'Landscaping really is my first and only love. I would not go so far as to say I'm grateful to Lady Orton, for it broke my heart to leave Edward as I did, but it was for the best, for both of us. Besides, broken hearts, I've discovered, really do mend. Especially,' she said with a small smile, 'when you can take the medicine that is Taravay. I truly do believe this is a special place.'

'Do you?' It was his turn to let a handful of sand run through his fingers, watching the glitter of the grains pour down like silver rain. 'Maybe you're right enough,' Murdo said, recalling his own thoughts, earlier that day. 'I came to Taravay eighteen months ago, with a broken heart myself. Difference is, you walked away before you walked up the aisle. I was under the mistaken apprehension that I had a wife.'

'You're married!' Jessica recoiled from him.

'No!' Murdo cursed his thoughtlessness under his breath, as shocked as she was by his declaration, which he had not in the least intended to make. 'I'm not married. I thought I was, but I was wrong. It's complicated.'

Chapter Thirteen

Jessica stared at Murdo, open-mouthed in shock, the embarrassed relief she had felt at her own confession quite forgotten. 'What on earth do you mean, you *thought* you were married?'

'I believed we were married, but it turned out that we couldn't be. It's a long story.' Murdo ran his fingers through his hair, a pointless gesture, for he had now cropped it so short it no longer flopped over his brow. 'I didn't mean to blurt it out like that. Only when you said that, about Taravay mending your broken heart, it struck me that it was doing the same for me.'

'Oh, Murdo. I've wondered so many times, about some of the things you've said, and I've wanted so many times to tell you about Edward, and now here we are, the pair of us—it's not in the least bit funny, but it's so ridiculous.' Jessica's smile wobbled, her eyes filled with tears.

'It is.' He managed a very small smile. 'I'm not married, Jessica, and never have been,' he said, taking her hand. 'Do you know, I've never once said that out loud, and it feels—it feels like a huge relief, to be honest.'

She edged closer in the sand. 'Do you feel you want to tell me more?'

'I think so.' He frowned down at their joined hands, then he nodded. 'She—Emily—she was already married when she married me.'

'Did you know? Oh no, no, that's a stupid question, of course you didn't know. What I should have asked was, did she?'

'She thought herself a widow, her husband tragically drowned at sea. He wasn't, as it turned out, but she was almost seven years my wife before she found that out, when he came back to claim her.'

'Seven years! You were married for seven years!'

'I thought I was married.'

'But, Murdo, you must have had a whole life, a home, friends—oh no! Do you have...'

'We didn't have any children, thank God.'

His grip on her tightened, his eyes fixed on their joined hands. She could see his thoughts flitting across his face, but she couldn't read them. Her own love affair seemed so trite in comparison to what he was telling her. She ached to hold him, simply hold him, but remembering that other time when she'd mistakenly offered sympathy, she bit her tongue and bided her time.

'It never bothered me for myself, that the bairns didn't appear,' Murdo said, lifting his head, but only to gaze at the sea. 'My own father set an example I had no wish to follow.'

'You're not the Laird, Murdo.'

'No.' He met her gaze with a tight smile. 'I'd like to think I'd have been a different parent if I'd been required to, but there's always that doubt, isn't there? Blood will out, that's what they say. What if I am my father's son, after all? Fortunately, as it turns out, I was never put to the test. But it bothered Emily a great deal. She's always wanted weans.'

'So when her first husband came back from the dead…'

'Ah no, it wasn't that she grasped the opportunity to fill her nursery. It's simple enough, Jessica. Emily loved him. She loved him first, and she loved him best. He'd been gone more than seven years, time for him to have been declared legally dead, our marriage legally valid. A complicated process, but one we could have seen through, if she'd wished it. But she did not, and I…'

Murdo released his grip on her, to curl his hand into a fist. 'I loved her too much to make her unhappy by getting in the way,' he said gruffly. 'Besides, it wasn't her fault. She didn't marry me under false pretences, she didn't mean to break my heart.'

'But she did,' Jessica said softly, as the answers to so many questions fell into place.

'She did.' He unclenched his fist. 'But like you said,

Taravay worked its magic. It took a while. When I first came here, I was demented with grief, not only for the loss of Emily but for the loss of my father too, though I didn't realise that, and it's taken you to point it out to me. That's what I meant about the timing of his passing the other day—yes, I did spot that you noticed. When I received the telegram informing me that he was dead, it was the same week that Emily had told me her husband was alive. I'd no idea when I came here that I would stay, but I'm glad I did. Taravay was my first love, after all. Now it's my only one. I've mended what Emily broke, but I don't ever want to go through that again.'

His poor heart. What a misguided woman Emily must be, to choose another man over Murdo. She would not—not, Jessica told herself quickly, that she would ever be required to. While he studied the sea, she studied him, her own heart aching at the thought of the torment he must have gone through alone here. For such a man to have confided in her after so long silently suffering, was humbling. The trust he had placed in her was humbling too. She would not let him down, she vowed fervently.

'Now you know my sad history.' Murdo broke the silence.

'Now I understand a great deal more about you. You're a very honourable man, Murdo.'

'Ach, all I did was what was right.'

'At a cost. And to lose your father, at the same time as you lost your wife.'

'I never told her.'

Jessica lifted his hand to her lips. 'You must have loved her so much.'

'I did, but it's over now.'

'Now you have your island,' Jessica said, firmly admonishing herself for the pang of jealousy, 'and I have my landscaping. We both have our first loves. You see, fate did bring us together.'

'Fate, and those letters of yours. I wonder who your Mairi was?'

'I've been so busy, I'd forgotten all about her.' Jessica cast a glance out to the sea. 'The tide and the weather have turned. We must have been here for hours.'

Murdo got up, holding out a hand to help her, and picking up her boots. 'You can sit on that stone to put them on.' He watched the sea as she did so, his hands dug deep in the pockets of his breeches.

'Murdo…'

'No, let's leave it, shall we? Let's think of this as a fresh start.'

'That's what I was about to say.'

He grinned. 'Great minds, and all that. You'd better hurry now, if you want to get back before the rain comes on.'

Jessica walked quickly away. Murdo watched her until she was out of sight, biting back the urge to call her back, for there really was nothing more to be said. There were white horses on the sea now, and the tide was rolling in fast. He should go back to his own croft, but he was unsettled, not only by his own unaccustomed outpouring, but by what Jessica had told him. Bloody feeble fool, that man she'd fallen in love with, not to have put up a fight. He wouldn't have given her up so easily. Not that there was any question of her ever being his to renounce.

He decided to go for a walk, over to the Atlantic side of the island to the cove where the seals gathered at low tide. There were no seals, and the sea was almost at its highest point, leaving only a stony strip at the head of the bay. He clambered down and picked up a handful of stones, skimming them on the water one after the other, using the full force of his arm. Then, sinking down onto the pebbles, he did what he'd been trying to avoid doing for the last eighteen months. He thought of Emily.

He conjured up her face, her smile, the way she seemed to float across the room rather than walk. He remembered the first time they had kissed, and he remembered how he'd thought his heart would burst with love and pride when they said their wedding vows. Seven years of memories he set loose, all the precious times he'd locked away in the back of his mind after the shock of her asking for her freedom and him agreeing, though it cost him dear. Seven years of happiness—or so he'd believed.

The sky turned grey then black, and the heavens opened. Rain like stair-rods pelted him, but he continued to stare out at the sea, remembering, the tears mingling with the salt spray that whipped at his face.

He'd lost track of time when he finally hauled himself to his feet, exhausted and drained, but the tide had well and truly turned. It all seemed so very far away now, Emily, his London life, the home they'd made together—as if the memories belonged to someone else. He could recall her face and figure easily enough, but she seemed lifeless, like a portrait rather than a person. So much time had passed since that day when she'd torn his heart in two, Murdo realised as he tramped across the sodden machair towards his croft, that he really had changed. Would he turn the clock back? No, he would not. What he felt for Emily now was a sad, sorrowful kind of affection, a long way from the love he'd thought would stay in his heart forever. He hoped she was happy.

It had been a very long dark winter. He'd mended his broken heart, but the scar was still tender. Never, ever again would he let anyone close enough to rip it open again. It was like spring unfurling inside him after a long dark winter. Ha! Jessica would like that one.

Jessica. His smile faded abruptly as Murdo opened the door to his croft and put a new peat on the fire before sitting down to pull off his sodden boots. Jessica, who'd had her own heart broken. Jessica, who was here on Taravay to heal, just as he was. Jessica, who could not be more unlike Emily if she tried. She was the—what was the word—aye, the antidote to Emily. A woman after his own heart—or maybe more accurately a woman who, like him, wanted to keep her heart safe. Though kissing her, holding her, as he had done in the sea this afternoon, that felt far from safe.

What Jessica was, Murdo reminded himself as he pulled the kettle back over the fire, was the key to the future of Taravay. So much more than a landscaper, she could take his thoughts and his ideas and identify all the steps, all the practicalities that were needed to turn them into reality. She knew what he, a man of finance, did not about what needed to be done in what order, and why one way of doing things might be so much more expensive than others. She gave him a confidence in his ideas that he'd been unwilling to confess had been lacking. He needed her more than he cared to admit. In more ways than one. Waiting for the water to heat, his mind drifted back to their kisses. To the softness of her skin. The way his own desire was reflected in her eyes. He'd never known that before. It was…

The kettle began to sing, and so too did his body. Cursing his aroused state, Murdo made himself a cup of tea. A fresh start, that's what he'd said they were making. Right then, a fresh start it was, and a time to draw a firm line under the past.

He'd write to Emily, and if it was her wish to do as his lawyer bade him, and make some sort of public declaration, then so be it.

Chapter Fourteen

Isle of Harris, Outer Hebrides

Donald Macneil poured the dregs from the pot into his cup. The tea was barely lukewarm and it was as weak as dishwater thanks to yet another of his housekeeper's economies, reusing the leaves. He swallowed it all the same, along with the burnt crust of the bread he'd toasted over the peat fire, for there would be nothing more to eat until dinner. He was sick of scrimping and saving. Sick of the wind that whistled through the gaps in the windows and the water that dripped through the roof and the way both made his old bones creak. He was sick and tired of not having any funds to remedy any of it. He was just shy of his eightieth birthday. Considering his abject living conditions, it was a miracle he was still alive. Surely, in his declining final years, he deserved better.

Cracking his knuckles, Donald reflected bitterly, as he did most mornings for lack of anything else to do, on the low blows that life had dealt him, and the twists and turns that had consistently deprived him of the good fortune he so richly deserved. Deprived by the actions of the woman who'd been promised to him from birth, who proved herself unworthy when she jilted him for another man. If she had not broken his heart, he would not have married his first wife— how was it they put it, on the rebound? And if his first wife had loved him more, she'd have given him a son, so that when she died, her wealth and her lands would have come to him and not returned to her family. His second wife now—ah, if ever a man was mistaken in a woman's character, then so it was with she. She had promised before all in the kirk to love, honour, and obey. It was her duty to forgive his sin of infidelity, which was technically not even infidelity, for though it had happened while they were promised, they had not yet been wed. It was true, he had succumbed to lust with another man's wife, but he had himself been between wives. And if he'd not been such an honest man, if he'd not taken a drop of two too much of the *Uisge Beatha* and freed his tongue to make a confession, his second wife would have remained in ignorance. But once he'd confessed, had she forgiven him and allowed him to become a better man for the cleansing of his soul? Not a whit of it. She'd made his life a misery, and she'd proved herself a poor housekeeper, and she had failed, just like his first wife, to provide him with a son. Even a daughter would have been bet-ter than nothing. Aye, he'd have settled for a daughter to look after him in his old age, but here he was, nigh on eighty, with an old crabbit housekeeper, a moulting, lame dug, a house that leaked like a sieve, and nothing else to call his own but a hatful of misery.

He was Donald Macneil of Harris, and he deserved better. Hoisting himself to his feet with the help of his stick, he glared out of the window at the dark clouds coming hurtling in from the Atlantic, his bones pro-testing at the very thought of taking himself out for a walk. He'd barely sunk back into his chair, when his housekeeper appeared with her tray to clear up.

'This came for you,' she said, taking a crumpled let-ter from the pocket of her apron. 'Dropped off from one of the Ness boats this morning. Will you be fine with herring and oatmeal again tonight? Not that it makes a whit of difference if you are not, for that is all there is.'

Donald, however, was too absorbed in his letter to either reply or protest. Frowning and narrowing his eyes the better to read his name, his primary concern was to make sure that it was not another demand for money, and it was with some surprise that he recog-nised the wavery script as belonging to a very old ac-quaintance—one he'd actually thought long since dead.

The contents of the scrawl were so interesting that he perused the letter three times in full, repeating it out loud, and exclaiming to himself at several points. *Well, well*, he thought, as he folded it up and tucked it into his pocket. So Laird Angus Macleod's son was not, after all, hiding on Taravay for lack of funds. Quite the opposite, in fact. Rumour had it that the fool had money to burn, and that he was planning to burn a fair whack of it on the island.

'Now what the devil would he want to do that for?' Donald asked himself, 'when Macleod himself had the place Cleared?' It had been quite the scandal at the time, but those who had sailed for the New World had had the company of a fair few from Harris on their journey, and after almost ten years, wasn't the deed over and done with and no going back? Here on Harris, the crofts had been given over to sheep. Over on Taravay—well, like as not, the sheep would have taken over the crofts.

'And as to the idea of a gardener!' Donald exclaimed to his dog. 'And a lassie, at that. Do you think he's got a wedding on his mind?'

His hound, rheumy-eyed like himself, had no opinion on this, but Donald, having mulled it over, found himself most unhappy with the idea. The boy must be… A frowning calculation made him shake his head in astonishment. Could it really be forty years? Odd, that he had not married, but it was best to ensure that state of affairs remained the case.

Without a shadow of a doubt, action must be taken

in response to this missive, but what and when and how required very careful thinking through. Any man with any sense knew that letting skeletons out of the closet never came without a cost. But not acting—no, there was no question of that.

Looking out the window, Donald saw that the rain had stopped, and the sun was making an attempt to shine through. The day, like his future, was brightening up. Calling to his dog, he pushed his hat down low on his head, wrapped himself up in an old plaid. The arthritic pair set out, the one snuffling for rabbits, the other snuffling for a way to redirect Murdo Macleod's fortune into his own pockets. After all, although he didn't know it, the lad owed him.

Chapter Fifteen

It was four weeks since Jessica had arrived on Taravay, and over a week since she and Murdo had poured their hearts out to each other. A fresh start, they had agreed, and indeed, Jessica thought, as she made her way to Taravay Beag on a beautiful afternoon, they had made an enormous amount of progress in that time. It was a pleasure to work with someone who respected her views and her expertise as he did, but who was also happy to challenge, to question, and to constantly push her to widen her horizons, rather than to close them down. They talked of nothing else but Taravay, and when Taravay slipped from their minds, and the silence stretched, when their hands brushed, or when they stood too close to each other to pore over a drawing, one or other of them would make the effort to break the spell. Jessica had given up attempting to explain it away. Murdo, like his island, entranced her. Murdo, like his island, was not, and never could be, hers.

The standing stone was about ten feet high, with a round hole about five feet up the face. It stood on the eastern tip of Taravay Beag above the cliffs, perched in a curious dip in the land, where the grass grew dark green, long and lush. How to make the most of the site without spoiling it, was the question in her mind as Jessica sat down with her back to the stone and took out her notebook. She closed her eyes just for a moment, relishing the warmth of the sun on her skin.

'Hello, sleeping beauty.'

She jumped up, completely disoriented, and Murdo caught her arm to prevent her stumbling. 'You made me start,' she said, 'I wasn't sleeping.'

'Just thinking with your eyes closed?'

'Exactly.' He was coatless, his shirtsleeves rolled up to reveal his tanned forearms, the neck of his shirt showing her a suntanned throat. His beard was now neatly trimmed to match his hair, a pale line on his cheeks marking where it had once grown wild. 'I never cease working, you know. My mind is a fermenting brew of ideas.'

Murdo laughed. His teeth were very white. His eyes crinkled up at the corners. The shadows under them were not nearly so pronounced. 'A very attractive brew.'

Her breath caught. 'Surprisingly attractive, that's what you said the first day we met.'

'It seems like months ago, but it was exactly four weeks ago today.'

'I know. I was thinking the same thing, only this morning. It seems so much longer.'

'Island time is different.' He touched her cheek lightly, catching a strand of her hair, pushing it back from her face. 'Jessica, after we talked about—you know, our fresh start? I decided it was time to write to Emily. There's a question of whether we make a formal announcement. Speaking for myself, I don't care, but she might. And I'd also like to know that she's happy.'

'What if she's not?'

'I've done all I can.'

'And you, Murdo, are you happy?'

'I'm certainly not the misery guts who met you off the steamer at Stornoway,' he said, smiling.

'They'd hardly recognise you over on Ness now.' Jessica reached up, flattening her palm over his short beard. 'Quite a transformation, while I, for my part, am dressed like a crofter's wife. If Edward could see me now, he'd wonder that he ever thought me a suitable match.'

'Edward is an idiot.'

'Ah no. He is a gentle, caring, man, who lives with his head too much in the clouds, that's all.'

'While you are very definitely of the earth. Or the sea, maybe? You look like a Selkie, with your hair loose like that.'

'What's a Selkie?'

'Funny now, that you should ask that, given where we are. Sit down beside me, and I'll tell you.' He took her hand, sinking onto the grass, and they sat together, their legs stretched out, her skirts feathering against his breeches. 'Have you happened to notice that the grass here is unusually long?' he asked her.

'I have, as a matter of fact. Why is that?'

'The sheep won't come here. Look over there, you see?' He pointed at a sheep with a pair of twin lambs staring at them from several yards away.

'Why not,' Jessica asked, 'is it cursed?'

'Not cursed, but a special, sacred place. If you look closely at the top of the stone, there's an old Celtic cross carved into it, so the chances are that it was put here by the early Christian settlers, and that's why the church was built nearby.'

'So it's a holy place? And the sheep simply don't want to come so close to the cliff edge?'

'That's one way of explaining it. But there is another.'

'What is that?'

'Well now. Long ago, way, way back, there was a young woman on the island, who was deeply in love with a man from Harris. A fisherman, he was, who would visit her here, perhaps in the croft I'm living in now—or maybe it was another croft on the same site.'

'Oh no,' Jessica said, her mind half on his story and

half on the man telling it, entranced by both. 'You're going to tell me that he drowned, aren't you?'

'Not at all. One day, as he sailed towards his love, who was waiting for him right here on this very spot, he heard a woman singing. Her song was so sad, so irresistible, he followed the sound, and there, on those rocks that are just peeking out below, she was sitting.'

'It must have been a lower tide than it is now,' Jessica said, shading her eyes from the sun to look.

'Ever the pragmatist. Indeed, it was low tide, I should have said. Anyway, there she was, a beautiful woman, her long dark hair her only clothing, and she was singing to the fisherman. Immediately he saw her, he forgot all about his true love, and he sailed towards her. And his little boat was smashed to pieces upon those very rocks.'

'Even though it was low tide?'

Murdo gave a snort of laughter. 'Maybe the tide had come in a bit by then.'

'So he swam towards her?'

'Oh no, he couldn't. It's believed to be unlucky for those who earn their living at sea to learn to swim— and that is true, unfortunately. So the fisherman was in the water, but he didn't drown. Instead, still singing her siren song, the Selkie—for that is what she was—dived in from the rocks and took hold of him, and swam out to sea, taking him for her own, and that was the last sighting the poor maid from Taravay had of her true love. But every day, without fail, she stood here, looking for him, hoping against hope for his return—when the tide was right, that is,' Murdo added with a grin. 'Eventually, she turned to stone. And the hole, right in the middle of that stone, is where her heart once was.'

'That is so sad,' Jessica said, smiling. 'And I don't believe a word of it. I think you made it up.' It was happening again. The shift in mood that made her breathless. The way he was looking at her, made it difficult for her to think of anything but kissing. 'I'm no Selkie. I can't swim, and as for singing a siren song, I'm tone-deaf.'

'I'm glad you're you and not a Selkie. I can't thank you enough for all you've done here, Jessica.'

He smelled of soap and the sea. Her body thrummed with his nearness. 'For my part, I can't thank you enough for the trust you've placed in me. We make a good team, don't we, Murdo?'

'A team? Yes, I like that. And we do.' He shifted, angling himself towards her, and took a breath. 'We work so well together, and we've made such incredible progress—beyond my wildest dreams, to be honest—I don't want to spoil it. But you must have noticed, no matter how much I try, I can't help wanting—thinking of you—in the most—the most inappropriate ways.' Murdo slapped his forehead with his hand. 'That sounds so bloody mealy-mouthed, but if I say any more…'

'It's not only you.'

He smiled wryly. 'I know, and that just makes it worse. Neither of us is looking for a soulmate—as far as I'm concerned, that's the last thing I want.'

'Nor I, never.'

'Exactly. And I'll be frank, Jessica, what I feel for you is nothing like my feelings for Emily. I'm not interested in protecting you or tending to you—which makes it sound as if Emily was one of your exotic plants—but what I mean is, you don't need tended and protected, and what I want…' He broke off, colouring. 'You know what I mean?'

Blushing, Jessica nodded. 'Do you think it's because I am so unlike Emily and you are so very unlike Edward that we want—that it's part of our recovery?'

'So you're a dose of medicine I'm obliged to take? That's a piece of sophistry that I find very attractive. What you are is key to the future of Taravay, and I don't want to risk losing you.'

'The success of Taravay is key to my future, and I most certainly don't want to risk losing my role in that.' Jessica wrinkled her nose. 'Perhaps that's the key to what we feel? It's Taravay that brings us together. Could it be as simple as that? And the fact that we're alone here—though that will come to an end soon.'

'It will.' Murdo frowned. 'I reckon a few more weeks

and we'll be starting work here, and I'll be able to do what you want me to do, and tell everyone what I'm hoping the future holds.'

'Only a few more weeks. Surely we have the self-control to resist each other for a few more weeks,' Jessica said.

'Surely we do.'

She had not noticed, she didn't know how it had happened, but they were leaning against each other. She could feel his breath on her face. 'If we wish to,' she said, knowing full well that her eyes told him she did not.

'If we wish to,' he agreed. 'But if we do not...'

'We are two rational adults,' Jessica said.

'I'm not feeling very rational at the moment.'

'Nor am I. What I mean is that, given what we've just said, there's no risk of things getting out of hand. It's safe.'

Her breath caught as his lips met hers, and she was lost in an instant as they kissed. Deep, dark, disturbing, raw. It was a kiss that obliterated everything, save for the kiss. The melding of their bodies, the scent and the heat, made her forget everything save the need to drink deep and deeper, to burrow close and closer.

They fell back on the grass, still kissing, his body half covering hers. She ran her palm over the bristle on his neck, and nipped his lower lip with her teeth. His hand brushed the side of her breast, and she inhaled sharply, her nipple peaking. Deeper kisses again, one of his legs between hers, her skirts in the way, but she could feel him, aroused. She tugged his shirt free from his breeches, her hand on the heated skin of his back, making him shudder. He cupped her breast, making her moan, his thumb stroking, circling her aching nipple, and she dug her fingers into his back.

Then he lifted his head, swore, breathing heavily, his eyes dark pools, staring into hers. 'That didn't feel particularly safe.'

Torn between embarrassment and frustration, Jessica tried to disentangle her skirts and sit up. 'Nor entirely free of risk.'

'We did call a halt though. I suppose that's something.' He rolled away, getting to his feet and holding out his hand to help her up.

'Yes,' Jessica agreed, though she wasn't sure that she could take any credit for it. 'I know you would not—and if you did, then I would—and—shut up, Jessica!'

Gently, he prised her hands away from her face. 'You're right, we should be reassured, but I think that's more than enough on the subject for now, don't you?'

She nodded. 'I should get back to work. I actually came here to sketch out an idea.'

'And I actually came here to tell you something rather interesting.'

'The plans for the jetty, have they arrived?'

Murdo laughed. 'Yes, but it wasn't that. Do you remember you told me about those letters written to your grandmother by Mairi?'

'Do you know who she is?'

'I think I might. I was looking for the family bible, and I came across the household accounts. They were signed by a Mairi Mackinnon.'

'Mackinnon? I wonder if she's related to my Norman? The Norman whose croft I'm living in?'

'It's likely. Not his wife though, for she seems to have left the job, and presumably Taravay, back in October 1825. I don't know where she went, but the accounts show a new housekeeper taking over in December that year. It could simply be a coincidence, but the timing fits.'

'I think I would recognise the writing,' Jessica said, excitedly. 'May I see them?'

'Of course.' He took out his watch, frowning. 'Though maybe tomorrow? I've a stack of things I need to do, letters and telegrams I want to have ready for Grahame in the morning. I'll meet you at the Castle after he's been, shall I?'

Chapter Sixteen

Early morning in any garden was Jessica's favourite time of day, and this morning, in what had once been the formal Taravay Castle gardens, was a perfect example. Last night's rain was drying into a hazy steam in the sunshine as she set out to meet Murdo, accompanied by a symphony of birdsong. Everything smelled lush and green. Usually when she was given a commission, it was to create something new without regard to what had gone before, and though she made a point, as her father had taught her, to reuse and replant as much as possible, her employers were more interested in the latest fashion. The trend for huge beds of garishly coloured flowers made her cringe, as did the formality of hedging, straight paths, poised garden statuary. It was a delight to have no remit here on Taravay, save to make the landscape fit for everyone.

Ideally, she would make no changes to what had been the formal gardens at all, spending the year documenting what was already growing, and assessing the effect of the four seasons, but that was a luxury she did not have. On the other hand, she thought, stooping to admire a pretty orchid tilting its face to the sun under a very overgrown hedge, here on Taravay there were, as Murdo had said, four seasons in a day.

Murdo. Yesterday, she had been so lost to everything save his touch, his body, his kisses, that she'd given no thought at all to where they were. If he had not come to his senses, she doubted she would have. Though surely she would not have made love in the open air? Would they have taken off their clothes? The idea was both shocking and thrilling at the same time. Edward would have been utterly appalled.

She drew up short, next to a mossy sundial. Edward. The love she had once had for him was wispy, ethereal, like the morning mist over the sea. It seemed astonishing that she had once believed he was everything to her. Jessica shuddered. To be everything to Edward or to any man, come to that, would have meant so much sacrifice on her part, it horrified her how close she had come to making it. Were it not for Lady Orton, she could have ruined her life forever, for looking back, it was astonishing how little she and Edward had actually conversed. Love had made her impractical, blind, and foolish.

She and Murdo talked all the time. How different he was now from the withdrawn, volatile man she had first met. How very different she was too. It was the respect he gave her, even when he challenged her, that had made her confidence grow and grow. In appearance too, she had changed, with her hair down and loosely tied, most of her petticoats abandoned, and in weather like this, like him, she wore no jacket, even rolling up the sleeves of her blouse. Of the earth, is how Murdo had described her yesterday. Yes, that's exactly how she felt, and it was Murdo who had set her free. Free to create something wonderful here, unconstrained by convention. Free to paddle in the sea, to roam the island with only the wild landscape for company, to speak her mind, and to let her body speak, without fear of being criticised or mocked. In fact, Murdo seemed to relish her lack of restraint. He had released her inner earth goddess.

Earth goddess! Hark at you, Jessica Smith! Laughing at her flight of fancy, she followed the path away from the sundial, pushing through tangles of shrubs and briars and ivy. Sheep, some with lambs, their winter fleeces mostly shed, grazed happily, unimpressed by her presence, moving reluctantly only when she came within a few feet of them. She found clumps of their wool snagged everywhere, an unclaimed resource perfect for protecting the more tender plants from frost.

The path took a twist through another huge overgrown hedge, and Jessica found herself looking straight down at the jetty. A pod of porpoises surfaced a few yards out, one after the other. She watched, entranced, as they arced gracefully out of the sea in succession, passing the buoy which marked Murdo's lobster creel.

Turning, she could see that the owner of the creel was waiting for her at the front door of the Castle. She hurried towards him, ignoring the fluttering in her stomach which grew more persistent as she neared.

'*Madainn mhath*,' he said. 'How are you today?'

'I'm looking forward to seeing those household accounts. Imagine, if Grandmamma's friend was the housekeeper here—what a coincidence that would be.'

'I might have it wrong, you know,' he said, 'Mairi is a very common name. Come on, they're in the office, through the baize door.'

'This looks like every estate office I've ever been in,' Jessica said when he opened the door to a very practical office and threw open the shutters. A desk took up most of the available space, and numerous cabinets and shelves stacked with ledgers occupied the remainder. 'You're fortunate that it seems to be watertight in here, else those old ledgers would be ruined, but they look to be in excellent condition.'

Murdo handed her a small book. 'Here is 1825, and there's quite a few going back in time on this shelf. Would you mind if I left you to it? Grahame hasn't been yet and I've some mail for him to collect. I'll catch up with you when he's been.'

'Yes, yes, that's fine.' Jessica was already sitting down at the desk and opening the ledger. The handwriting looked familiar, but it was the signature at the end of each week which convinced her, the distinctive curl on the tail of the *m* was exactly the same. She had found her grandmother's correspondent. Norman Mackinnon's mother, aunt, cousin, sister? She'd like to find out. Why did she leave? Was it the appeal of a big city? And how did she and Grandmamma become friends?

Musing on this, Jessica began to browse the shelves. As well as the housekeeper's accounts, there were larger ledgers recording the quarterly rents. The year of the Clearance was 1870, and here it was, a double red line drawn under August of that date. Then in a different hand, one rent for the next two quarters, which must be Norman. The last ledger was four years later, an entry for March that year and nothing else, so that must be when poor Norman died leaving the Laird alone here, save for his housekeeper. Norman must be buried in the graveyard.

Frowning, Jessica sat back down at the desk. Something about the dates niggled at her. Opening a drawer, she found a scrap of paper and an old pencil. 1870, the island was Cleared. Eighteen months ago, in 1877, Murdo had returned. He'd been married seven years, he'd said, which by her reckoning made it the same year as the Clearance. Was it a coincidence? Surely it must be. Had the Laird known his son was getting married? If so, then surely he'd have been pleased, hoping that the next generation of Macleod's was secured. But if he had disapproved of Murdo's choice…

She dropped the pencil, horrified. All that Murdo had said of his father made a despot of him. A despot would not take well to a marriage he hadn't endorsed. Would a despot Clear his island to spite such a son? It was a sickening notion, but if it had occurred to her, then it must also have occurred to Murdo. She tried to recall everything he'd said of the event, but all she could remember was that he'd been adamant—it was not his fault.

Poor Murdo. Whether it was true or not, the doubts must be there. Speaking of which, where was Murdo? Checking her watch, she was astonished to discover that almost an hour had passed. Hurrying back outside, she could see Grahame Macfarlane sitting on the jetty, his boat tied up, the sail down. Shading her eyes from the sun, she scanned the shoreline, but she couldn't see Murdo. Perhaps he'd forgotten a piece of mail and returned to his croft for it.

Pulling shut the Castle door, Jessica made her way quickly to the walled garden, preoccupied by the implications of what she'd found. The sound of voices drew her up short in the doorway. In the potting shed, poring over her drawing of the island, was Murdo. The man with him was a stranger, dressed entirely in black, save for his white stock, a wide-brimmed hat sitting on top of a startlingly bright red head of hair.

Murdo saw her first, and beckoned her in. He was scowling. 'Jessica,' he said, 'let me introduce you to the Reverend Roderick Muirhead. Reverend, this is the renowned landscaper, Miss Smith, whose work you have been studying.'

'*Madainn mhath*,' the man said in what to her ears sounded authentic Gaelic. 'Miss Smith. How do you do?'

He was tall, about the same height as Murdo, though much more slimly built. His hands were large and knobbly, the wrists thin. He had a long neck with a protruding Adam's apple that bobbed up and down when he spoke. With a great effort, Jessica managed not to direct her 'how do you do' to it, lifting her gaze to his face. He was much younger than she had initially thought, not more than twenty-one or -two, and his skin was milk-white, mottled with freckles, his eyes pale blue. His grip however, was firm, and the look he gave her was not in the least bashful.

'Do I detect a Lowland accent?' he asked her.

'I was born and raised in the Borders, not far from Dumfries.'

'Ah, the final resting place of the great Robert Burns. As a man of God, I should not express too open an admiration for him, and there are indeed some of his poems that I would not consider fit for women and children, but my *Kilmarnock Volume* is one of my

dearest possessions. I do not think that he wrote spe-
cifically about gardening, but of farming—ah, yes.'

Reverend Muirhead cleared his throat and, to her
utter astonishment, declaimed:

'My father was a farmer upon the Carrick border O
And carefully he bred me in decency and order O
He bade me act a manly part, though I had ne'er a
farthing O
For without an honest manly heart, no man was
worth regarding O.'

'Of course, it's a song rather than a poem, but I'm
afraid I'm tone-deaf.'

'As is Miss Smith, she tells me. But I presume you
did not bully Grahame Macfarlane into bringing you
here in order to recite poetry at us, Reverend Muirhead.'

The minister blushed. 'I persuaded Mr Macfarlane
to bring me here because I felt it my duty to visit the
island, Laird Macleod, and because I was intrigued by
Miss Smith's presence.'

'I don't use that title,' Murdo snapped. 'And as to
Miss Smith's presence here, you can stick your fire
and brimstone lecture up your...'

'Murdo!'

'Ah now...' Reverend Muirhead held up his hands.
'You've taken what I said quite out of context, Laird—
Mr Macleod. When I said I was intrigued, I referred

to the nature of her work here. I was informed that she would be restoring the gardens of Taravay Castle.'

Murdo muttered something in Gaelic.

'Indeed,' the Reverend said, 'it was Mrs Macfarlane who informed me. Not a kind nickname, she has been given, but she takes it in good part.'

'So you speak Gaelic, then?' Murdo said. 'But you're not from here.'

'I'm from Oban, on the west coast of Argyll. My father is a fisherman and so too was I, until I answered the call to serve God.'

'If you've come here in search of a lost sheep for your flock, you're wasting your time. Unless it's real sheep you want, which we have in abundance, though good luck with herding any of them up. They've been running wild here for nine years.'

Why was he being so rude? Jessica cast him a frowning look, but the Reverend Muirhead seemed not at all offended.

'I would not be so presumptuous, Mr Macleod. This is my first posting, and I am very well aware of how young and inexperienced I am.'

'Doubtless there will be many over on Ness who will wish to guide you. Who was it prodded you into coming here?'

'I came of my own volition, I assure you. I am curious, as I said.' Reverend Muirhead took his hat off, releasing a wild tangle of bright orange curls that made him look absurdly young. Despite this, to Jessica's admiration, he seemed not in the least intimidated by Murdo's mood. 'When I arrived in Ness three months ago, there were many who were happy to tell me how I should conduct myself. Local worthies, I think is the English phrase. "The Old Minister did it this way", they'd say to me, "but the Old Minister did it that way". I was wet behind the ears, I admit that I still am, and the Old Minister's shoes are a big pair to fill. In some cases, I could see it was the right thing for me to follow the advice I was given. In some instances though, I'm deciding—slowly, mind—that I will make changes. I've an open mind, Mr Macleod, that's what I'm trying to say.'

'And to what purpose have you brought your open mind to Taravay, if you're not here to preach at me?'

'The Reverend has already said, he's interested in your plans,' Jessica intervened. 'Now that he's here, don't you think it would be a good idea to...'

'I'm busy, and I doubt Grahame Macfarlane will relish frittering away his day here, waiting on the Reverend's convenience.'

'I am sure he can spare half an hour,' Jessica said, 'and I am more than happy to...'

'Fine. I'll let you get on with it then.' He turned to go, then changed his mind, addressing the minister again. 'Miss Smith is a landscaper of great renown with an impeccable reputation. I will not have her good name muddied. Do you understand me? She's vital to the success of this venture, and I am very lucky that she has agreed to carry out the task, for she had many, many other offers, I'll have you know.' After a moment's hesitation, he held out his hand. 'Good day to you, Reverend,' he said, before turning his back and stalking off.

Painfully embarrassed by this vociferous defence which, she suspected had completely the opposite effect than what Murdo intended, Jessica gave the minister a wary smile. 'He really is very busy,' she said.

'And I really am curious, Miss Smith, as to what you and Mr Macleod have been working on. Will he reside here, move back into the Castle? Does he hope to repopulate the crofts? The good people of Ness deserve to know one way or another for they are quite in the dark.'

'Since he's given me permission, then let me show you.'

Pulling her biggest drawing of the island towards her, Jessica began to sketch out Murdo's dream for the minister. He listened attentively, nodding at salient points and asking sufficient informed questions to make her talk on. 'Well,' he said, when she finally drew to a close, 'that is quite a project you have here. I cannot understand why he has kept it from the people most concerned…'

'He has his reasons,' Jessica interjected hurriedly.

'He will tell people in his own good time, but until that point, Reverend Muirhead, I must ask you to keep what I have told you to yourself.'

'I would say nothing that was not positive.'

'You must say nothing at all. I am sure you will be a most excellent advocate when the time comes, but until then…'

'I don't understand. This presents an exciting future for Taravay and by association many of the people over on Ness.'

'Exciting, but very different from what once was. It involves a great deal of change.'

'And as I've discovered for myself, there are some who don't like change,' he said wryly. 'Very well, I will keep my counsel for now.'

'You had better go,' Jessica said, checking her watch and realising with dismay that almost an hour had passed.

The minister frowned, picking up his hat and twisting it around in his hands. 'Mr Macleod obviously places a great deal of trust in you.'

'Yes.'

He nodded, studying her openly. 'Before I go, I feel obliged to question the propriety of your presence here. An unmarried woman, a single man, quite unchaperoned. Inevitably, there has been talk.'

'Were I a man, there would not have been.'

'That is true. But you are not a man.'

'I am a woman who has had to work doubly, if not trebly hard to prove myself, compared to any man,' Jessica said, trying not to let her anger or panic show. 'My presence here is to provide practical assistance to Mr Macleod in realising his long-held dream for this very beautiful but currently deserted island, nothing more. I am married to my work, besides being thirty-five years old and well beyond the age of taking a husband. And that information,' she finished tartly, 'you have my permission to pass on to whoever you may choose.'

'Thirty-five!' Reverend Muirhead exclaimed, for the first time sounding like the very young man he was. 'Practically a *Cailleach*.'

'Oh no, that is too harsh. However, you have said quite enough…'

'She's said more than enough. Grahame Macfarlane is waiting to sail,' Murdo said, startling them both, 'and Miss Smith has work to be getting on with.'

'Then I will say my goodbyes and express my thanks. Miss Smith has been most enlightening. Let me assure you of my support when you are—if you wish…' Jamming his hat onto his bouncing red curls, Reverend Muirhead bowed, backed out of the potting shed, and hurried off.

'Buffoon,' Murdo muttered.

'No, he's not. I liked him, and he is eager to be your ally, Murdo. Why were you so rude to him?'

'Did he offer to rescue you and your morals?'

'No, he didn't, but the way you were behaving made it seem as if I needed rescued.'

'I can't believe he said nothing.'

'Well he did, but I put him straight. I told him that I was here to help you realise our dream, and that I was married to my work, and that I was too old to be thinking of taking a husband.'

'You're only thirty-five.'

'Ancient, in the eyes of someone who can't be more than twenty-two, though he carped at my calling myself a *Cailleach*.'

'I wish I'd never taught you that word.'

Jessica sighed in exasperation. 'Is that all you have to say?'

'If he'd dared to question me about the propriety of your being here…'

'I'm very glad he did not. I wanted to put an end to any speculation, not fuel the fire, for heaven's sake. I told him he was welcome to pass on what I'd said.'

'I bloody well hope you made it clear that he wasn't welcome to pass on anything else you told him.'

'Yes, of course I did. You've made it very clear, I know perfectly well that you want to tell people in your own time, though why you should eschew such an advocate as he was willing to be…'

'Because I choose to!'

'Murdo! What on earth is wrong with you? You were in a perfectly good mood this morning...'

'Grahame Macfarlane had no right to bring that man here. I'd like to have sent him packing but I'm not so stupid, despite what you are obviously thinking.'

'What I'm thinking is that you missed an opportunity...'

'I told you! I'll tell people when I'm good and ready.'

'Look, I know that you're worried that they won't like so much change, but look at this,' Jessica said, pointing to the drawing on her desk. 'Yes, there are questions that we still have to answer, and as to timescales—but, Murdo, most people will be delighted with the opportunities it offers. Can't you see that?'

'I don't want to talk about it right now.'

'Has something happened? Something you're not telling me?'

He stared at her for a long moment, then took a scrap of paper from his pocket. 'I went back to the Castle after I left you here with Reverend Muirhead.'

She took the paper, recognising her own scribbled dates and questions with a sinking feeling. 'It took me only a few moments to check Mairi Mackinnon's handwriting. It is her.' She paused, feeling sick, but Murdo simply continued to stare at her, his mouth a thin hard line. 'I was curious about Norman, and I wanted to find out when he'd died so I was flicking through the rent books and the dates—the dates struck me as—it seemed such a strange coincidence.'

'It's no coincidence.'

'What do you mean?' she asked in a whisper.

'Since you're so determined to know, it's exactly what you've surmised yourself. I came here to inform my father that I was getting married. He did not approve of my choice. He told me that unless I changed my mind and waited for him to choose a bride for me, then I was dead to him.'

'Oh no.' She reached out for him, but he jumped back. 'Oh, Murdo, what a thing to say to you. As if you would ever give up the woman you loved.'

'*You* gave up the man *you* loved when you were instructed to. And if you had not done so, your employer would have, out of spite, blackened your name and done her best to spoil that career and your future. Which is exactly what my father did. He Cleared Taravay out of spite, to ensure that when I eventually inherited, there would be nothing left. There, are you happy now?'

'Of course I'm not happy! I can't believe he would act in such a wantonly cruel and wicked way.'

'No more could I. I've done my best to put it to the back of my mind, for the temptation to shoulder his guilt, as you can imagine, was difficult to resist.'

'But it wasn't your fault.'

'I am aware of that, but I was the unwitting cause,

and all, as it turned out, for nothing, as I have neither a wife nor a thriving island.'

'I'm sorry. Oh, Murdo, I'm so sorry.'

'I don't know how many times I've told you I don't want your pity. *I'm* sorry I confided in you. I thought you'd be pleased to find out who your grandmother's correspondent was. I didn't expect you'd go sticking your nose into what doesn't concern you.'

'Murdo!'

'Just get on with what you told your precious Reverend Muirhead you are here to do, and leave me alone.'

Chapter Seventeen

Shocked to the core, her knees like jelly, Jessica dropped into her chair in front of her desk. It took her a moment to work out that she was as angry as she was hurt. Murdo's attack on her was not only a bolt out of the blue, it was utterly unfair. She hadn't been prying. In fact if he hadn't been spying on her, picking up that stupid scrap of paper she'd left behind, he wouldn't even know what she'd deduced. Yes, probably—yes, almost certainly—she'd have asked him about it, but she'd have done it carefully, tactfully, choosing her time. This forced a wry smile from her. Murdo was many things, but he was rarely tactful. He was, however, usually a great deal more mindful of her feelings—or he had been of late—which forced her to the conclusion that he'd deliberately meant to hurt her. Which hurt her even more, and made her absolutely furious!

She threw herself to her feet and stalked out to the walled garden, but although she meant to pace out the beds she had planned, a simple but useful task, she couldn't concentrate. She had always prided herself on her even temper, and the nature of her work meant that, although she could reason and object to suggestions she disagreed with at times, she could never give vent to fury. Not that she'd ever felt the need. Even in that horrible interview with Lady Orton, she'd been ashamed, mortified, frightened, not angry. And as for Edward, the most tender, gentle, caring man, there had never been a cross word between them. Mind you, they had never actually discussed anything controversial. What if he'd asked her to give up her work if they had married? How would she have reacted then?

Ignoring the drizzle that was now hazing the sky, Jessica sank onto her favourite bench, frowning. Why *hadn't* Edward raised the issue of her work? Because he had assumed there was nothing to discuss? Because he knew *she* assumed she would continue, and he was simply waiting until they were married to inform her otherwise? That was what Lady Orton had implied, and it felt, unfortunately, very like the truth. At least with Murdo, she knew where she stood. Though where she stood right now was very much in his bad books.

She closed her eyes, lifting her face to the rain, enjoying the soothing softness of it on her skin. They were a team, Murdo had said, and they had been, until today. Today he'd abandoned her with the Reverend Muirhead, leaving *her* to explain *his* plans, ranting at her when she'd done so and unfairly accusing her of having forgotten his wish to keep them to himself, and then accusing her of spying on him. Hot tears leaked from her eyes, mingling with the rain. So much for her belief that he had changed. So much for her belief that he thought of her as an equal. Ironically, she had ruined it, not by giving in to her attraction to him but because of her curiosity and fascination with him. It was so unfair. She hadn't done anything wrong.

Wasn't this precisely how Murdo felt about the Clearances here? What the Laird had done was manifestly unfair as well as spiteful and vicious. Murdo had done nothing wrong, but he had been the trigger. It wasn't his fault, yet she could see, quite clearly, why he struggled to accept that.

Her anger fading, Jessica resumed her pacing. Murdo had paid such a price for doing the honourable thing. He'd been true to himself, true to the woman he loved, and what he'd got for it was a ruined marriage and a ruined island. Finally, she understood why it was so important to him to make his dreams for Taravay as near to perfect as possible. He didn't want to make another mistake. His father had punished him for failing to be the son he wanted, refusing to accept Murdo's love. Then Emily had rejected his love, and even though Jessica understood she'd been true to her own first love, she couldn't help thinking her mistaken. Though if she'd been true to Murdo…

Would Murdo be here on Taravay, or would he have left the island as it was, and continued with his life in London? If he had stayed in the City, then Jessica wouldn't have met him. And even if she had, Emily's Murdo would not be Jessica's Murdo. Not that he was *her* Murdo, absolutely not. He was his own man and she was her own woman, and neither of them wished it any other way, not ever. Taravay had brought them together, their isolation had brought them closer, but Reverend Muirhead's visit had been a stark reminder that they would not be alone forever. Perhaps, she thought desolately, it was for the best that Murdo had put her in her place. Tears filled her eyes again. It wasn't that she cared about him, not in that way. He wasn't essential to her happiness. She'd allowed his moods to affect her own far too much.

The rain had become a downpour without her noticing. She was already soaked to the skin, and the sky was so dark it was pointless to return to the potting shed. The sky lit up with a jagged streak of lightning, followed a few seconds later by a crack of thunder. Stirred, restless, anxious, unsettled, Jessica decided to brave the storm. A gust of wind seized her skirts as soon as she left the shelter of the walled garden. The rain drummed down on the path. Another flash of lightning lit up the stormy sea, and the thunder which followed reverberated through her.

Enthralled, relishing the raw power of nature, she

battled her way down to the jetty where the waves were pounding the pier, the swish of pebbles being cast up onto the shore beside her, mesmerising. Where did the gulls go in bad weather? She couldn't see a single bird in the sky, in the sea, or on the shore. She hoped Grahame Macfarlane had made it safely to Ness. Salt spray showered her. The wind howled. The lightning cracked and the thunder competed with the waves for the loudest roar. Tempestuous, like the owner of the island. Thrilling, despite the danger, like the owner of the island. Captivating, like the owner of the island.

Her mood lifted. She would not be defeated. She would not be intimidated. She would not fail herself. She would not fail Murdo. She would not fail Taravay.

He knew, even before he'd left the walled garden, that he'd been grossly unfair to Jessica, yet Murdo kept going, storming out and hurrying headlong towards Taravay Beag in a rush to get as far away from her as possible. He shouldn't have left her alone with Reverend Muirhead. He shouldn't have ripped up at her for pointing out, perfectly sensibly and rightly, that the man would make a good ally. And he shouldn't have taken her to task for simply putting two and two together, precisely as he had done. He'd given her all the dates himself. He knew how curious she was about the Laird—about his father's reasons for Clearing Taravay. Everybody was curious about that, it was perfectly natural. So why had he let fly like that?

It was drizzling as he reached the causeway, the sky darkening, white horses cresting on the sea which had turned from blue to iron-grey, suiting his mood perfectly. He'd never lost his temper with Emily, not once, not even when she'd told him they were not married. Stark disbelief, he'd felt, then utter devastation that he'd ignored by rolling his sleeves up and getting down to the business of sorting out the mess. It was something he was proud of, that he'd been practical, that he'd kept his feelings to himself, sparing Emily the guilt and the worry. He'd done the same when that telegram had arrived, telling him that his father was dead. Not a trace of what he was feeling had he revealed to the mourners at the Laird's funeral. Only when he was alone here, had he given vent to his pain.

He stopped, staring down at the Lewis-facing beach, remembering how enchanting Jessica's delight at being in the water had been. And contagious. Just over there, they'd kissed, a kiss that he'd felt he'd been waiting for from the moment he met her. Just there, sitting in the soft sand that was stained dark with rain, she'd confided her broken heart to him, and he'd confessed to his own. He'd said things to her he'd never said, some of them not even to himself. From the moment he met her, he'd found himself opening his mouth and voicing whatever was in his head without thinking first. He'd put it down to having been alone here for so long, but it wasn't that. It was her.

She'd forced him to take a good look at his feelings for his father. His father, not the Laird. Murdo smiled ruefully at this. That was her doing, and she'd been right, what's more, when she'd pointed out that he had tried to love the old despot. It had felt like a fresh start, standing in front of the grave and saying his goodbyes and accepting once and for all that he'd never be able to make things right between them. He'd felt as if he was, finally, entitled to take on Taravay and to make it his own, and that was Jessica's doing.

She was always on his side. She loved Taravay almost as much as he did. She'd taken his precious plans and she was helping him to realise them, and to improve them too. He'd encouraged her to voice her own thoughts and ideas, to question and to challenge him, and then he'd slapped her down for it. When he'd seen her today with the that minister, the pair of them talking their heads off, for some reason it had really got his goat. He wasn't jealous, that wouldn't make any sense at all, but it had felt very like it. He *had* been raw though, knowing that she'd pieced together the puzzle of Taravay's Clearance. It put his father in a malevolent light, and for himself—no question, he'd been on the defensive for no reason, as she'd pointed out.

Face it, Murdo said to himself, *you've been wrong every step of the way with Jessica today, and it would serve you right if she'd had enough.* The thought of losing her made his heart sink. He pictured her face when he'd walked away, just a few hours ago. Stricken, she had been. Galvanised into action, heedless of the rain which had started to tip it down, Murdo turned back the way he came. He had to find her, do a good bit of grovelling, and find a way to make it right.

She wasn't in her croft. She wasn't in the walled garden. He was wondering if she was in the Castle, for he'd left it unlocked, when he saw a figure down at the jetty.

'Jessica!' Either she didn't hear him, or his voice was caught by the wind which was whipping round her skirts. The spray was drenching her. Murdo cursed himself viciously, striding down the path towards her.

'Jessica!' She turned, just as huge wave crashed into the jetty, and Murdo lunged for her, pulling her to safety. 'What the hell were you thinking? You could have been swept away.'

She'd been smiling when she turned, but at his words and his tone, made harsh by fear, her smile faded and she tried to push him away. 'Then I'd have spared you the bother of taking me back to Lewis.'

He tightened his grip on her, his worst fears realised. 'I didn't mean it. Not any of it. I'm sorry. I'm so sorry. Please don't go.'

She stopped struggling. 'It's hardly the weather for

a sail. I was enjoying the storm. I'm not planning on going anywhere at the minute.'

The relief was overwhelming. 'Thank the stars. I don't know what came over me. Jessica, I'm so sorry.'

'You hurt me.'

'I *know*. I meant to, because—because it hurt me, that you'd worked out I had made the wrong choice.'

'The wrong choice? You followed your heart.'

'And look where it got me. I won't be doing that again.'

'But you have, you've chosen Taravay. Your heart belongs here.'

'I didn't think of it like that, but you're right. You're the only person who knows what this island means to me. I couldn't feel any worse, thinking of how I spoke to you. I'll understand if you can't forgive me.'

She studied him for a moment. He could see her debating with herself, and he felt her bracing herself before she spoke. 'You made me feel that I'd forgotten my place.'

He'd been wrong, when he said that he couldn't feel any worse. It was a slap in the face, but he deserved it, well and truly. 'The worst thing I could have said, I see that—no, I must have known that. I know sorry isn't nearly enough but I am, deeply. I need you, Jessica. What I mean is, Taravay needs you. I mean, I need you to help me make Taravay—ach, what I mean is, please don't go.'

'I'm not going. I need Taravay too, Murdo. My work here is the foundation for my future as much as yours. It's going to take a great deal more than a dressing-down from the volatile owner to make me want to run away.'

'Volatile! That's one way of putting it. I promise you I won't ever speak to you like that again. We're a team. I won't forget that again in a hurry.'

'If you do, I'll remind you. You made me so angry, and part of it was with myself for not speaking up.'

'I didn't give you a chance. I am so sorry.'

She laughed lightly. 'Please stop apologising. It's making me think that some other Murdo has taken over your body.'

'A changeling. Maybe it's a change for the better.'

'I prefer the original.'

She smiled one of her transforming smiles, the one that went to his head and his groin. Her hair was lying sleek on her head. There were raindrops on her lashes. Her blouse was transparent, clinging to her contours, making her seem so slight, so frail, when he knew her to be so strong. 'I can't bear the thought of losing you,' Murdo said.

Jessica stilled. 'Because of Taravay, you mean?'

He gazed deep into her eyes. 'Yes,' he said, telling himself that it was the relief of being forgiven, the wildness of the weather that was stirring him. 'Because of Taravay,' he said, pulling her closer.

She wrapped her arms around his neck. 'Yes,' she said, tilting her mouth towards his.

'Oh, Jessica,' he whispered, pulling her tight up against him. 'Yes.'

She tasted of rain and the sea. Her skin was cold, her lips warm and soft. He wrapped his arms tightly around her, feeling the heat of her skin against his through their sodden clothing. Their kisses were hot, deep, getting hotter, deeper. He wanted to lose himself in her, he wanted to clothe himself in her, he wanted to be deep inside her, he wanted to feel her clinging to him, every fibre of her being clinging to every part of his. Jessica, Jessica, Jessica. Her name was a whisper in his head as they kissed and kissed, making him ache with longing, making him hard with desire, stirring a fire inside him that felt as if it were engulfing him.

What actually engulfed them was a rogue wave crashing at an angle into the jetty and showering them with seawater. They staggered back to the shore, breathless, wordless, and there they stood holding hands, gazing out at the sea. The rain had stopped, though the sea still heaved and roiled, and the skies had cleared to inky-black, peppered with the first stars. 'It's late,' Murdo said inanely.

'I don't know how it got so late,' Jessica agreed, equally inanely.

'You should get out of those wet things before you catch a chill.'

'You too.'

They held hands as they climbed up the path to her croft, but it was only when they reached her door that they looked at each other. She was flushed, smiling, and shivering. He wanted to wrap her in his arms again. He touched her cheek gently, afraid that words would spoil things. She caught his hand, pressed her lips to his palm, and nodded, just as if he'd asked her as he'd wanted to, if all was well. He kissed her softly on the lips. There was no need for words after all. Then she opened the door, waved, and disappeared inside and Murdo began the tramp back to Taravay Beag. When he arrived at his own croft, he realised he'd been humming to himself.

Chapter Eighteen

The last three days had passed like a dream. The sun had returned to Taravay, and so had harmony. Jessica smiled with contentment as she ticked another item off her list. It was still growing, with more tasks added than completed every day, but they were making real progress. She was expecting several quotations from suppliers in the post, and checking her watch she calculated that Grahame Macfarlane would be due around now, so she decided to make her way down to the jetty to meet him. There was already a fishing boat tied up, but the man Murdo was talking to was a stranger. Seated side by side on the jetty, the pair of them were deep in conversation, so she decided not to interrupt, returning to the potting shed.

Half an hour later, the hairs on the back of her neck prickled. Jessica looked up, already smiling, getting to her feet, already knowing that it was Murdo. '*Madainn mhath.*'

'*Madainn mhath*,' he said, setting a bundle of letters down on the table and holding out his hands.

She took them, stepping closer for the gentle kiss which they allowed themselves every morning. A chaste enough kiss, lips to lips, hands clasped together, nothing more, but it did not feel chaste. She drank in the smell of him, sea and sunshine, then she took a step back, just as he did, and they released each other, and they smiled, one of those special smiles. And then they both pretended it hadn't happened.

'Who was that?' Jessica asked, picking up the post and shuffling through it.

'Finlay Murray.'

'Your childhood friend?'

'The same.'

She tried to hide her surprise, cutting the seal on a letter with her gardening knife and pretending to read it.

'Has anyone ever told you, you're as easy to read as a book? Go on, ask me.'

She set the letter down, shaking her head. 'If I'm so transparent, I don't need to.'

'I sent a message with Grahame Macfarlane asking Finlay to come over,' Murdo said, drawing up his chair. 'I wasn't sure he would, but it seems he was as keen to make his peace as I was. Is the tea in that pot still hot?'

'No, and it's revoltingly strong, just the way you like

it,' Jessica said, pouring the tar-like liquid into the tin mug she kept for him to use. 'Go on?'

He shrugged, took a sip and gave her an appreciative grin. 'When I came back for the funeral, it was Finlay who sailed me over. He assumed, as most of them did, that I knew what had happened here. He asked me, what are you going to do about it? Nothing, I told him, because that was what I thought at that point.' Murdo paused, took another sip of tea, and shook his head. 'From that, he assumed that I didn't care, and I assumed, as soon as I'd seen the state of the place, that he blamed me—which he mistakenly did. And being modern Nineteenth Century men, we let all that fester away and didn't talk to each other again. So I arranged for Grahame Macfarlane to bring my supplies and collect my mail, and of course Finlay took that as a personal snub and—well, it's cleared up now, so he and Grahame will be sharing the sailings here, which will suit Grahame very well, I reckon. There,' Murdo said, setting down his empty mug, 'did that answer the question you didn't ask?'

'Mostly.'

'Ah yes. I did indeed let him in on our plans. And he is indeed very supportive. In fact, you'll be delighted to know that he shares your own view that we should be letting everyone on Ness into the secret sooner rather than later.'

'Murdo! We still have so many important things to decide.'

'What? Haven't you been urging me almost since you set foot on Taravay to tell people...'

'Yes, yes, but that was before...' She broke off, shaking her head. 'It's just a surprise, that's all. And,' she added, when he said nothing, 'I know that you want everything to be perfect, which I completely understand because...'

'Because even though my father put me in an impossible position, there have been times when I've thought I made the wrong choice, and this time I want to get it right.'

'Yes.'

Murdo picked up his empty cup, stared into it, then set it down. 'It's not only that. There's the fact that it took me the best part of a year, wandering about here like Robinson Crusoe, to take my head out of my ar... to take my head out of the sand, and start making amends. But the main reason is, I thought I'd have to explain, you see, why he did it, and that by explaining, then it would be easy for people to think, as my father did, that Emily was a big mistake.'

'You loved her.'

'I did.' He drummed his fingers on his leg, frowning down at them. 'My father's objections to Emily were not to her person but to her bloodline, or lack of it. As a Macleod of Taravay—dear God, how often did he remind me that was what I was—he was insistent that it was my duty to marry into what he called "genuine Highland blood". I was sure that if he met Emily he'd change his mind, but he refused.'

'Are you telling me that you do regret defying him?'

'No, and I'm not saying that I wish I'd never married Emily—or not married her,' he said with a ghostly smile. 'There was a letter from her today, actually. She is very happy, and she's very grateful to me for "facilitating the transition", is how she puts it. She has no desire to publicise the change in our circumstances because everyone who matters to her already knows, and she wishes me well. Oh and she is expecting a child. And you needn't hold your breath as if you're waiting on me to explode. I am pleased for her, but nothing else. Strictly speaking, I didn't need to tell you any of this. To be completely honest, I probably wouldn't have if I'd been in any way unsure of what I felt, but I'm not.'

'Thank you, then, for confiding in me. I'm honoured.'

Murdo smiled wryly. 'You're welcome. It was odd, like reading a letter from someone I knew a long time ago. I'm not the man who married Emily. I'm the man who has recovered from marrying Emily. I don't regret it, but I won't put myself through it again. Does that make sense to you? Do you feel the same?'

'I don't regret it, but I won't put myself through it again?' Jessica bit her lip, frowning. 'Do you know, I think that might be exactly how I feel. Murdo, does Finlay know anything about your life in London?'

He shook his head. 'No one here does. When I was living in exile, any communication with Taravay would have been too painful. At first, when I was younger, I was ashamed too, that my father had deemed me unworthy, so I think I was determined to show him that I was perfectly happy without him or Taravay.'

'You must have missed the island and the people terribly.'

'I was young, there was a whole world out there. It was more a case of not wanting my father to find out that I'd been in touch with anyone, for their sake as much as mine. And don't forget, Jessica, Finlay is ages with me. He was getting on with his own life. I'm simply glad we've made our peace. Which brings me back to what Finlay and yourself have both been saying. I think it's time we started making plans to share Taravay's future with the Niseachs. Talking to Finlay today made me see that I've no need to explain myself. He showed no interest in the whys and wherefores of what my father did, and he assumed that what I'd been doing here alone was working it all out, so I didn't disillusion him. It's what I said to you countless times, back when you first came here. It's not the past that matters, it's the future. So have a think about how we might go about that.'

'I will add it to my list.'

'Aye, me too.'

As Murdo got to his feet, Jessica also pushed back her chair. 'I'm so pleased for you. You should be pleased with yourself too, it's a big step forward that you made today.'

'Ach, it's been a long time coming, and it's not as if we did any soul-searching. I save that for you,' he said awkwardly. 'You won't believe me, but I'm not usually the soul-searching type.'

'No more am I. You know more about me than I did, before I came here.'

'Then that makes the pair of us.'

Somehow, they were clasping hands again. The air between them stilled as they looked at each other. 'Island life,' Jessica said. 'Being alone, with no one else to confide in.'

His hands tightened on hers. 'That's it,' Murdo said.

She knew in her bones it wasn't true, but she had to believe it, for to attribute it to Murdo was far too dangerous. 'Friends,' Jessica said, clutching at a more believable straw. 'Moving from estate to estate, garden to garden, I don't really get many chances to make friends, or the opportunity to keep them. And now that my mother has gone…' She had no one. A chasm of future loneliness opened up. 'I will be free to travel wherever I like. Europe, perhaps, that would be a new challenge.'

'Your work here will keep you at least another year, if you're wanting to see it through. I hope you will.'

'Of course I will.' A year, transforming this wonderful island, it was a dream come true, but for how many more weeks would she be alone with the owner, who was already transformed? Whatever it was that existed between them would come to a natural end. As she had always known it would, Jessica reminded herself sternly, pinning a smile to her face. 'Taravay is the key to my future too.'

'It will be strange, having people here, which we will sooner rather than later, if not to stay then to visit,' Murdo said, echoing her thoughts.

'We can't make your dream a reality without them.'

'There are times when I wish we could.'

Her breath caught. She stepped closer to him, at the same time as he urged her towards him. 'Me too,' Jessica said. 'But we cannot.'

'No.'

His lips grazed hers. Their tongues touched. Their mouths opened into a soft, deep kiss. Sun-warmed. Yearning. Hands clasped, keeping the most tantalising distance between them, they kissed, and for long moments the world was lost. When it ended, dazed, they gazed at each other, both gave a slight shake of the head, a small smile, then they stepped apart.

'We really should get back to work,' Jessica said, her mind on anything but gardens and plants.

'We should. Indeed we should. I have to admit though, it's not what I'm thinking of, right at the moment.'

'Nor I.'

Murdo gave a snort of laughter, running his fingers through his cropped hair. 'Do you have any idea what that does to me? No, don't answer that, it must be perfectly obvious. I'll take myself out on the boat and away from temptation. I haven't checked my creels for a few days.'

But he made no move to leave, and their eyes met again, and they stepped into each other's arms again, and this time the kiss was rougher, deeper, rawer. This time, when they dragged themselves apart, they were both flushed, breathing hard.

'Lobster,' Murdo said, making for the door. 'Have you ever tasted it?'

Still completely flustered, Jessica shook her head.

'It's early in the season, I've had nothing but crab so far, but if there is one I'll cook it for you.'

And with that, he left. Jessica watched him hurrying across the walled garden, hesitating in the doorway, then deciding not to turn back. She put her fingers to her tingling lips. Her body was thrumming, churning, burning. She poured herself a cup of cold, viciously strong tea and drank it in one gulp, choking on the leaves. Then, with a deep sigh, she resolutely pulled her notebook towards her and picked up her pencil.

Chapter Nineteen

Jessica stepped through the open door of the Castle. A lamp was lit in the vestibule, and when she reached the Hall, there were several more, interspersed with candles in tall, tarnished sticks, lighting the way towards another open door. She followed the trail, entering the dining room. The curtains were drawn. A peat fire burned in the large grate. Two large candelabra were lit at one end of the table, where two places had been set with beautiful porcelain and silver cutlery, both inscribed with a coat of arms. There were crystal wine glasses and a claret jug of wine. There was a loaf of bread on a board, and a cheese.

Thanking the stars that she'd found the time to bathe and change, Jessica stood on tiptoe to check her hair, which she had pinned up for the first time in weeks, in the tarnished mirror above the mantel.

'Dinner is served, Madam.'

Murdo set a covered salver down on the table and stood to greet her, and her own greeting caught in her throat. White shirt and stock showed off his tanned face. The black leather waistcoat was neatly fastened over his flat belly and narrow waist. And below, not trousers but a kilt made of a tweed woven in the most beautiful muted colours that reminded Jessica of the moorland they had crossed when travelling from Stornoway. He wore no sporran, but the buckle on his belt and the pin that held his kilt down were silver and adorned with polished agates. Long knitted stockings showed off his strong calves and well-polished boots completed the ensemble.

'I've struck you dumb,' he said. 'Did you think I was one of the Castle's ghosts?'

'No one would mistake you for anything other than flesh and blood,' Jessica said, her own flesh and blood extremely agitated.

'Nor you.' He took her hand in his, bowing over it and pressing a soft kiss to her palm. 'You look very lovely tonight.'

She blushed wildly, only just refraining from saying, 'oh, this old thing', and in fact very glad indeed that she had donned her one and only silk gown, even if she had left off most of the petticoats. 'You look magnificent. And so does this room.'

'Don't look too closely, it will spoil the illusion.' He ushered her to a chair, then sat down at the head of the table beside her.

'Truly, Murdo, when you said you'd cook me lobster, I thought you'd leave it on my doorstep. I didn't dream that you'd go to so much trouble.'

'It's a very small thank you. Besides, we've been living here for a month now, and we've not once had dinner together. I thought it was time to remedy that.'

'You've done so in style.'

He poured them both a glass of wine. 'I'd hoped for champagne but there was none in the cellar—I don't know why I was surprised at that, mind. There's nothing but potatoes and butter to go with the lobster, and some bread and cheese, all of which came from Ness, I hasten to add. *Slàinte Mhath*, Jessica. Good health.'

'That was perfect,' Jessica said, eating a last sliver of cheese with a contented sigh. 'I am very glad you didn't leave the lobster on my doorstep. I'd not have had a clue how to go about eating it, never mind cooking it.'

'There's no skill to that. We used to boil them up in a bucket on the beach, along with crab. The biggest challenge was getting the stove in the kitchens to light, it must be about fifty years old, and the copper pan I used is probably older still. I reckon I'll need to— ah but no, I'm not going to talk about work tonight.' Murdo poured the last of the wine and touched his glass to hers. 'We should do this more often.'

'I would be delighted to. I've never dined in such lavish surroundings.'

'Aye, with the place covered in cobwebs, the mice running around inside the wainscotting, and the silver tarnished,' he said, his smile fading as he saw her expression. 'Come, you must have eaten in far finer establishments than this.'

'In the Servants' Hall.'

'You're not a servant.'

'I'm like a governess, betwixt and between stairs. It's the Servants' Hall or alone in my quarters. I am certainly never invited to dine with my employers.'

Murdo tossed back the remnants of his wine. 'I had no idea.'

'Why should you?'

'You deserve to be treated with respect.'

'By and large, I am accorded the greatest of respect for my talent, but my blood is of the common sort.'

'I remember,' Murdo said, scowling, 'that first day. "I'm green-fingered, not blue-blooded", you said. I don't give a damn about such things.'

'That's because…'

'What? Because I've been born with a silver spoon in my mouth? Is that what you were about to say?' He pushed his chair back to douse one of spluttering candles.

'It's late.' Disappointed at the turn the conversation had taken, Jessica got to her feet. 'I had better go. I like to make an early start.'

'Ach, don't let us end on this note. You're right, I am

privileged, and though I've worked hard for my money, I can't deny that my name and my education too, have given me a leg up. It seems wrong to me though, that you're not given the same respect when you've worked every bit as hard as me, and your knowledge is a damn sight more practical. What's more, I'll be willing to bet you're not paid half of what you're worth. I know what you're charging me and I'll most certainly be doubling it...'

'Murdo, please don't,' Jessica protested, her face burning. 'I am charging you the going rate.'

'Do they try and reduce your fee, when they find out you're a woman? I bet they do.'

'Sometimes, but I never accede.'

'That must have cost you?'

'Occasionally, in the past, but my reputation protects me. I make a good living.'

'You should be rich. You deserve to be rich.'

'If we make a success of Taravay then I will certainly be able to command a higher fee in future.'

'I think you sell yourself short. I think if you reviewed the way you come up with your fee, there's a lot more you could legitimately be charging for. I could take a look...'

'Please don't! It's not necessary.' In the tense silence that followed, Jessica bit back the urge to apologise for snapping at him. *It doesn't matter*, she wanted to say, but it did. 'I'm thirty-five,' she said stiffly. 'I am well accustomed to fighting my own battles.'

'I don't doubt it. I only offered because for once, I felt that my expertise was superior to yours. I don't know how many times over the past few weeks you've given me a lesson in how to go about something. I only wanted to help, and I certainly didn't mean to patronise you.'

'Now I feel about the size of that leftover bit of cheese.'

'Don't be daft. You're used to having to prove yourself even more, because you're a woman.'

'Yes. I'm sorry, I know you don't think of me in that way.'

'I'm loath to contradict you, but right now, that's exactly how I'm thinking of you.'

She lifted her gaze from the carpet to meet his eyes and found herself speechless.

'It's a lovely night,' Murdo said. 'Would you like to take a look at the stars?'

She nodded, following in his wake as he led her out of the dining room, but instead of heading outside, he made his way up the central staircase. His kilt swung gently as he climbed. A step behind him, she was mesmerised by the tantalising glimpses it gave her of the bare flesh at the top of his stockings.

'Hold on to the rail and keep your eyes on your feet now,' he said, opening the door of the turret.

She didn't care that he had noticed her appreciation. They were no longer at odds, quite the opposite, and that was all that mattered. Then, as she emerged at the top of the turret, it was not Murdo but the view that made her breathless. The sky was inky-black, the air unexpectedly warm, sweetly smelling from the damp ground. The moon was a slither in the sky, while the stars were enormous, glittering and glinting, spread out above them like a carpet of twinkling diamonds. Standing beside Murdo at the parapet, she could hear the sea, a rhythmic shush, shush, shush, like a lover's whisper. It was almost as dark as the night sky, streaked with the silver crest of a wave every now and then. Bats swooped in graceful arcs just below them, snapping up the insects.

'It's utterly beautiful,' Jessica whispered.

'I think so,' he said, smiling down at her and sliding his arm around her waist to pull her closer. 'Watch,' he said, pointing out to the Atlantic coast. 'It's getting to be a bit late in the year, but if we're lucky we might see the Northern Lights. Conditions are perfect.'

She had no idea how long they waited, their gazed fixed on the horizon, their bodies nestled together, awareness of each other a fluttering tension each time one of them moved, a hand smoothing, her head on his shoulder, his cheek against her hair, their hips grazing. A shooting star blazed across the sky, followed by two more in quick succession. And then at last it happened.

A sudden blaze of green light high in the sky that rippled and faded, followed by another of bright purple. Silver, teal blue that turned to turquoise, then the bright green of algae became the golden colour of ripe wheat before it faded. Jessica watched, utterly mesmerised, as the lights shimmered. The lines of colours were shaped like waves, morphing into jagged lines like lightning streaks, and then back to softer curves.

When it was over, it took some moments for her eyes to adjust. The stars which had seemed so bright seemed dimmer. 'I've never seen anything so wonderful,' Jessica whispered, turning into Murdo's embrace. 'Thank you.'

She lifted her face, because the kiss had been simmering between them ever since they stepped out into the night. She must still have been dazzled by the Northern Lights, because when their lips met she could have sworn stars exploded. Ridiculous. Delicious. She wrapped her arms around his neck and pressed closer. He murmured her name, his fingers curling into her hair, and their kisses deepened.

She was leaning against the wall of the turret, safely away from the parapet, even though she didn't recall moving, and they were still kissing. She slid her hands under his waistcoat, feeling the heat of his skin, the sharp intake of his breath, his belly tensing. He was pulling the pins from her hair, running his fingers through it, kissing her throat, the swell of her breasts above the neckline of her gown. She slid her hands around to his back, down to the swell of his buttocks, pulling him closer. His lips met hers again, and their kisses became urgent. She could feel his arousal through his kilt, through the silk of her gown and thin undergarments. He smoothed his hand over her breast, making her nipples ache for his touch through her chemise. She arched her back, pulling him closer, relishing the groan that she drew from him, the way he said her name, a drawn-out plea.

Murdo swore under his breath, dragging his mouth from hers, his hands on her shoulders, breathing deeply. 'We're in danger of falling over the edge,' he said raggedly.

She laughed, a strange strangled sound. 'We've moved away from the parapet.'

He muttered something else in Gaelic. 'I wasn't talking about the parapet. It was too much. I shouldn't have...'

'You didn't—you must be aware that I know—that I'm not exactly an innocent.' Now her toes were curling inside her shoes. She made a helpless gesture. 'I meant that I—I'm not usually so forward.'

'Nor am I.' Murdo caught her hands in his, forcing her to look at him. 'Did I go too far?'

Not far enough, were the words that sprang to mind, but she managed to bite them back. 'No, but I think this conversation is in danger of going too far, don't you? It was effects of the stars, and the Northern Lights, and the wine and the lovely dinner. All of it was perfect.'

'Almost too perfect. I'll walk you to your croft.'

'Thank you, but I think it's better that I make my own way.'

He looked as if he might object, then he changed his mind. Telling herself she was relieved, Jessica lifted his hand to her cheek, kissing his knuckles. 'Goodnight, Murdo. It really was perfect.'

She went carefully down the turret stairs, and then hurried down the three other flights. The lamps were still burning in the Great Hall, but the candles had burned out. The night air was chill now, and there were clouds gathering, covering the stars. She hastened onto the path, pausing halfway to her croft to look up. As she had expected, he was still there, watching her. She lifted her hand, turned, and continued on her way.

In the morning, there was a note on her desk in the potting shed.

'I forgot all about this last night, as I got distracted by something or, more accurately, someone!' Murdo had written.

I managed to find Norman Mackinnon's grave for you. It was in the churchyard but tucked away in a corner. The inscription is in Gaelic, but I've translated it for you.

Intrigued, Jessica unfolded the separate piece of paper. Sure enough, there was Norman Mackinnon's name and the date of his death, 1874, just as she had surmised from the accounts book. He'd been a very old man of eighty-four when he died. It was the words which followed that caught her attention:

Also in memory of Mairi, daughter of Helen, much loved sister of the above Norman, who died of cholera in Glasgow in September 1839. Her heart will always be on Taravay.

'I think this confirms we've found your Mairi,' Murdo's note continued.

What I wonder though, is who added that, so long after her death and against the convention here of separating men and women. Norman would surely have had a stone erected at the time in the women's cemetery. Could it have been my father? Something for me to puzzle over if I can't sleep, which I'm pretty sure I won't after tonight. Not all the fireworks were in the sky. M.

Chapter Twenty

'I think that's as much as we can do for now.' Murdo closed his notebook and stretched his legs out in front of him. 'Another week at the most, and we'll have everything we need to take to Ness. I can't say I'm looking forward to it. I'd far rather pass on the gist of what we're planning to a few people and let it make its way around. Catriona the Foghorn, Reverend Muirhead, and Finlay, between them they'd have just about everyone covered.'

'And all the detail would get muddled, and before you know it the Niseachs would be up in arms because you were turning over the estate to grouse shooting parties and demanding a tithe on the lobster creels,' Jessica said.

'Now there's an idea, why didn't I think of that.' He held his hands up. 'You know I'm joking.'

'People will want to come to Taravay to imagine the changes for themselves.'

'I hadn't really thought of that.'

'No more Robin and Robina Crusoe.'

Murdo gave a snort of laughter, then his smile faded. 'I'd been thinking it will be a month or so before we have enough supplies to start sorting out accommodation for the labourers, a few more weeks after that before any sort of real work can commence.'

'It will be good to see Taravay busy again,' Jessica said, half-heartedly.

'We'll have time, while the visitors are only here by day, to get used to it, I suppose,' Murdo said, sounding equally half-hearted. 'Let's forget about it for now. The sun's back out, it's set to be a lovely evening, will we take a walk and talk about something other than business?'

'That would be lovely. You go ahead, I'll join you in a minute, I want to finish my own notes,' Jessica said.

She watched until he left the walled garden, but instead of picking up her pencil, she dropped her head onto her hands. She ought to be delighted at the pace of their progress, and she was, but she was also—what was she feeling? Afraid of failing? She was nervous, but confident, so it wasn't that. It felt like fear, panicky butterflies. She knew perfectly well what it was too. It was fear of their time together coming to an end. Fear of an abrupt ending to something that had only just begun. Something she feared—yes, that was the right word—was beginning to become a bit too important. And she was afraid that others might perceive what she didn't want to admit, that she already cared for Murdo more than she ought to.

'And so it's a very, very good thing that we've got such little time,' Jessica informed herself, getting up. 'And it's a very, very stupid thing for me to waste any of it when I could be out there with Murdo.'

Thus rebuked, or telling herself that she was, she closed the door of the potting shed and went out to find him. He was standing above the jetty, his hand shading his eyes from the sun. 'There's a boat heading this way,' he said. 'I think it's Grahame Macfarlane.'

'Is something wrong, do you think? A telegram?'

'No, it looks as if we have a visitor, rather sooner than expected. There's a stranger in the boat with him.'

As Murdo watched Grahame bring the boat in, his stomach was churning, though for what reason, he had no idea. The closer the boat got to the jetty, the more certain he was that he'd never seen the old man before, yet the nearer they got, the more uneasy he felt. What was Grahame thinking, bringing a visitor to Taravay so late in the day? Beside him, Jessica was silent, frowning, obviously equally concerned about night falling and being left with a stranger on the island. He had the distinct impression that she was no more looking forward to sharing Taravay than he was. It was contrary of them both, for populating Taravay with new islanders and visitors aplenty was what they were both working so hard towards. They'd been too much alone, he knew that. He was getting too used to having her to himself. Too used to having her there all the time. Too used to her company. It would be good for the pair of them to have a dose of reality. A slow drifting apart, that would be easier to manage. Not that he was expecting it to be difficult. He'd always known she was going. He'd miss her for a bit, but Taravay was what mattered, and Taravay was his forever.

'I've brought you a visitor, Murdo.' Grahame Macfarlane's voice cut into his thoughts. 'I did try to persuade him to wait until tomorrow, but he insisted you'd be happy to accommodate him tonight.'

Murdo caught the rope and began to make the boat fast, casting glances at the old man, but he was absolutely certain he'd never met him before.

Grahame jumped onto the jetty to help tie up. 'His name is Donald Macneil,' he said under his breath. 'He arrived this afternoon from Harris, and began kicking up a bit of a fuss about being brought here immediately. Said that he was one of the old Laird's oldest friends, and he'd only just found out that his son was on Taravay. My wife offered him a bed until the morning, but he said that at his age he could never be sure he'd see another morning, so...'

'Am I to be kept waiting all night for you to whisper together like a pair of gossiping fishwives? Give me a hand and help me out, and then you can get yourself back to that interfering wife of yours.'

'I can wait half an hour or so and take him back,' Grahame offered.

He would happily have jumped at this, but Murdo's gut told him it would be a mistake. 'Go off home. I'm sorry you've been dragged out twice in one day. Would you ask Finlay Murray to bring the mail and our supplies in the morning, give you a bit of a break. I'm sure he'll be glad to do it.' He made his way to the side of the boat. 'Welcome to Taravay, Mr Macneil.'

'Am I now? I hope so.' The old man gripped his arm to steady himself, but his step from boat to jetty was solid enough. He must have been tall in his younger days, for even with his stooped shoulders, he was less than a head shorter than Murdo himself. He was scrawny, with a hawk-like nose, but his jaw was square, he had good cheek bones, and his hazel eyes, though rheumy, had thick dark lashes, in contrast to his bushy grey brows. 'Have you looked your fill then?'

'I have, and I'm afraid I have no idea who you are.'

'We've never met.' Donald Macneil slapped his arm. 'You've done well for yourself though, I heard. And this,' he said, nodding at Jessica, 'must be the gardener. Come here, and let me take a look at you.'

'This is Miss Smith, and she's a landscaper of great renown, not a kitchen maid for you to inspect.'

'No need to get on your high horse.'

'Mr Macneil.' Jessica stepped forward and held out her hand. 'How do you do?'

'That very much depends, young woman. Though now I look at you, you're not so very young. You'll not see thirty again, that's for sure.'

'I don't see how…'

'You are quite right,' Jessica interrupted him, 'I am thirty-five. Most people take me for younger.'

'Well I'm in my eightieth year, and I've enjoyed the company of my fair share of women in my time, let me tell you. Skin like yours, anyone would take you for a Highlander, but it doesn't wear well in the sun.'

'Then it's as well we don't see too much sunshine here on Taravay, isn't it?'

Murdo's snort of laughter had the uninvited guest glaring at him. 'What do you think you're at, keeping an old man standing about in the cold? At my age, a breath of wind from the wrong direction could see me off.'

'You've caught us unprepared for visitors, Mr Macneil. There are only two crofts fit for living in, and Miss Smith has one of them. You're welcome to mine, but it's on the other side of the island. I can fetch the pony…'

'No need for that. I shall stay in the Castle.'

'It was closed up when the Laird died.'

'Not even two years ago, that was. I'm sure your gardener can get me a room ready, and in the meantime,

I'll take a dram or two with you, just to keep out the cold. We can eat later.'

'Did I not tell you that Miss Smith is a landscape gardener, not a servant,' Murdo snapped.

'You're the Laird and she's the only woman on the island. Don't tell me she has you fending for yourself?'

'I choose to fend for myself, and I'm good at it.'

'I hope so, in that case. I've a delicate constitution. I can't stomach herring in oatmeal, if that's what you're planning. A wee bit of beef, some venison maybe, and some nice fresh eggs. There'll be a good claret in the cellar too, unless you've drunk it all. Angus Macleod was known for keeping a good cellar, though not known for sharing it much. And for breakfast…'

'Taravay Castle is not yet a hotel,' Murdo snapped, throwing the rope to Grahame and waving him off. 'You'll take what you're given.'

'Not yet? By God, is that what you're planning to throw your money away on?'

They had reached the top of the steep path. 'What the hell,' Murdo said, coming to an abrupt halt, 'do you know about my money? And what business is it of yours, how I choose to spend it?'

Donald Macneil gave a wheezy laugh. 'How do you imagine anyone knows anything about anyone in these parts? You've been sending enough telegrams to open a new office here on Taravay. You've money to burn, by the sounds of it.'

'You're not from Ness.'

'No, I'm from Harris, I've lived there all my life, but I've friends over yonder,' he said, pointing in the direction of Lewis, 'and they keep me informed of what's what here.'

'I'll ask you again, why exactly are you here?'

'Well now, as I've already said to you, that is a subject that might require a dram or two.'

Murdo hesitated. He'd come across a good few liars and fraudsters in his business dealings, but though his instincts told him Donald Macneil was a chancer, there was something about the man that made him wary. Whatever he had to say was unlikely to be good news. 'Come on then,' he said gruffly, heading towards the Castle. 'I'll find you a bed, but it will likely be damp, and I'll be finding myself one too. No offence, but though you might claim to know all about me, I know nothing about you, so I'm not letting you out of my sight. I'll feed you, and I'll even find a few drams for you to have, then you can have your say, but you'll be leaving in the morning with Finlay Murray.'

'If I were you, lad, I'd wait to hear what I have to tell you, before you go issuing instructions. It is of a confidential nature,' Donald Macneil said, looking significantly at Jessica. 'We can dispense with the gardener.'

Murdo's hackles rose, but he could tell from the glint in the man's eyes that he was being tested. 'Miss Smith…'

'Has a great deal to be getting on with.' Jessica once again pre-empted him. 'So I'll bid you good evening, Mr Macneil, and goodbye, because I don't expect to see you again.'

She didn't extend her hand to the man, Murdo was pleased to see, nor did she insist on assisting with the domestic tasks that Macneil had assigned to her. He wondered how often in the past she'd been forced to defend her position against the ingrained prejudice of others. She had already turned in the direction of her own croft, walking with her usual swinging gait. He'd been looking forward to their evening walk, and the dinner he'd planned for both of them would now be shared with this inquisitive stranger.

'Thirty-five, not yet wholly past bearing you a bairn. I hope that's a complication you're taking care to avoid.'

A fresh pang of unease gripped his belly as he turned back to the old man. 'If you don't keep your slanderous thoughts to yourself, you'll be swimming back to Ness in a minute when I throw you off the jetty.'

Donald Macneil raised one of his craggy brows, shaking his head. 'I sincerely hope it's not marriage you have in mind. A gardener, and you calling yourself a Macleod of Taravay. You'd have Angus Murdo spinning in his grave.'

'I call myself Macleod of Taravay because that is who I am.'

'Well now, we'll see about that.'

Chapter Twenty-One

Jessica spent a sleepless night, unable to stop herself from checking the lights in the Castle, wondering what on earth was going on. It was none of her business, she told herself, but she couldn't help feeling excluded, put firmly in her place by Donald Macneil, even though Murdo himself had defended her. She had taken an instant dislike to the man. He was what her father would have called sleekit, a man interested only in furthering his own cause at any cost. The fact that he had deprived her of an evening alone with Murdo hardly helped endear him to her.

She woke curled up in the chair by a smouldering fire as dawn began to break on a grey day, and managed to immerse herself in her work sufficiently to exclaim in surprise when her father's watch told her it was almost noon. Where was Murdo? Why hadn't he come to find her? Had his visitor left? What on earth had the old man had to say that was so important? And perhaps even more perturbing, why had Murdo allowed him to stay, and in the Castle of all places, where he had not slept himself since he had left the island at eighteen. It wasn't her place to be worried, but she was. There was something wrong, she was sure of it.

The morning's mizzle had softened into a damp murk. Pulling on her cloak, Jessica left the walled garden. There was fresh milk, bread and eggs on her doorstep, so Finlay Murray had been and gone. Had he taken Donald Macneil with him? She dithered, trying to decide whether to walk in the direction of the village or Taravay Beag when, looking over at the Castle, she saw that the door was wide open. Now thoroughly concerned, she hurried over, calling Murdo's name as she entered the Great Hall. There was no sign of him or of the visitor. Had he forgotten to close the door? Calling his name again, she checked each of the rooms on the ground floor, but all were as dusty and unused as before, save for the dining room, where the remains of a peat fire was in the grate, and the remains of a decanter of whisky on the table with an empty glass beside it.

There was only one room on this floor she had not checked. Hesitantly, she opened the door of what she knew to be the Laird's study, though she had never been inside it. Murdo was seated behind a large desk, which was strewn with papers. Books from the shelves lay in stacks on the floor. He was still wearing yesterday's clothes, and he had not shaved, as he now did every morning, to neaten his beard. 'Murdo?'

He blinked, staring at her, uncomprehending.

'Are you ill?' she asked, for he was indeed pale under his tan, and his eyes had that haunted look she had not seen for weeks.

He shook his head, his expression dazed, as if he'd sustained a blow to the head.

'Has that man gone?'

'After breakfast. He had four eggs and most of a loaf of bread,' he enunciated carefully.

Jessica eyed the tumbler half hidden by a stack of books. It was full of whisky. 'How much of that have you had?'

'Not. A. Drop.' This was said with a ghostly smile. 'Tried. Couldn't. I need to find the family bible.'

'I think you need to go to your bed.'

He slammed his fist onto the top of the desk, making Jessica and a number of the books jump. 'I've not touched a bloody drop. *He* had his fill. Must have the constitution of an ox, the old—the old…' Suddenly he dropped his head into his hands, swearing.

Utterly at a loss, Jessica crossed the room, thinking to comfort him but at her touch he jumped up, growling at her. 'Leave me alone.'

'Murdo! What on earth is wrong with you?'

'Wrong? Oh, nothing, nothing at all, except I've no bloody idea who I am or what I'm going to do. He'll be back. I need to find the bible.'

'I'll help you.'

'I've already looked everywhere. If I don't find it...' He sank back down onto the chair, his face in his hands once more. A huge sob wracked his body. 'Taravay is all I've got now. I've got nothing else, no one. If I can't find that bible...'

'Murdo, you've got me.' Horrified by the way he seemed to be crumbling before her, Jessica put her arms around him. He struggled to push her away, but she held him tightly until the fight went out of him and he burrowed his head into her shoulder and sobbed. Silent tears for his anguish and hurt ran down her cheeks as she kept her hold, whispering over and over that he had her, that all would be well, that they'd find the bible, though she had no idea why it was so important, and not a clue how she would make all well, not having any notion of what had gone so horrendously wrong.

It felt like an age, but it was over in a few minutes. His sobs stopped, but his face remained pressed into her, his arms linked behind her back. 'I'm sorry,' he said, his voice muffled.

'Please don't be. I've no idea what that—that slug of a man said, but...'

'That slug of a man,' Murdo said, freeing himself from her embrace and dragging a handkerchief from his pocket, 'is my father, according to him.'

Jessica's jaw dropped. 'What did you say?'

He scrubbed at his eyes, keeping his face averted. 'Based on what he told me, I'm his bastard son.'

'No! No, he's lying. That's not possible. No, no, no, Murdo…'

'Please.' He held his hand up to quieten her. 'It's a long story, and my head is thumping.'

'Would you like a cup of tea? Oh dear heavens, that is such a stupid thing to suggest when you must be feeling—I don't know what you are feeling.'

'Wrecked. Reeling. And now I'm mortified too. You must be thinking I'm…'

She put her hand over his mouth. 'I'm thinking that maybe a cup of tea is exactly what you need after all, and then a sleep.'

'Tea, but I can't sleep. I need to find that bloody bible.'

'Why?'

He took her hand between his, clasping it tightly. She could see him debating with himself, then he nodded, letting her hand go. 'It will help me make sense of it if I explain. *You'll* help me make sense of it.'

'Are you sure?'

'Yes,' he said with more conviction. 'I want to.'

A lump rose in her throat, but she forced a smile. 'I shall go forth and conquer the stove in the kitchen. If I'm not back in half an hour, you'll know I've failed.'

'I have every faith in you. But bring the tea to the drawing room, not here.'

Murdo waited until Jessica left the room before he dropped his head onto his hands again. *Reeling* and *wrecked* didn't even begin to describe how he was feeling. It was the same thing all over again, just as he'd felt eighteen months ago before he came here. He thought he was in control. His plans for the future were taking shape. And then a bolt from the blue, and his world was falling apart again. This time though, he wasn't sure he had the strength to recover from it.

But it wasn't the same, he realised. This time, he wasn't alone. This time Jessica was here. Jessica, who had held him while he cried like a bairn, and instead of mocking him, she'd offered him tea and sympathy, and told him that she had every faith in him, all the while looking as if she was ready to roll up her sleeves and do battle on his behalf. This idea made him laugh. He rubbed his eyes again and ran his hand through his hair—he couldn't get used to it being so short. How long had she been gone? How long would it take her to master that blasted stove? He didn't want her to find him here, still wallowing.

He heaved himself up and made his way to the drawing room, pulling back the curtains on a day that was—for now any road—sunny and dry. He opened the long windows to let the fresh air in and pulled two chairs over with a table between them. He was down, but he wasn't out and he wasn't alone. The relief of that gave him a wee bit of a pause. Hadn't he decided, on the long road to recovering from Emily that he'd never let himself rely on anyone again? If you needed someone too much, they could hurt you. He still had the wounds to prove it, though actually, they must have healed a good bit of late, for when he poked at them, as he was doing now, they didn't hurt. Well, there was the problem, wasn't it? He couldn't go forgetting how much it had hurt. Mind you, Jessica was not Emily, that was for sure and certain. He was depending on her right enough, to help him make Taravay his own, but he knew fine, they both did, that this—this idyll, yes, he liked that word—this idyll was only, could only be, temporary.

Though if Donald Macneil was telling the truth, he remembered, bile rising in his throat, Taravay was not actually his after all. Murdo curled his hands into fists. The old goat was lying, he must be lying, and the bible would prove it.

'Tea is served.' He turned round, hurrying to take the tray from Jessica. She smiled at him. 'It's tea with no strings,' she said.

'Don't be daft. I know you too well to think I can get away with a forbidding silence. Haven't I tried that a number of times, and eventually given in to your picking away at me?'

'I don't pick away.'

'Ah no, Jessica, it was a poor joke, don't look so stricken. Sit down and I'll tell you the whole story, or as much as I know of it. I meant it when I said I wanted to. All that probing that you do, painful as it might be sometimes, it eventually helps.'

'I'll take that as a compliment.'

'Oh, it is, trust me.'

Chapter Twenty-Two

'I don't know how much, if any of it, to believe,' Murdo concluded half an hour later. 'But my instincts are that there's more than a few grains of truth in it.'

Jessica, shocked to the core, veering wildly between outrage and disbelief, had forced herself to remain silent while he recounted what Donald Macneil had told him. Seething with questions and anger, she tried to piece the story together. 'It sounds like a fairy tale, there are so many twists and turns.'

'You're not wrong. That's the second time I've heard it recounted, and I'm still struggling. The very idea of my father—of the Laird—falling madly in love and eloping with another man's betrothed, for a start.'

Jessica poured the last of the tea into Murdo's cup. It was now cold and tar black, exactly how he liked it. 'I can't believe it. I simply can't believe it.' She got up, leaning out of the low window to breathe in the sea air. Weeping and wailing wasn't going to help Murdo. He needed practical advice. 'Right,' she said, sitting back down again, 'first of all, let's make sure I have his story straight. Henrietta, your father's first wife, was originally betrothed to Donald Macneil. When she jilted him and married your father...'

'The Laird.'

'Your father,' she continued firmly, 'the Macneils of Harris, and in particular Donald Macneil, took it as a personal slight. But your father and Henrietta were happily married for six years. In the meantime, Donald Macneil had recovered from his broken heart and married someone else. Then, six years after they were married, Henrietta died.'

'Macneil didn't know what happened, but we know from the gravestone that she died in childbirth, along with the child.' Murdo smiled grimly. 'I remember saying to you at the time that had the child survived, my father—the Laird might not have put himself to the trouble of marrying again.'

'And I remember telling you not to wish your life away,' Jessica said vehemently. 'Don't let Donald Macneil's half-truths and lies destroy you, Murdo. Where would I be without you? The confidence you have in me, the trust and the faith, they are the foundations for my future too.'

'You're right. I'm wallowing in my own misery.'

'Oh no, I didn't say that. If it had been me, I'd have drunk that decanter of whisky dry, and I hate whisky.'

Murdo drained his tea. 'You're one of the strongest

people—men or women, mind—that I've ever met.
I'm glad you're on my side.'

His smile warmed her, as it always did. 'Always,'
Jessica said.

'Second only to whatever garden you've given your
heart to.'

Her smile faded. Whether he meant it or not, it was
a warning she would be a fool not to heed. 'Of course,'
she said, stacking the tea-tray. 'Now, where were we?'

'The Laird…'

'Your father…'

'Married Margaret, my mother, nearly ten years
after Henrietta died, to get himself an heir. Another
established fact, but now we come to Macneil's version of the marriage. According to him, my mother
was miserable, cut off from her family on Skye, and
her husband showed little interest in her beyond the
one reason he'd married her for.'

'Poor woman,' Jessica said. 'I've seen it myself, in
several of the aristocratic families I've worked for.
Once they have provided the heir, the wives become
redundant though, happily for me, a few of them then
take an interest in the garden.'

'But after three years of marriage, my mother had
not provided the heir.' Murdo winced. 'I know from
my own experience that when a woman wishes for a
child—have you never wanted children?'

Jessica shook her head, appalled at how many dreadful parallels this story was drawing for Murdo. 'I suppose I assumed that if Edward and I had a child, then someone else would look after it while I worked. I'm too ambitious to be a devoted mother. That sounds both naive and utterly selfish, but it's the truth.'

'Emily longed for a child, while I—well, I've told you my feelings. She blamed herself, but as it turns out, the problem likely lies with me, given she's now expecting. Don't look so heartsore,' Murdo added, 'I really am happy for her. For myself—Taravay is my legacy. Provided Taravay is mine, of course.'

'We will prove it,' Jessica said fiercely. 'Taravay is the basis for my future too.'

'Well then, let's get on with proving we're both entitled to be here. The next part in Macneil's tale is the one I find the hardest to swallow, I must admit. The meeting in Stornoway between him and Margaret, his setting out to seduce her because of that old grudge he had against her husband.'

'She was unhappy, she was unloved, and she was lonely,' Jessica said. 'All he had to do was show a bit of interest in her. And if she was desperate for a child too...'

'You're making me think you believe the man!'

'He tells a persuasive story, but men like that always do. *Sleekit*, that's the word that sprang to my mind the moment I saw him, but you can see he'd have been a handsome man—he still would be, if he'd wash and tidy himself up. And sleekit men often have charm.'

Murdo cursed in Gaelic. 'A fine father, I would have.'

'He's not your father,' Jessica protested automatically, but her own words had sown a seed of doubt. There couldn't be two men further apart in character, but in features there *were* similarities. The eyes, with those thick dark lashes, the jaw. 'No, he's definitely not your father.'

'Definitely not? Are you thinking…'

'It's a good story, it's believable. That's why men like him are so successful,' Jessica said hurriedly. 'I can imagine it would be relatively easy for him to seduce your mother, and I can also imagine that if he thought he had been too successful, that she was with child and it was his, that he'd be terrified of the consequences if the Laird found out. He was about to be married for a second time himself, though your mother almost certainly didn't know that, and her husband was the Laird of Taravay.'

'So when they agreed, as he said they did, that my mother would pass the child off as the Laird's…'

'Macneil would have been beyond relieved, and happy to take nothing more to do with it.'

'Until he was widowed for a second time, living in penury on Harris, and discovered that the son he'd never owned was rich,' Murdo said bitterly, getting up to stare out of the window. '"My own flesh and blood", he said, "I knew the minute I saw you that you were the fruit of my loins". Dear God, as if he thought I'd be stupid enough to think he cared for me. Turning up out of the blue after all these years. How convenient! All he's interested in is my money, and all he wants from me is to give him enough to keep him in the comfort he reckons he's entitled to. It's blackmail, pure and simple, not some far-fetched father and son reunited sob story.'

Jessica listened, the horrible sick feeling in the pit of her stomach telling her what Murdo already seemed to know, that Macneil's story was very plausible indeed.

'"I'm your poor suffering father", the man said.' Murdo continued, almost as if Jessica wasn't there. '"It's your duty to bail me out, and in return I'll keep our secret to myself". Blackmail.' He turned at that, snarling. 'I knew when I saw him in the boat last night—was it only last night!—I knew that he was trouble. Something you might find lurking under a stone you don't want to turn over.'

'Murdo, we don't know for sure. Even Donald Macneil cannot possibly be certain...'

'Ach, but we're both thinking it's probably true, aren't we? You said yourself, when you were looking at that portrait of the Laird out there, that I was nothing like him.'

'I said you must take after your mother.'

'That I will never know, for there's not a single portrait of her here. I told you we were never close, didn't I? Well that was an understatement. She used to avoid me. That's what I remember of her when I was a bairn, that every time I sought her out she'd turn away.'

'Murdo, she was miserable.'

'And maybe loaded with guilt, every time she looked at me, the cuckoo in the nest.'

'Stop it.' Jessica gave him a shake. 'Now you *are* wallowing. We don't know if any of this is true, and even if it is, there's only one bitter old man's word against a whole history of you living here as the legitimate son of the Laird.'

'Dear God, do you think he knew? No, he couldn't have, he'd never have accepted another man's by-blow for his own. On the other hand…'

'Stop it!' Jessica gave him another shake. 'You're tired, you're emotional, you've had a shock, you've been up all night, you're in no fit state to be coming to any conclusions.' She reached up to smooth his furrowed brow. 'You need to rest.'

He nestled his cheek into her palm, his eyes closing. 'We missed our walk last night. I was going to make us dinner here.'

'You can make me dinner tonight. You need to rest now.'

He caught her hand, pulling her towards him. 'I'm not tired.'

* * *

It was comfort he needed, Jessica told herself, comfort and solace, as Murdo wrapped his arms around her. She could give him that, at least, she thought, as she lifted her face to his. They both needed this. To prove that they were united in whatever lay ahead. To prove their love for Taravay. To make up for what they had missed last night. And to simply forget everything else, for now.

Their lips met, and she did forget, for he kissed her passionately, urgently, and she kissed him back, equally urgent, clutching him close, wanting to obliterate everything except the two of them, together, united, crushing the threats, pouring all the agonies she had been feeling for him into her kiss and her touch. Locked together, they kissed, tongues and lips, hands frantically seeking skin. She tugged his shirt free, relishing the shudder that went through him as she ran her hands over his belly, over his nipples, the rough hair on his chest. He kissed her throat, her neck, loosening the buttons of her blouse, his mouth on the swell of her breasts, making her nipples peak, ache for him. They fell to the floor together and there were more kisses, and he tugged her blouse open, and his mouth found her nipples through her chemise, making her cry out, moan, her hands on his back, pulling him down towards her.

Skin. His skin was heated. Her hands roamed over

it, making his muscles ripple. His shirt was gone. Her chemise had somehow also disappeared. He lay over her, cupping her breasts, stroking, licking, sucking, setting her on fire, clenched, tense, urgent. He lifted his head, a silent question, and she pulled him back down towards her, answering with kisses.

She cared about nothing now, but keeping him even closer. He was wanted. He was needed. She needed him so much. She kissed him, pouring her thoughts into her kisses, murmuring yes, when he said her name, yes, when he touched her, yes, when he took her nipple in his mouth again and the tension inside her built, and then yes, yes, yes, when it broke suddenly, violently, a storm of passion that had her clinging, shaking, her face pressed to his chest, until it passed, and shame swept over her. She was lying half-naked on a drawing room floor and *that* had happened when he hadn't even touched her *there*.

'Don't,' Murdo said softly, pulling her closer. 'Don't you dare apologise.'

Her face was burning, but his words drew a strangled laugh from her. 'I don't know—I didn't mean—I wanted to make you feel better.'

'You did.' He smoothed his hand down her back. 'You have.'

She could feel him, fully aroused, pressed against her leg where her skirts had rucked up, and her body responded yearningly.

'Ah no.' He shifted away from her. 'We're neither of us in a frame of mind to be sure what we're doing.' He got up, pulling her with him, and kissed her mouth softly. 'I say that mind, but it's not what I'm feeling. I don't think I've ever wanted anyone so much.' Frowning, Murdo picked up her blouse and handed it to her, before pulling on his own shirt. 'What I mean is— I'm not meaning—I know you don't want—no more than I do.'

'No, no, of course not. I didn't think that. It's the same with me.' Jessica hurriedly buttoned her blouse and shook out her skirt. 'The situation is—I mean what happened last night, and then talking about it. Oh, Murdo, it's all so awful.'

'I can't argue with that, but there's no point in us going over it again. The family bible is key to this. Though where it is, and why it's not where it should be, in his desk, I have no idea.'

The mystery of this struck Jessica as odd. Had the Laird hidden the bible for a reason? 'It's simply been misplaced,' she said, unconvincingly.

'Maybe.' He stifled a yawn. 'I'm sorry, Jessica, I think this is all catching up with me. I need to sleep, right enough.'

'Of course you do, I totally understand. Then later, we'll come up with a proper plan to find that bible.'

'Thank you.' He hesitated in the doorway, frowning. 'I'm not kidding myself, am I? I don't know what it is, I never mean things to go so far between us. Am I taking advantage?'

'You know you're not. Stop fretting,' Jessica said. 'You're in no fit state to think rationally. Get some sleep.'

'You're right.'

The door closed behind him. Jesicca waited until she heard the sound of the main door creak open and then closed before she sank down onto a chair. It was the situation. Alone here on an island, two adults, with so much in common, of course they were attracted to each other. That's all it was, nothing more, and if she was starting to think it could be anything more, she should remember why she was here. What she was feeling was love for Taravay, because Taravay was so fundamental to her future. And because this beautiful island had wormed its way into her heart. Yes, she loved Taravay, that made a great deal of sense, and it also made sense that she cared about its owner. The owner whose heart was given to his island, only and forever.

Was it actually his island? It must be. Without Taravay, Murdo would be distraught. He'd had his heart broken. He'd mended it. She would not allow anyone to break it again. Especially not that parasite of a man, Donald Macneil. Taravay belonged to Murdo. And Jessica was going to do everything in her power to help prove it.

Chapter Twenty-Three

Murdo had never felt less like sleeping. It had taken every ounce of his self-control *not* to finish what he and Jessica had started. They had turned to each other for comfort, that's what they'd concluded after the event, but what he'd felt in that moment, holding her, touching her, kissing her, was about as far from comfortable as it was possible to get. He forgot everything when she was in his arms, everything except her. It felt so—so natural, as if it was meant! And that, he told himself as he tramped across Taravay towards his croft, was a very dangerous and wrong-headed way of thinking. He couldn't afford to let himself start believing Jessica meant anything more to him than—than…

His mind veered away from attempting to put whatever it was he did feel for her into words. What he didn't feel was love. With regard to that, he felt himself on more solid ground. It wasn't love he'd been wanting to make with her. He'd made love to Emily, and it had been nothing like the storm that overwhelmed him when he had Jessica in his arms. In fact, he thought, frowning out at the Atlantic as he crossed the spine to Taravay Beag, he couldn't really remember what it had been like making love to Emily. A sign, then, that his heart was well and truly mended. And a reminder that he was not interested in having it broken again. No danger of that, absolutely none at all, for what he felt for Jessica was…

Ach, he was going round in circles, like a dog chasing its own tail! Whatever it was, it was not love, and that's all that mattered. What was he doing, wasting his time thinking about feelings any road, when he should be focusing his mind on finding that bloody bible? Jessica was a distraction. Maybe too much of a distraction? The state he was in, he wasn't quite in control of himself, and no wonder. No wonder either, that he'd turned to her in such a fervour. Maybe he *had* needed comfort after all? Maybe what he should do was stay away from her for a spell? The fact that he didn't want to—quite the opposite—made his mind up for him. Although they'd agreed they'd come up with a plan together for finding the bible, hadn't they? No, he could do that himself. In fact, that was what he was going to do right now. Get back to the croft, make a plan and get on with it, leaving Jessica to concentrate on her own work.

But what if he couldn't find the bible? What if Donald Macneil really was his father? Then Taravay would not be his, and all their plans, his and Jessica's, would be in ruins. His gut clenched. Jessica's future depended on her work here on Taravay. Without him, there would be no future for Taravay, and as for Jessica—yes, she would pick up other commissions, but not the prestigious kind she'd be offered with Taravay as her masterpiece. How many times had she told him that Taravay was the key to her future? And to his. Taravay was all that mattered. What he urgently needed to do was prove that he was the rightful owner.

Back at his croft, Murdo made himself a pot of tea and set about writing a list of possible places to search for the bible. His head ached. His eyes were gritty. The long night was finally catching up with him. He'd rest for five minutes, just sitting here with his head on his folded arms.

You're a Macleod of Taravay, and ye must act like one. Don't ever forget that. Don't ever let anyone tell you otherwise.

Waking up with a start, Murdo peered into the darkness, heart pounding, sure that he'd heard his father's voice. The Laird. Not his father. Or were they one and the same? Outside night had fallen. He stood up and opened the door to peer out at the stars.

You're a Macleod of Taravay, and ye must act like one. Don't ever forget that. Don't ever let anyone tell you otherwise.

That was it! Murdo struck his forehead with his

hand. He'd been thinking about it all wrong. Whether or not he had Donald Macneil's blood in his veins was irrelevant. The Laird had been certain that Murdo was a Macleod of Taravay, even if he also deemed him an unworthy one, and if the Laird had believed him to be his legitimate heir, then that belief would be formally documented in more than one place.

There were no fresh supplies on her doorstep when Jessica rose the next morning, bleary-eyed from a restless night. She dressed quickly, thinking that something must have happened to detain Finlay, but en route to the walled garden, she was surprised to see a crate sitting on the jetty. In over a month, she could not recall Murdo ever missing a delivery. Had something happened to him? Telling herself not to be ridiculous, that he must simply have overslept, she hurried down to collect the small packet of mail, deciding to walk out to meet him, rather than await his usual morning visit.

Her anxiety rose as she made her way across to Taravay Beag and saw no sign of him. Could she have missed him? He could be in the Castle, or at the abandoned village, or any number of places. But no, he wouldn't have gone anywhere without picking up his post, and he had never before left her without something for her breakfast.

'Murdo?' Hesitantly, she opened the door to his croft. The fire was out. There was a pot of tea on the table, but it was stone-cold. 'Murdo?' His bed was un-made. She refused to allow herself to check to see if the sheets were still warm and instead picked up the piece of paper by the empty teacup on the table. It was a list, very similar to the one she'd made herself last night, of places he planned to search for the bible. Had he made a start? But where?

Now thoroughly uneasy, she left his letters and tele-grams on the table and went back outside. The sky was lowering, but it wasn't actually raining. Not yet. If he wasn't over on the other side of the island, the only other place he could be was the church. Could he possibly be thinking that the bible had been buried with the Laird? And even if it was, did she really think Murdo was about to exhume his father? 'For heaven's sake, Jessica!' Preposterous idea.

Castigating herself under her breath, she pulled the croft door closed and set off towards the church. She saw him from a distance, a tall figure, coatless, his hands dug deep in the pockets of his breeches, and her heart lurched. He was safe. Not that she'd thought oth-erwise. Not that she'd been really worried. And she'd definitely not truly believed that he'd be ransacking a grave. Though he was staring intently down at the headstone, and as she approached, slowly now, she could see his brow was deeply furrowed. She stopped, desperately wanting to find out how he was, to tell him inanely that all would be well, but at the same time, reluctant to disturb him. Was his failure to meet Finlay's boat because he wished to avoid her?

'Jessica.' To her relief, Murdo waved her over. '*Madainn mhath.*'

'I picked up the post and left it in your croft,' she said, joining him.

'Has Finlay been already? I've lost track of the time. I had an idea in the middle of the night. I thought I'd follow it up at first light, but I went to my bed and fell into such a sound sleep I only woke about an hour ago. I'm sorry, I hope you helped yourself to something for breakfast.'

Unwilling to confess that she'd been too concerned to eat, Jessica shrugged. 'I wasn't all that hungry this morning.'

'Me either,' he said ruefully. 'Were you worried about me?'

Too worried. Irrationally worried. Because...

No! Jessica screwed her eyes shut. No, no, banish that thought! She would not be so stupid, she could not be so stupid as to have fallen in love with him.

'Jessica?'

She smiled tightly, forcing herself to meet his eyes. Whatever she had been stupid enough to do, at least she could keep it from Murdo. 'I thought, when I realised that you were here, that you were so desperate to find the bible that you might consider exhuming the Laird's coffin. I realise that's a ridiculous thought.'

'Good God,' Murdo exclaimed. 'I never for a moment—ach but no, why would he do such a thing?'

Why indeed? A much more important question than the state of her heart. 'Murdo, this man here,' she said, indicating the gravestone, 'believed he was your father. He raised you as his own, and a man like the Laird, so proud of his heritage, would never have done that if he'd had the slightest doubt about your true parentage.'

'I know that, though maybe my failure to live up to his expectations is proof of my bastard blood.'

'Don't say that!' She caught at his sleeve, giving him a shake. 'You have integrity. You have principles. You have honour. Did you inherit that from Donald Macneil, a bitter old man who came all the way from Harris to blackmail you? I don't think so.'

'Did I get my ruthless streak—and I have one, it's why I am such a successful businessman—did I get that from the Laird who Cleared his lands to spite his disobedient son?'

'You are your own man. It's not bloodline that counts, it's who you are inside here that matters.' She laid her hand on his heart. 'And inside here, you are—you are…' To Jessica's horror, tears welled up. 'You are a good man, Murdo. You should be proud of yourself,' she said, turning away from him.

'Jessica, don't cry.'

'I'm not crying.'

He gave a little snort of laughter, pulling her into his arms. She knew she should resist, but she couldn't. She let her head rest on his chest, comforted by the steady beat of his heart, wrapping her arms around his waist. She loved him so much. So very much. There, she had admitted it to herself. There was no taking it back. She was such a damned fool.

Resolutely, she blinked back her tears and let him go. 'I'm sorry. I'm tired. I didn't sleep much last night. I was also racking my brains, trying to think where the bible might be buried.'

Murdo studied her for a moment, frowning. 'Yesterday, when I asked you if I was taking advantage...'

'I told you that you were not. It's nothing to do with—with that.' Her cheeks were burning now, but she forced herself to hold his gaze. 'If I'm worried about anything, it's Taravay. Donald Macneil's story is likely a pack of lies, and he has no proof whatsoever to back it up either, but if he starts spreading rumours...'

'Aye, I know. We can't risk it.'

Once again, to Jessica's relief, she had managed to divert him. 'So the bible...'

'Well here's the thing, Jessica. That's what I realised in the middle of the night. We don't necessarily need the bible.'

'We don't? But what other proof is there?'

Murdo indicated the church. 'It's in there. Come on, I'll show you.'

* * *

Astonishingly, Jessica had never set foot inside the little church. It was a simple affair, with a flagstone floor, a narrow aisle separating two sections of boxed pews, and a plain altar made of very dark wood.

'The parish registers are in here,' Murdo said, opening a creaking door to a small room where a lectern, several chairs and trestles which she now knew were used for coffins took up most of the space. The registers were lined up in a row on a shelf in a cupboard, a gap showing at the end of the row, the missing leather-bound book already open on the lectern. 'There,' Murdo said, indicating a neat line, 'do you see?'

The entry was for April 27, 1838. 'Murdo Angus Macleod,' Jessica read. 'That's you, but I can't read the rest, it's in Gaelic.'

'A son born to Laird Angus Murdo Macleod,' Murdo translated, 'and his wife Margaret, on April 18, 1838, and baptised this day in the parish of Taravay by the Reverend Angus Macfarlane.'

'April 18. That means your birthday is on Friday.'

Murdo grinned. 'This is the only gift I need or want. Whatever Macneil claims, I am the legal owner of Taravay, and this proves it.'

'It does.' She traced the words again, a slow smile dawning. 'Oh, Murdo, your plans are safe.'

'Our plans. Nothing and no one can prevent you now from becoming the toast of the landscaping world.'

Jessica burst into a peal of laughter. 'I shall be crowned landscaper of the year, and awarded the much-coveted golden trowel. And no, before you ask, there is no such thing, and there is besides, the small matter of actually completing the work.'

'But we can, now. We can tell the world—or at the very least, the Niseachs—about the revitalised Tara-vay we have planned, and we can set the wheels in mo-tion, order supplies, employ builders and engineers and gardeners. We can do it, Jessica. Isn't it wonderful?'

'Wonderful,' she said, and she meant it, because he looked so very delighted, and because this was what she wanted too, to make sure that his precious Tara-vay, the love of his life, was his. 'Truly wonderful,' Jessica said, because it meant that her future too, was hers to make, and that's what she wanted more than anything in the world.

'I know,' Murdo said, his hands tightening around hers, 'it means Taravay will no longer be ours alone, but we always knew that would happen.'

'We did.' A lump rose in her throat as she looked at him, wondering how long she had been deluding her-self about her true feelings for him. 'It's for the best, don't you agree?'

He took his time answering, long enough for her to imagine, stupidly imagine, that he might be feeling exactly the same as she did. 'I think it might be,' he said eventually. 'There's so much to do, we'll not be needing any distractions.'

'Is that what I am?' The words were out before she could stop them. She pulled her hands free.

'Don't be like that, Jessica.'

'I'm not—whatever you're thinking, I'm perfectly fine, and I'm delighted that the ownership of Taravay is no longer in dispute, and now I'm going to go and…'

'Well I'm not perfectly fine, and I don't think you are either.' Murdo caught her hand again, pulling her back towards him. 'It's not your fault that you are a distraction. I think about you too much. When I'm not with you, I'm wondering what you're doing, what you're thinking, and when I'm with you, I'm wanting to—aye well, I don't need to spell it out. And before you say anything, I know fine and well that it's not only me, but that only makes it worse.'

Did it? If Murdo felt as she did—for a moment, a tiny moment, Jessica allowed herself to dream. His next words brought her crashing down to earth with a thump.

'I know that your career is the only thing that really matters to you,' he said, 'and as for me—well you know, because I've been painfully honest about it, that I've no intentions of letting myself get too—too attached.' He broke off to swear under his breath. 'Too attached! As if I'm a limpet and you're a rock. What I mean is—what I'm trying to say is—we need a dose of reality—that's what I'm trying to say. We've been too much alone, and we're in danger of letting all that we have in common, all we have shared during our time here—which I'll admit is a lot—we're in danger of thinking that it amounts to more than it is.'

Cheeks blazing, Jessica took a step backwards. 'Are you trying to warn me off, Murdo? I assure you—as I have done repeatedly since the start—that I want nothing more from you than…'

'I'm not Lady Bloody Orton telling you that you've ideas above your station, for the love of God! From the first minute I met you, you were telling me that all you wanted to be was the best landscaper, and I'm delighted that I'm now able to give you the opportunity to prove that. I know you don't want anything more from me, and I don't want anything more from you, but this—this whatever it is between us, it has to end, and I don't want it to end badly for either of us.'

'You mean it's best that the world gets in the way, before our feelings do?'

'Exactly, though we wouldn't be that daft, would we?'

'No, of course not.'

'I don't mean to upset you.'

'I'm not upset. Truly. And I am truly delighted that you've found the register and the proof you need.'

'All I need to do now, is decide whether to pay Donald Macneil off.'

'Give in to blackmail?' Jessica exclaimed. 'Surely not?'

'You don't think he might possibly be telling the truth? That I am his natural son?'

Despite the evidence that lay in front of them, she did have doubts, and it was obvious that Murdo did too. 'It is possible, but surely, at the end of the day, all that matters is that you are Murdo Macleod of Taravay. And don't you dare forget it,' she added firmly.

'Thank you.' He made to take her hand, then changed his mind. 'I'd better get on. What about you?'

Suddenly, what Jessica needed desperately was to be alone. 'I'll stay here for a bit, maybe look through the registers and see if I can find Mairi.' She pulled a register out at random, and began to leaf through it, biting her lip. It seemed an age before he left, closing the door softly behind him. She waited, listening to his footsteps as he walked back up the aisle, hearing the creaking of the church door as it closed, and only then did she sink down on the flagstones and give way to a bout of tears.

Chapter Twenty-Four

By morning, Jessica had regained her composure and sense of perspective. Everything Murdo had said yesterday made sense. Taravay was the key to her future and to his. Yes, she was in love with him, but it made no difference. Admitting this much to herself was a huge relief. She loved him so much, and so very differently from the way she'd loved Edward. She loved Murdo for all his flaws and imperfections—in fact she loved him even more because of them. She loved him because he was the first person in her life who accepted her, with *her* flaws and imperfections, and didn't want to change her. She loved him for the strength and confidence he'd given her, and because he'd never questioned her ambition—quite the opposite. Murdo didn't care that Jessica was a gardener, and unlike Donald Macneil, he certainly didn't look on her as a very shallow step above a glorified servant. She loved Murdo because he understood how essential her work was to her, and because he wanted her to succeed, because he was actively helping her to succeed. She loved him for so many reasons, but Murdo did not love her and would never love her—would never permit himself to love her. Murdo was afraid to love again, and who could blame him?

She loved him, but they were destined to live separate lives, so she would keep her secret close, tucked safely in her heart. And she would make the most of what time they had left together, she resolved as she carried the pot of tea to the walled garden. As work progressed on Taravay, she would wean herself off him, so that when she had to leave, when her work was done and her reputation secured, it would not be so painful. Her heart would be bruised, but she would protect it, save it from breaking in two. She would have her memories, and Murdo—Murdo would never know, so Murdo too, would be safe.

'*Madainn mhath.* Am I disturbing you?'

Her heart leapt. Jessica ignored it. Murdo was in a clean shirt under his leather waistcoat, his cheeks freshly shaved, his cropped hair still damp. 'Perfect timing,' she said, 'the tea is like tar and almost cold, so just as you like it.'

'Thank you,' he said, accepting the mug she offered and sitting down opposite her. 'I've been talking to Finlay about how best to reveal our plans. I'm thinking of opening up the Castle and issuing an invitation to everyone to come over. You could do some tours, talk them through some plans, I could show them the village, sound out any who might be interested in taking on a croft, or know someone else who is.'

'I think that's a wonderful idea. In fact, I had some thoughts of my own.'

As usual, when they were talking about Taravay, the time flew and their ideas sparked off each other, and as usual, as they sat together, it was there between them, that other unspoken conversation, the invisible bond that drew them inexorably together. His hand brushed hers as he reached for a pencil. Beneath the table, their toes touched, or their knees. Those moments when their eyes met, and the look went on too long, and they moved towards each other, then hurriedly moved away, leaving one or other of them to pick up the thread of the conversation, both of them pretending it hadn't happened.

'So we're agreed,' Murdo said, draining his mug, 'we'll open Taravay to the world—or at least to the Niseachs—in a week's time? Am I asking too much of you?'

'I think you should be asking that question of yourself.'

Jessica closed her notebook in a businesslike manner. Her pencil fell to the ground, and Murdo picked it up, handing it to her across the desk. Their fingers touched, twined. Their eyes met.

'Jessica.'

'Murdo?'

'Yesterday, I'm thinking I made a bit of a meal of it. We're not daft, neither of us. We know why we're here—haven't we just proved it?'

'Yes. We have. Taravay.'

'Taravay.' He nodded. 'So when I said you were a distraction, I didn't mean we should be avoiding each other.'

Somehow, the desk was no longer between them. 'No,' Jessica said, 'how can we?'

'Do you know, when you smile you're like a different person.'

'So are you.'

He lifted his free hand to touch her cheek. 'All these hours in the open air, and your skin's like milk.'

'My mother was the same.' She smoothed her palm over his cheek, down to his neatly trimmed beard. 'Yours is the colour of a chestnut.'

They were so close she could almost taste the faint aroma of tea on his breath. Her skirts were brushing his legs. Her heart was hammering. As his lips touched hers, her eyes closed. Such a soft kiss, the first she had given him since…

She stepped back, crashing into the desk. He steadied her, but immediately let her go. 'I forgot,' Jessica said, scrabbling to regain her composure. 'Yesterday, in the church, I found something of interest in the register.'

'Yes?' Murdo was straightening his waistcoat, avoiding her eyes. 'Mairi?'

'No, Henrietta.'

'Henrietta—you mean the Laird's first wife?'

'You're father's first wife,' she corrected him. 'She didn't die in childbirth as we thought, but of scarlatina—I recognised the word. What was odd though, was that there was no mention of the infant who is buried with her.'

'You could have missed it. It may simply have said with her infant, in Gaelic. Most likely dead of the same disease that took its mother, poor wee mite.' Murdo was at the door now. 'Probably too young to have been baptised, which is why there's no name. Sometimes they waited a few months, just to make sure the bairn was healthy.'

'But you were baptised within a few days of being born.'

'The Laird was quick to claim me, right enough.'

'Your father,' she persisted.

Murdo pursed his lips. 'I've decided to pay to have some work done on Donald Macneil's house over on Harris. I'll settle an income on him, as soon as I can too, but in the meantime I'll give him a bit of a sweetener. I know, you think I'm giving in to blackmail and he deserves nothing, but we really can't afford him to spread rumours, and...'

And he is probably my father. The words lay unspoken between them. She longed to contradict him. She wished she could find him something that proved otherwise. 'I understand,' Jessica said.

'I thought you would. It's—it's an odd feeling,' Murdo added after a moment, 'not knowing for certain who you are.'

'But you do know who you are. You are Murdo Macleod of Taravay.'

He smiled wryly. 'I hope so.'

It was late when Murdo sailed himself back from Port of Ness, having spent a good two hours laying down the law to Donald Macneil, tying up his terms in legal knots that he knew very likely could not be enforced, but which he hoped the other man did not. Was Macneil his father? There was a physical resemblance, but though he'd searched his soul while they were talking, he'd felt nothing but anger at the man's sudden and unwelcome appearance in his life. Macneil made no show of affection, offered neither regrets nor apologies. His purpose was to make his own last years as comfortable as he could, at Murdo's expense. You had to take your hat off to the man's barefaced gall. Comfortable enough, he'd be now, to live to a hundred, and the fact was, it was a small price to pay for Macneil's silence and to salve his own conscience too, if Macneil was telling the truth.

Murdo had no more desire than the old man to continue their acquaintance. Sleekit, that was how Jessica had described him, and it certainly fitted, though at one time that decrepit old dog must have had charm enough to be a scheming seducer. Murdo struggled to dredge up his few memories of his mother. Why had she been so much in the background during his early years? Was it because the Laird had been so determined to shape him in his own image he wanted no other influence to be brought to bear? She had spent a great deal of time in the garden, he recalled suddenly. And there had been once, in the glasshouse, she'd shown him how to take a cutting from one of her succulents. How could he have forgotten that? Her hand guiding the knife held in his hand, helping him tamp down the soil. He could remember the damp, moist air, and the smell of her soap—was it lavender? Those succulents Jessica had discovered, they had been planted by his mother, surviving all those years untended, against the odds. Unlike his mother. Poor woman. Had Macneil really seduced her? If so, she must have lived in terror of being discovered.

A pod of porpoises were leaping up alongside the boat, such joyful creatures with their beaks seeming to smile with exhilaration as they carved through the water. Though the day had been grey and drizzly, it was turning into a lovely evening, as it so often did here, the skies clearing to a soft blue speckled with inoffensive fluffy clouds, like sheep painted by a child.

He rounded the Butt of Lewis, and Taravay came into view. As ever, Murdo's heart swelled at the sight of it. He was Macleod of Taravay. Whether he carried the Laird's blood in him or not, Angus Murdo Macleod had been a father to him, in his own despotic way. He was entitled to Taravay. Taravay was his.

And soon Taravay would also be restored to the people of Ness. Today he had employed an avidly cooperative Catriona Macfarlane, giving her the freedom to engage whatever other help she needed, to take on the task of cleaning some of the Castle's main rooms. His plan was to let people in, to wander at will and see for themselves there was nothing more sinister in residence than the mice and the spiders, and Catriona would evict as many of those as she could over the next few days. She would start work tomorrow, sailing over with her husband. From tomorrow, during the day at least, he and Jessica's time as island castaways would be at an end. What would he do with himself when the island was transformed? Funny, he'd not given it a thought. Taravay was his home, but could he live there permanently without a purpose? Jessica would be gone, off to transform someone else's landscape, to help realise someone else's dream.

Jessica. It didn't sit well with him, the thought of her sharing her ideas, laughing, disputing, planning with someone else. But that was foolish. Anyway, with someone else she'd be different. Not his Jessica. Not that she was *his* in any real sense.

The porpoises had abandoned him. The sun was starting to sink over on the far side of the island. Jessica would be in her croft now, most likely surrounded by her books and her precious notebook, writing lists, planning orders, or maybe thinking of him? The urge to go to her was too strong. Resolutely, Murdo concentrated on tying up the boat, unloading, before turning his feet towards his own croft and his mind towards the upcoming visit from the people of Ness.

Chapter Twenty-Five

'Close your eyes,' Jessica said, 'and don't open them until I tell you.'

'I don't normally like surprises,' Murdo said, smiling as she took his hand.

'Hopefully you'll like this one! Keep them firmly closed. Watch the step here. And there. Now you can open them.' She let go of his hand. 'Happy birthday,' she said in carefully rehearsed Gaelic.

The rockery she had created in the far corner of the glasshouse was small. The little boulders and rocks were carefully selected for their glinting stripes of agate, with small fossils embedded in them, the predominately grey and white tones of those she'd gathered from the Atlantic side of the island a stark contrast to some of the orange and yellow sandstone ones she'd found on the beach near the jetty. The broad, meandering stream of little pebbles and shale emerging from an upended terracotta pot looked, just as she had hoped, like a waterfall meandering gently from the top to the bottom of the little garden. And set carefully into the rocks were the succulents that Murdo had told her his mother had grown, dressed with silver sand from Taravay's beach.

Beside her, Murdo was silently studying his gift. 'I know it needs more plants,' she said nervously.

'It's wonderful.'

'Oh.' Seeing him so moved brought tears to her own eyes. 'Good.'

He laughed gruffly. 'Not good, it's perfect. I don't know how you found the time. Or how you managed to get the larger stones up here.'

'My trusty wheelbarrow. And I worked after dinner. It doesn't get dark until late now. Do you really like it? When you told me that these plants were your mother's…'

'I absolutely love it. A fitting tribute to my mother and to Taravay.'

Jessica beamed. 'Exactly what I hoped for. I've been on tenterhooks for the last three days, terrified you'd stumble on this by accident, but fortunately you've been so busy elsewhere.'

'It's been non-stop, hasn't it. Catriona and the other women have worked wonders at the Castle.'

'She's enjoying every minute of it. If you're looking for a housekeeper for the hotel, I think she'd bite your hand off.'

'And Grahame has already offered his services. He

was an apprentice engineer in Glasgow before he met Catriona. I said I'd put in a good word with…' Murdo broke off. 'Enough of business, it's my birthday, and we have the island to ourselves for the evening. Would you like to take a walk?'

'Actually, because it's your birthday, I was hoping you would take dinner with me,' Jessica said. 'Don't worry, I didn't cook it myself. Catriona prepared it. I thought we could watch the sunset first, and then dine at the Castle, but if you have other plans?'

'I can think of nowhere else I'd rather be, and no one else I'd rather be with. If we're going to catch the sunset though, we'd better go now. We can watch from the turret.'

Jessica made a face as she checked her father's watch. It was already after eight. 'I don't know where the time has gone, I meant to change for dinner.'

'You look lovely as you are.'

His words, that strange smile, the way he looked at her, really looked at her, made the air itself seem to tense. 'If your taste is for someone that's been dragged through a hedge backwards,' Jessica said, sounding breathless.

'Windswept and interesting,' Murdo said, pushing a strand of her hair behind her ear. 'And lovely, inside as well as out. Thank you again for my present, it's the most thoughtful gift anyone has ever given me.'

'I'm glad you like it.'

'I love it.'

His lips brushed hers. She caught her breath. She heard him do the same. He curled his fingers into her hair, and she slipped her arm around his neck. Their lips softened into another kiss, soft, sweet, gentle. Then it ended, though they both knew it wasn't over.

They walked hand in hand to the Castle, climbing up to the turret without the need to say anything. They stood at the parapet, looking out to the Atlantic coast of Taravay as a glorious sunset played out, just for them. Gold streaked across the sea as the sun sank, and the sky turned amber, then rosy, then dark-pink and crimson, and they stood silent together, holding hands, waiting.

When the sky turned inky they kissed again, and this time it was different. Darker kisses, dangerous kisses, with the sharp edge of the stars that glittered above them. Kisses that made their breaths ragged, that made their hearts hammer, that made their blood feverish. Kisses that had them staggering together towards the door of the turret, that had her braced against the door, Murdo pressed against her, and still it wasn't enough.

'Is this a mistake?' he asked, his hand on her breast, her nipple aching at his touch.

'No.' She slipped her hand under his waistcoat, splaying her fingers over his back. 'Unless—are you sure you want to?'

'Yes. Oh, Jessica, do you...'

'Yes. Yes.'

More kisses as they made their way down the narrow stairs. More kisses on the landing, where he lost his waistcoat and she tugged his shirt free, and he shivered as her hands roamed over his chest, his belly, and she shivered too as his muscles clenched at her touch.

It was almost dark on the top floor of the Castle, the only light coming from the lamp they had left at the door to the turret. The bare boards of the landing creaked as they stood wrapped in each other's arms, kissing, stroking, kissing more fervently. She was on fire. She couldn't think straight. Yes, she could. She wanted this. Only this. 'Don't stop.'

'I don't want to.'

She burrowed her face in his bare chest. She didn't remember him taking off his shirt. His skin was burning. She licked his nipple. He groaned, tugging her back upwards to kiss her again, tongues tangling. His hands on her blouse now, yanking at the buttons, pulling it open, then his mouth on her breasts, and it was she who moaned.

He swept her up into his arms, carrying both her and the lamp, down the next flight of stairs before kicking open the door of a bedchamber. It was a massive room dominated by a large bed of dark oak adorned with the Macleod crest, incongruously made up with a selection of ill-matched blankets and cushions. 'The King's

Chamber,' Murdo said, setting her down, 'made ready for a visiting king who never arrived, and to my knowledge never used, until I slept here the other night.'

The shutters were open. The windows faced out over the sea. Jessica opened one, leaning out to hear the familiar sound of the waves breaking on the shore. He would ask her again if she was sure. Was she? She hadn't planned this. She had dreamed of it, but she hadn't planned it. She may never get another opportunity. She would never know what it would be like to make love to the man she loved.

He slipped his arms around her waist, kissing her neck. '*Do* you want this, Jessica?'

She turned in his arms. 'More than anything.'

He hesitated for a moment, thoughts she couldn't read flitting across his face. Then he smiled, a dangerous smile, and picked her up, placing her on the bed. Slowly, he undressed her, kissing every bit of newly exposed flesh, his eyes fixed on her body, drinking her in, in a way that ought to have embarrassed her because she had never been studied so blatantly, with such evident desire. It made her shiver with expectation, the slash of colour on his cheeks and the sureness of his touch, his own clothes discarded as carelessly as hers were removed so carefully. His mouth on her breasts. His body beside her on the bed now, their limbs naked and entwined, kissing, pressed together urgently. Then he moved, and his mouth was on her breasts again, then on her belly and then, to her astonishment and delight, lower, such intimate kisses that sent her spiralling out of control, had her clutching at his hair, had her calling his name, wave after wave of pure pleasure pulsing through her body.

She had never, ever, ever wanted anything so much now as Murdo inside her, and just when she thought she would die of wanting, he was there, exactly where she needed him to be, tilting her towards him, easing himself inside her so slowly, so deliciously slowly, all the time looking at her, his eyes fixed on her, so that she could not doubt the effect she was having on him, his need, his wanting etched on his face. They moved, slowly at first, then faster, a faultless rhythm that made her cry out again, that made her tighten around him, that had her clutching at his shoulders, urging him on, until with a wild cry he freed himself from her just as his own climax took him.

And then there were more kisses. No words, but more kisses. Soothing. Tender. Loving, on her part. His arm lay heavy on her thigh. Their legs were tangled up together. They lay side by side like this for so long, she felt for the first time in her life that she understood what it was to be two halves of one entity. It was that thought that made her gently disengage herself from his arms.

When Jessica moved away, for a split second Murdo felt bereft. He wanted to stay like this, entwined in the aftermath of their lovemaking, kissing, holding each other, too dazed by the wonder of what they had shared to need words. The strength of his desire brought him firmly back down to earth. Passion was one thing, but this was something else. Something dangerous. Something he would not risk, because it might just be the end of him.

Jessica was edging out of the bed. He was distracted by the curve of her buttocks, the long length of her legs, the glimpse of her left nipple, but as she picked up her chemise and began to wrestle it over her head, his mind took over from his body. 'What's wrong?'

'Nothing,' she said, rummaging for the rest of her clothing. 'I'm worried your birthday dinner will be ruined, that's all.'

She wasn't looking at him. Her voice had a strange pitch to it. Was she already filled with regret? Had his own overwhelming desire allowed him to ignore some sign from her that she didn't mean what she said? But it had felt so damned right.

Murdo cursed inwardly, moving over to the edge of the bed. 'Jessica?' His tone was sharper than he'd meant. She started, stumbling halfway into pulling on a petticoat. 'Jessica,' he said, more softly, 'did I misunderstand?'

'Misunderstand?' She dropped the petticoat and, to his surprise, threw herself at him. 'No, no, no.'

He wrapped his arms around her. She laid her head

on his shoulder. Her hair was like silk. Her skin was like cream. 'You don't regret…'

'You mustn't think that.'

She smoothed her hand over his hair, pressing a kiss to his brow, and his face was crushed between her breasts. To his embarrassment, he was immediately and unmistakably aroused. He shifted backwards on the bed. 'I'm sorry.'

But she seemed to have forgotten all about whatever it was that had propelled her out of bed. She shifted between his legs, smiling that smile of hers. 'Don't you want dinner, then?'

He didn't understand what was going on in her head, but when she smiled at him like that, he didn't care. 'Not yet,' he said, falling back onto the bed and pulling her on top of him. 'Do you?'

She leaned on her elbows to look at him. Her hair fell over his face. Her breasts, covered only by her chemise, were pressed against his chest. 'No, not just yet,' she said, smiling and leaning forward to kiss him. He slid into her so easily, and she gave such a delightful sigh, that he was immediately lost.

Chapter Twenty-Six

The sun was already shining when the first of the Ness folk arrived on Taravay, many of them in the little fishing boats Jessica now knew were called *sgoths*, a design unique to Port of Ness. She watched from just outside the walled garden as Murdo, dressed in his usual garb of shirt, breeches, and leather jacket, but with his sleeves down and a stock around his neck, greeted the first of their visitors. The usual flutter of her heart was accompanied by the churning of butterflies in her stomach. This was such an important day for him and for Taravay, she couldn't bear for it to be anything but perfect. She knew that almost everyone who could make the short journey would come, she knew that they would make all the right noises, but she also knew that what really mattered was what they said later amongst themselves, and for that she and Murdo would be relying on Catriona, Finlay and perhaps the Reverend Muirhead.

She and Murdo. They were a team, he'd said that

several times over the last three days, as if he needed to stress that was all they were. The butterflies in her belly fluttered their wings hard enough to make her feel sick, but it wasn't merely anticipation. Three days ago, that night on Murdo's birthday, had changed everything between them, and not for the better. It hadn't happened straight away. Everything had been perfect at first, from Murdo's pleasure in the little succulent garden she had created for him, to the sunset they had watched together, to their lovemaking. Even now, thinking about that made her shiver with delight. It had been so perfect. So different. *Wonderful* was an understatement, and she knew that Murdo had felt the same. Well no, not quite the same. For Murdo, there had been passion but not love.

Wrapping her arms around herself, Jessica swallowed the lump that clogged her throat every time she let herself dwell on this. Had he guessed her own feelings? Was that why, after the second time they'd made love, he had begun to distance himself from her?

They'd been lying entwined, sated, lost in the bliss of the aftermath, or so she'd thought. He had kissed her hair. He had stroked her back. And then his hand had stilled. Nothing more, just the stilling of his hand, but it made her look up. And he'd said, just as she had said to him after the first time they had made love, that they shouldn't let dinner spoil, that it would be a shame to let Catriona's efforts go to waste. But neither of them had eaten much, and conversation between them had been stilted. That was the first time she had asked herself, had he guessed? She still had no idea. She couldn't bear it if he had. When they said goodnight, he had kissed her cheek, and she'd jerked away from him, and she must have misread, in the darkness, the hurt in his eyes. And through that long, tormented night, she had resolved that if Murdo hadn't yet guessed that she loved him, she was going to make certain he did not. She couldn't bear him worrying that she wanted more from him than he had offered, more than he ever wished to give anyone again. She couldn't bear for him to pity her. So she put a guard on every word she said, every action she made. He noticed, how could he not, and he did the same, and now the invisible thread which had drawn them together from the moment they met was stretched further and further every day.

Did she wish she hadn't given in to temptation? Did he? Had their lovemaking ruined everything? It had been a stark reminder, that aftermath, of the hurt she was storing up for herself. It was for the best, she'd told herself so many times in the last few days, because it was clear Murdo was protecting himself as well as her. Boundaries had been drawn, and she was glad of it. Taravay was what mattered. Thank heavens for Taravay.

Below her, a small armada of boats were queuing to tie up at the jetty. Finlay was in charge of imposing order on the chaotic scene. Murdo was leading a group of islanders up the hill. Jessica fixed her welcoming smile in place. From that first day they'd met on the pier at Stornoway, Murdo had placed an enormous trust in her. She wasn't going to let him down.

'It is a wonderful thing that you are planning here, Miss Smith. I am delighted to see such a good turnout.'

'Reverend Muirhead.' Jessica, who had been enjoying a solitary moment by the standing stone, turned and smiled. 'It is Murdo you should be complimenting. My contribution has simply been to assist him in realising his dream.'

'Mr Macleod gives you a great deal more credit than that. He's been singing your praises all day.'

'Has he?' To her embarrassment, she could feel her cheeks flushing. 'I'm very fortunate to have an employer who places such trust in me.'

'Employer? You know it's funny, but you're such an integral part of Taravay, that I had not thought of you as an employee, nor of your taking on work elsewhere. I suppose, mind, that you'll be here a good year or so yet, in order to complete what you have started?'

'Yes.' The word, to her own ears, sounded far from wholehearted. She was not, until now, aware that she had doubts. When had that feeling of dread crept up on her? A whole year on Taravay with Murdo becoming increasingly distant was painful to think about. She couldn't possibly be contemplating leaving before that though. She was simply tired.

'Miss Smith?'

Jessica started. She'd quite forgotten the minister's presence.

'I don't want to be presumptuous,' he said, 'but is there something wrong?'

'It has been hectic these last few days. Weeks. It's so important to Murdo that everyone sees what he plans in a positive light.'

'Ach, there will be detractors, there always are. Some people resist change, they want to stick with the old ways, but I'm fairly certain they will be very much in a minority.'

'How can you be so sure?'

Reverend Muirhead laughed gently. 'Are you imagining that all this,' he said, with a sweeping gesture to the island, 'is a well-kept secret? Telegrams, as you must know, are public property, and though Grahame Macfarlane is a discreet enough man, his wife is a different kettle of fish.'

'So Murdo shouldn't be worried?'

'No, no, not at all. It's a sad fact that the Hebrides is losing its people, Miss Smith, and not all of them choose to leave. There's plenty of Highlanders from much further afield than Ness or even Lewis who will jump at the chance of a new life here.'

'That will be a huge relief to Murdo.'

'And you, Miss Smith?'

Aware of his pale blue eyes on her, Jessica recalled her initial opinion of the minister, that he was an astute observer and older than his years. 'It will do my reputation a great deal of good to be so closely associated with the rebirth of Taravay.'

'Taravay reborn. I like that. If only some of the other islands could also be reborn, but alas, the combination you have here, of wealth and skill and commitment is a very rare one, for I don't think it's putting it too strongly, Miss Smith, to say that you have given your heart as well as your considerable talent to Taravay?'

'No,' Jessica said sadly, 'it's not putting it too strongly. Taravay most certainly has captured my heart.'

'Yes, I thought as much.'

'I meant the island, Reverend Muirhead.'

'Indeed,' he agreed blandly. 'Such a beautiful place, and you've had it all to yourselves too, it would be a wonder if you did not find yourself falling in love.'

'We—that is, Murdo—is hoping a great many other people will fall in love with the island,' Jessica answered, putting a heavy emphasis on the last two words. For a minister, the Reverend Muirhead was an excellent fisherman.

'And I'm sure they will, as you have,' he agreed, turning his gaze towards the sea.

Was he giving her a meaningful look? Or was she

reading too much into his words. Reverend Muirhead was one of those men who knew the value of silence, but if he was waiting on some sort of confession, he'd wait a while.

The waves crashed. The sun continued to shine. At last, the minister spoke. 'It is a wonderful view you have here.'

'It is.' Relieved, Jessica launched into her speech about making the most of the vistas, and to her further relief the minister was happy to be distracted, listening carefully, and when she was finished, requesting access to the church.

'For we have one very similar on a small island just off Oban, where I was raised.'

Happy to oblige, for she had taken a liking to the man despite his earnest ways and probing questions, Jessica led the way, telling him of her search through the registers for Henrietta's child.

'Mr Macleod is in the right of it,' he agreed, as she opened the door to the church. 'Sadly, baptism is often postponed where a child is poorly, and even more sadly, the burial is often not recorded. My goodness, but this is almost exactly the same as the church back home. A beautiful setting for a wedding, don't you think?' Without giving her an opportunity to reply, he continued, 'The registers will be held in here, I assume?'

Reverend Muirhead led the way down the aisle, looking about him in delight. 'I have a real sense of

God's presence here. It's a terrible thing for me to say, but I don't get that sensation in every church I visit, though perhaps that is my fault and not God's. I should not be talking in such a way to you, Miss Smith. It's a bad habit I have, to say what is on my mind to those I feel I can trust, even when I don't actually know them very well. I took to you and to Mr Macleod straight away, though he did not take to me. My goodness, look at these registers, they are in wonderful condition. May I?'

'Please,' Jessica said, both bemused and endeared, 'feel free to take a look. I'm afraid I have to get back, would you mind if I left you here on your own?'

He was already delving deep into one of the old ledgers. 'I have to get back myself in an hour, but I'll be fine.'

Thinking that there was every chance Reverend Muirhead would forget all sense of time, Jessica made a mental note to make sure he was not stranded, and set out for the other side of the island

It had been a long but very successful day, Murdo thought as he stood in the doorway of the Castle, watching the last of Taravay's visitors finish the remnants of the tea and Catriona Macfarlane's griddled scones, some of the men draining the last of their dram of whisky, in preparation for sailing home. There had been a few references to the Clearance, and at least twice he'd heard someone say that the Old Laird would be spinning in his grave, but the list he had of people who were interested in working on the improvements, working on the island when the improvements were complete, or wanting to come and live here, was satisfyingly long.

'You're no Matheson, that's for sure,' one of the most elderly visitors had said, shaking his hand, referring to the man who had built Lews Castle in Stornoway, and the current owner of the Isle of Lewis itself. 'It's clear you've the best interests of the island and its people in your heart, and for that we will all be thankful.'

'Thank you,' Murdo said, delighted. His first thought, to tell Jessica the encouraging news, was quickly followed by the sickening lurch of his insides that happened every time he thought about her. Three nights ago, the most passionate encounter of his life had taken place, here in this very Castle. Nothing he had imagined—and he'd imagined it a lot—came close to the reality of what had occurred between them that night. Nothing had ever felt so right, so natural as making love to her, and in the aftermath, holding her close. Simply holding her, and not wanting to let her go. Not ever. Which was why he had let her go, a bit too abruptly.

He was not in love with her. He would not let himself consider the possibility. But the possibility had him on edge, so he had hardly swallowed a morsel of the food Catriona Macfarlane had left for them to eat. He could not, must not love Jessica, because Jessica loved her work more than anything. She was here on Taravay now, but she would not be here forever. But he kept thinking of the way she'd kissed him, the way she'd held him, the way she'd looked into his eyes the whole time they'd been tangled up together, as if he was her heart and soul.

He was imagining it. Sure, they had proved their bodies were made for each other, but that was passion, not love. Abstinence, that was the cause of it, he'd decided, that was what had made it seem so special. He had not made love in almost two years. And then there was Taravay, the island he and Jessica both loved, the island that had brought them together, that was key to their very different futures, that bound them. It was all of those things, but it wasn't love. He couldn't let it be love. So he wouldn't call it anything. And as for Jessica, she too had seemed on edge as they ate that night, watching him covertly, saying little, frowning off into the distance. And over the next few days it carried on, both of them not wanting to talk about what had happened, talking only of Taravay, and given there was so much to do, that was easy enough to achieve.

But now, as he shook hands with people and bade them goodbye and thanked them for coming and assured them he'd noted down their requests and suggestions, instead of being thrilled, all he could think about was the wall he'd built between himself and her, brick by brick over the last three days, until he felt he couldn't see over it, and he didn't know how to fix it, or even if he should. She'd be leaving eventually. It was better that he taught himself a new way of feeling for her.

All the same, a prickling on the back of his neck alerted him to her presence, and there she was, her hair in a neat chignon, wearing a jacket and matching skirt over a blouse he didn't think he'd seen before, but walking with that carefree stride he'd recognise anywhere, towards the walled garden. He missed her. Now, that was a bloody stupid thing to say when he saw her every day, countless times. But he did miss the freeness of their conversation, the pleasure of her unguarded presence, the constant clamouring of his body for hers. Something that had become even more persistent since that night.

Maybe they shouldn't have made love. No, he would have that memory forever, he couldn't regret it. But he wasn't in love with her, and she wasn't in love with him. It was time they started behaving like responsible adults again, not giddy adolescents. They had so much to talk about after today. If he waited until the morning, it wouldn't all be so fresh in his mind. So after everyone had gone, they could go for a walk and review the day. Ease some of the tension.

Thus resolved, Murdo spent the next hour waving

off the many boats, feeling a happy sense of anticipation. He was talking to Grahame Macfarlane, the last to leave, when Catriona came hurrying down with Jessica in tow.

'At the coo's tail as ever, my wife,' Grahame said, helping Catriona on board.

'I wanted to make sure that the Reverend Muirhead has not been left behind,' Jessica said. 'I left him in the church, engrossed in the ledgers.'

'I've not seen him leave,' Grahame said.

'That's because he's still here.' Catriona pointed as the minister came scurrying along the path, hatless, his red hair bobbing, clutching a large box.

'My apologies,' he called, breathless. 'I come bearing gifts. Or at least, *a* gift. For you, Mr Macleod.'

'Where on earth did you find that?'

'You remember, Miss Smith, I mentioned that there is a church on an island near my home that is almost exactly like the one on Taravay? It was when I was looking through your ledgers—they really are most interesting—well it was then, that I remembered there was, under the altar a most ingenious hiding place, and I could not resist taking a look in your church.'

'And you uncovered this?' Murdo said, frowning down at the locked casket.

'It looks like a bible box.'

'That's exactly what it is,' Murdo said, 'I recognise it.'

'Odd, that it was hidden like that, though if it is very

old, I suppose it was put there for safekeeping.' Reverend Muirhead held out his hand. 'Thank you again, Miss Smith, for showing me the church. A wonderful place for a wedding, as I told you.'

'What the...'

'Rebirth, Mr Macleod, that is how Miss Smith described your plans. Weddings, baptisms, and indeed funerals, they are all part of the future here. Good day to you both, I hope to see you soon.'

'That man,' Murdo said, glowering as Grahame's boat headed out to sea, 'is an oddball. What the devil were you about, letting him rummage about in the church like that?'

'He's a man of God, of course he wanted to see the church. Murdo, whatever that box contains, remember that you are legally Macleod of Taravay.'

Whatever that box contains. So Jessica thought that damned box was every bit as ominous as he did. The evening he'd been looking forward to, a walk, a reconciliation, sharing the well-earned excitement of their success, tasted like ash in his mouth. He wanted to hurl the box into the sea, and hurl himself into her arms. With a heavy heart, Murdo turned his back on Jessica and began to walk up the hill. 'Come on then,' he called over his shoulder, 'we might as well get this over with. I think I might know where the key is.'

Chapter Twenty-Seven

The key to the box was in the top drawer of the Laird's desk in his study. 'I don't know why,' Murdo said, brandishing it, 'but I've always known this was important.'

Jessica sat down nervously on the opposite side of the desk. Murdo was looking extremely apprehensive. She cursed herself for having left the far too curious minister alone in the church. Whatever the contents of this box revealed, she felt horribly responsible. 'Remember,' she said, 'you are legally…'

'Aye, so you keep saying.'

'You don't have to open the box.'

'What, are you thinking the devil himself will fly out of it?'

'By the looks of it,' she snapped, 'I'm not the only one. Oh, Murdo, I'm sorry.' She leaned over the desk, but he snatched his hand away as if she had scalded him. 'I'm sorry,' she said again.

'Ach no, I am.' He sat back, running his hand

through his hair. 'I was looking forward to tonight. I thought we could take a walk, bask in our success. I know I've been like a bear with a sore head these last few days.'

'Today meant so much…'

'Aye.' He drummed his fingers on the desk. 'No. I mean that's true, we've been busy and today meant so much, but I won't pretend it's only been that.' He met her eyes briefly. 'I think you know that as well as I do.'

'You believe what happened was a mistake,' Jessica said flatly, feeling as if her heart was being squeezed.

'No, I don't.' He moved his hand towards her, then yanked it back. 'But I think it would be a mistake to repeat it, don't you?'

She clasped her hands together, willing herself not to let him see how upset she was, for his tone was gentle. He didn't want to hurt her. Murdo felt exactly as she had surmised. 'Would it be better—would you prefer it if I left?' she asked.

'Left? Now, before our real work has even started? What makes you ask such a question? Of course I don't want that, any more than you can wish it. Taravay is the key to your success, Jessica, and you are vital to Taravay. Of course I don't want you to leave. Truth is, I can't bear the thought…' Murdo pushed his chair back, but he didn't get up. 'I know how important this is to you. I'd never do anything to get in the way of that, or jeopardise that, do you understand me?'

For the first time in her life, Jessica was conflicted. She loved Taravay. She loved her work. She loved Murdo. Which did she love more? It was an impossible question, and irrelevant too, given that Murdo had more or less told her, as bluntly as he could, that he didn't love her. 'I know what Taravay means to you too,' Jessica said, 'and the last thing *I* want is to get in the way of its rebirth.'

'Muirhead liked that phrase, didn't he?'

'He thinks it will be a wonderful success, Murdo. And so did almost everyone I spoke to today. Which is why I am asking...'

'I don't want you to go, but I think—it's like we said, isn't it? We knew that once we were no longer alone here, things between us would change. We always knew it was a fleeting thing, the situation—ach, all the things we've said. We knew that, didn't we?'

'Yes,' she said, because she had no option but to agree, because that was the answer Murdo so obviously wanted from her. 'Yes, we did.'

'What we did—that night Jessica, I could never regret it. It was—it was magical. Like nothing I've ever—but the consequence is that it's put an end to the closeness we shared. I hate the way we're so awkward with each other now, don't you?'

'I can't stand it.'

'Nor can I. It's daft, but this morning I was thinking how much I've been missing you. Even though I see you all the time…'

'But it's like we were talking at each other and not to each other.'

'That! Exactly that.' He smiled sheepishly. 'So I'm not daft, then?'

'Not daft.' She smiled back at him. His hand reached across the desk. Her fingers twined with his. 'I've missed you too.'

It was there between them again. She saw it in his eyes. He leaned forward, pulling her towards him. Her elbow hit against the box, sending it sliding across the desk. They both jumped back.

Murdo swore. He glowered at the box, as if he'd happily smash it to pieces. Then he put the key in the lock. It turned easily. He took the bible out and laid it on the desk. It was a large book, leather-bound, gilt-edged, embossed with the Macleod coat of arms. His hand was shaking visibly as he opened it. Jessica watched, her heart in her mouth as he flicked through the cover pages to the family tree. His face was shuttered as he ran his finger down the generations, relaxing marginally as he stopped reading.

'I'm there all right, same as the baptismal records.'

He turned the tome towards her, and she read it for herself, in the ornate script, Murdo's name, his date of birth, with a direct line to Laird Angus Murdo and his wife Margaret. Jessica smiled. 'So you see, there was nothing to worry about after all.'

'No, apparently not.' He was distracted, peering into the box, pulling out a sheaf of letters and shuffling through them.

Jessica studied the family tree. There could be no doubt now that Murdo was the legitimate heir. And here was Henrietta, the Laird's first wife, and here at last was the record of her child. 'Seonag,' she articulated carefully, 'isn't that Johanna?'

Murdo, frowning down at one of the letters, nodded. 'Johanna, Seonag, Joan.'

'A little girl. You had a half-sister, and she was born three years before her mother died. So not an infant. Three years old, buried with her mother, yet there is no name recorded on the gravestone and no date of death here. Isn't that odd, Murdo?'

He made no reply. His face was ashen. The letters were spread on the desk in front of him, but he was staring off into space.

'Murdo?'

'Not odd at all,' he said, his voice barely more than a whisper. 'Because she didn't die.'

'What?'

'My sister. Half-sister. Except she's not. Which means I'm not.'

'You're not what? Murdo, you look as if you're going to faint. Shall I get you...'

'I don't want anything. Nothing.' He jumped to his feet, pushing past her. 'Get out of my way.'

'Murdo!' Jessica got to her feet, running after him.

'Leave me alone! Just get out of my sight and let me be.'

Stunned, Jessica watched as he ran across the Great Hall, threw open the door and pulled it shut behind him. All her instincts were to follow him, but the look on his face made her shiver. Instead, she made her way slowly back to the study. She picked up the three letters, noted that they were all written in English, and with a sense of dread, she began to read.

12th October, 1843

Angus, it is with a heavy heart that I write this, knowing that I am soon to depart this world. I have examined my conscience so many times over the last six years, and so many times I have been on the brink of a confession, but the truth is, I am too weak a woman to face your wrath. Yet I am also too frightened to go to meet my maker without telling you the truth. I have been an unfaithful wife. Murdo is not your son. My marriage vows were broken not for love, but in a wrong-headed though genuine attempt to give you what you have so long desired, an heir for Taravay. My failure to bear you a child has been the source of much grief for us both. Your contempt for my failure drove me to take desperate measures, and to lie

with another man with the purpose of conceiving a child. I do not blame you for this, Angus, you made it clear when our marriage was agreed that obtaining an heir was your only reason for our union. I shall not name the natural father of my child, for fear of retribution. He is a selfish creature who had a purpose quite other than he claimed, but then so too did I. My child was conceived in deceit, but delivered to you with love. Murdo has none of your blood in his veins but you have claimed him as yours from the moment he gave his first cry. My one solace, as I depart this world, never to see my son grow to be a man, is that you will take good care of him. I beg you, Angus, though you will never forgive me, not to vent your anger on your son. For Murdo is your true son. You have moulded him in your image, and I know that you will ensure that he becomes what you wish and need, a true Macleod of Taravay. Please have the minister pray for my eternal soul, for I know you will not.
Margaret

Athole Gardens, Glasgow,
September 1839
Your Lordship,
It is with regret that I write to inform you of the death from cholera two days ago, of our house-keeper Mairi Mackinnon. I have served as Cham-

bermaid under Mrs Mackinnon for three years. The fever took her very sudden. I am sorry to tell you she did not die easy. I am writing because she begged me most fervently to tell you this. I use her exact words, as she urged me to do. Your daughter is well and happy and loved. She lives in the town of Thornhill. Neil and Bella Scott are her adopted parents. She knows no other. Mrs Mackinnon also begs that you tell her brother of her passing, and that you mark it on a gravestone. You owe her that much, she said to tell you. Hoping this finds you in good health.
Most sincerely,
Elizabeth Buchannan

The Manse, Thornhill,
January 1871
Dear Lord Macleod,
I discovered your letter of March last year amongst the papers of my predecessor. The Reverend Brickell suffered a long illness which unfortunately left him unable to deal with a great deal of parish business. In answer to your query, it is with regret that I write to inform you that the people into whose welfare you enquired, Neil and Bella Scott, have both gone to meet their maker. I have made enquires at your behest, and can confirm that the couple did have a daughter, Joan, but that she has now married and left the area. I

note that your letter wished the matter to be resolved with some urgency, and can only apologise for the lengthy delay. Should you wish me to make further enquiries on your behalf, please consider me at your disposal.

In the meantime I am your most humble servant,
Reverend Hugh Williams

Chapter Twenty-Eight

Seated at the base of the standing stone, Murdo watched the dawn break, streaks of burnished amber appearing through a sky of iron-grey. The sea was pewter, the crests of the waves were silver. His heart was leaden. His soul was black. Who was he? He had no idea at all. He was not Emily's husband. He was not the Laird's son. He was not Macleod of Taravay. He was a man who had nothing, not even an identity. Even his heart belonged to another.

Jessica. He loved her. Pointless to deny it now, since he had nothing left to lose. He loved her. He loved her so very much more than he'd loved Emily. He loved her because she made him a better man, a different man. Because she was what had been missing from his life, and he'd known it instinctively from the moment he met her. She saw him for who he was. But who was he now? An unwanted and unloved bastard, that's who he was. It would break his heart to leave, but what choice did he have? Jessica must never know how he felt. He'd spare her any guilt. Jessica would be happy and have both her career and Taravay, and for him, that would be enough. It would have to be.

He'd speak to her calmly and quietly. He wouldn't let her see what he felt or how much he was hurting. He didn't want her feeling guilty. He didn't want to provoke her to tears. He didn't want her pity. He would do the right thing. He'd put someone else's happiness first before, he could do so again.

All night Jessica had paced, tossed and turned, her mind in a turmoil. The Laird was not Murdo's father, but was in fact her mother's father, her own grandfather! She couldn't believe it. The idea was so utterly preposterous that she returned to the Castle to read the letters again, but the facts were laid out for her, it was indisputable. She stared at the portrait of the Laird in the Great Hall, but could see nothing of her mother in him, and felt nothing for him herself. She had his blood in her veins, but it didn't change her, and it didn't make her think any better of him. Worse, in fact, for the man had callously sent his daughter away to be adopted. How fortunate for her mother that Neil and Bella Scott had taken her on. They were Jessica's real grandparents, not that glowering despot up there on the wall.

Dear heavens, thank the sun and the moon and the stars that the man was *not* Murdo's father, because if he had been—her mind shied away from the thought. She was not in love with a relative. She was in love with Murdo. Where *was* Murdo? While she was shocked by the contents of the letters, they made little difference to how she felt about her family. Poor Mama was dead. But Murdo must be in a turmoil. Where on earth was he?

She sat alone in the Castle, listening to the rafters creak and the mice scurry, waiting on him returning. By morning, she could wait no longer. She found him by the standing stone, bleakly gazing out to an iron-grey sea that merged seamlessly with the ominous sky. When he turned towards her, eyes deeply shadowed, his expression tormented, she had to suppress the urge to burst into tears. 'Have you been here all night?' she asked.

He shrugged. 'Walking around, for part of it. Thinking.'

She edged closer to him. 'The Laird did as your mother asked. He raised you as his son. In a way, it proves he loved you even more.'

'Because he knew all along that I was a bastard?'

She couldn't help but flinch at his harsh tone. 'Don't say that.'

'It's what I am.'

'Legally...'

'Oh aye, legally I'm the Laird's son, though there's not a drop of Macleod blood in my veins.'

'You're the same person now as you were a day ago, a week ago, a month ago, Murdo. Nothing has changed.'

His fists clenched. 'Everything has changed. Whatever it says on paper, I've no claim to my name, and no claim to Taravay.'

'But that's exactly what it does say on paper. You are the Laird's son, his legitimate heir.'

'Jessica, did you read those letters properly? The child, Joan, that the minister refers to, daughter of Neil and Bella Scott, is Johanna, the Laird's daughter, whose birth is recorded in the bible. You are the Laird's granddaughter.'

'Bella and Neil Scott were my grandparents. The Laird has nothing to do with me. I still find it difficult to credit the connection. It does finally explain, mind you, why Mairi Mackinnon wrote to my grandmother all those years ago. Why would the Laird send his daughter away though? The only reason I can think of was because she was a daughter, and not a son. And Macneil said that the Laird loved Henrietta. Perhaps when Henrietta died, my mother reminded him too much of what he had lost? What is it? Why are you looking at me like that, Murdo?'

'Jessica,' Murdo said, 'your mother was the first-born.'

'Yes, but she was a female.'

'Here on Taravay, it is the firstborn child who inherits, whether they are male or female. It's not uncommon in Scotland.'

'What? My mother—no, that can't be right, that would mean…'

'Your mother was the firstborn,' Murdo said. 'You are her only child. Taravay isn't mine. It's yours.'

'No!' She staggered, and would have fallen had he not caught her. 'No, that's not possible.'

'I'm afraid it's not only possible, it's a fact. So you see, whether the Laird acknowledged me as his son or not doesn't matter.'

She stared at him, shaking her head violently. 'I don't want it. Taravay is yours. It has to be yours, it's the love of your life.'

'If it's the money for the work you're wondering about, I've decided to establish a trust fund to pay for everything. It's the least I can do.'

'What?' She wrenched herself free. 'I don't want your money. I don't want your island. Taravay is yours! How can you be so calm about this?'

'I've had all night to think about it. It's done and dusted, Jessica, there's no point in my railing at fate. I have to do what's right, no matter how much it pains me.'

His words rang a bell. Hadn't he said something along those lines before, when talking about him walking away from Emily? And was he really as calm as he was pretending to be? No, there was a pulse beating at the side of his neck, she could see it. 'Murdo,' Jessica said, striving for calm too, 'the Laird wanted Taravay to be yours. It's why he acknowledged you. Why he did nothing with that letter your mother wrote on her deathbed. You were only five years old then, but he raised you as his son, just as she begged him to.'

'Aye, until he decided, once and for all that I wasn't fit for purpose and disowned me.'

'He didn't.' She was beginning to panic. Murdo's expression was hardening. 'Your name is on the family bible, in the parish register...'

'Did you look at the date on that letter from the minister at all?'

'I can't remember. Why does it matter?'

'It was written in January 1871, in reply to a letter received in March of the previous year.' Murdo waited impatiently, but Jessica could only shake her head. 'March 1870 was when I informed the Laird of my marriage. It was the date of our final rift. So that very same month, the Laird finally decided to fetch his true heir back. Only he was too late, so he Cleared the island out of spite because he had been doubly thwarted.'

'Oh no! Oh, Murdo, no.'

'Aye, you have the full picture now. What are the chances, eh? If only the other minister hadn't been ill, he'd have been bound to track down your mother, and what a pleasant surprise she'd have had, wouldn't she, to discover herself the heir to an island.'

'My mother would not have wished—she had no idea—my father would not have given up the gardening career that he loved to move here.'

'Would he not have? That's where you get it from then?'

'What do you mean?'

'He was driven, just as you are. What would have happened if your mother had wanted to live here?'

'I genuinely don't know,' Jessica retorted, flustered.

'It hardly matters any road,' Murdo said. 'Your mother never had the choice, for she never knew. The Clearance happened, but fate intervened, and sent you to here to help repair the damage done. You always said you thought you were meant to be here, didn't you?'

'I didn't mean this. I don't want this. I will refuse— I do refuse—don't, Murdo, please don't.'

'Don't do what? Point out what you're legally entitled to? Point out that you're not only green-fingered but you're blue-blooded after all.'

'I don't care about that. I thought you didn't care.'

'I don't! You could have been born under a hedge and I wouldn't give a damn. You're the one that's always had a bee in your bonnet about your lineage or lack of it. I thought you'd be pleased.'

'Pleased! To discover that I've stolen Taravay from

under your nose? Well I won't. As far as I'm concerned no one need ever know about those letters.'

'But *I* know, that's what matters.'

It was the way he said, it, with such finality, that cut short her protestations. Looking at his face, his mouth stubbornly set, his fists clenched, and his eyes—his gaze was fixed on her, but he wasn't seeing her. 'Murdo, I don't care who your father is. No, that's not actually true. I'm very glad that your father is not the Laird, because that would have made you my uncle. Had you considered that?'

He swore, aghast. 'No I had not, but,' he continued doggedly, 'you are the Laird's granddaughter and therefore the owner of Taravay. I have no right to be here now. As I said earlier, I will establish a trust to allow you to carry on and implement your plans.'

'They're *our* plans, Murdo. It's your dream. Taravay needs *you*, Murdo.'

He folded his arms and turned away from her, gazing like a marble statue out to sea. 'I'm leaving, and that's an end to it.'

Something snapped inside her, seeing him so implacable, so determined, and so stupidly stubborn. 'Of course you are, it's what you always do, isn't it? You walk away.'

The statue immediately transformed into a furious man. 'How dare you! What the devil do you mean by that?'

Nothing. I take it back, she wanted to say, but she was fighting for her life, so she stood her ground. 'The Laird wouldn't accept your choice of bride so you walked away. Your wife loved another man more than you, so you walked away.'

'What, would you have had me stay, when she didn't want me?'

'Of course not! But you ran, Murdo, you packed up all your feelings and you fled, both times. You sacrificed yourself for someone else. I know, because you told me, that you didn't let Emily see how hurt you were, and I'm willing to bet that you didn't let the Laird know either.'

'I chose to walk away, I didn't run, there's a world of difference. And what's the point in weeping and wailing when you're not wanted?'

'But you *are* wanted. Never mind about Taravay, *I* want you.'

He flinched visibly, taking a step backwards. 'No.'

His denial lit a fire inside her. 'No? Do you think I don't know what's in my own heart?' Jessica flung at him. 'Well I do. I love you.'

'You're feeling sorry for me.'

'Oh, Murdo, I'm not. I'm in love with you.' The relief of being able to say it was overpowering. 'I love you with all my heart and all my soul, and I don't want you to leave.'

But her heartfelt words put him even more on his

guard. 'You think you do because of the other night, but...'

'I made love to you the other night because I'm in love with you.'

'You love your work. Your career. Taravay.'

'Stop talking about Taravay! I'm talking about what I feel for you, and it's a—a damn sight more than what I feel for a landscape, or even this landscape.' The truth was stunning, and stunningly simple. 'It doesn't mean I don't love my work, but does one have to exclude the other?'

His lips firmed. 'You've been very certain up until now that it did.'

'I thought it did, because love, marriage—for a woman it involves sacrifice. But I've never asked myself, does it have to be that way, because I've never felt like this before.'

'No!' He put his hand up in front of him, backing away from her. 'You're saying this because you're feeling guilty. You think if you marry me, then you can give me Taravay back.'

'This isn't about Taravay! This is about me. About us. I've just told you I love you, for heaven's sake.'

But he shook his head adamantly. 'You don't want to get married and I understand that.'

'I want to be with you.' Aware that her hands were clasped together like a supplicant, but even more aware that her pleas were falling on deaf ears, Jessica wanted to shake him, to go on bended knee to him, desperate to find some way of showing him what seemed suddenly so blindingly obvious to her. But he wasn't listening, and she was horribly aware that she wouldn't have another opportunity, because he was set on leaving, and when Murdo was set on a purpose it was impossible to stop him.

'I love you,' she said, her last throw of the dice. 'And if you love me…'

She broke off. The question hung in the air for an agonising length of time. The waves crashed, the wind was picking up, and Murdo stood, arms crossed, mouth set, gazing somewhere over her head. She felt as if she was shrinking before his eyes. 'I see,' she said finally, her voice a whisper.

Only now did he speak. 'I'm sorry.'

Mortified, hurt and angry, Jessica gathered together the remnants of her pride. 'I don't want your pity,' she said, throwing his own words at him. 'In fact, I'm sorry for you, Murdo Macleod. At least I have the courage to admit what I'm feeling. I suspect it's not that you don't love me, it's that you won't let yourself. You're scared of having your heart broken again, and I can understand that perfectly, because frankly I'm terrified too.'

He was listening now, she could see that, but she also knew it was too late. 'I would have taken the risk. I'd rather have failed than not have tried to find true happiness. But you have made your decision for your own reasons and I hope you find happiness one day, Murdo, I truly do.'

She took his unresisting hand in hers, pressing a kiss to his icy-cold knuckles, then she turned her back on him. She couldn't bring herself to say goodbye. She walked away, refusing to allow herself to look back. She walked, faster and faster as the rain began to fall, hurrying along the spine of the island, in search of the sanctuary of her croft. And there, burrowed deep under the bedclothes with her pillow over her head, she lay wide-eyed, listening to the sound of her heart breaking.

Chapter Twenty-Nine

Murdo's sense of righteousness carried him to his boat. Instinctively, he did not head for Ness, having no desire to speak to anyone, nor to explain himself, and instead sailed north, finally landing on Rona. Like Taravay, the island was unpopulated, though this was thanks to the remoteness of the location, and not due to a Clearance. If the weather turned, he could be marooned here for days, he thought morosely as he perched himself on the pebble-stoned beach, gazing back at the Atlantic towards his own beloved island. The island which was no longer his. Right now he couldn't care less about Taravay. It was the woman he'd left behind there who occupied his thoughts.

Jessica. She'd all but torn his heart from his chest when she told him she loved him. It had cost him everything he had to say nothing, only the absolute certainty that he was doing the right thing by her had kept him silent. So why did it suddenly feel like the biggest mistake of his life? What was she doing now? He had lied to her. He'd left her. But he had saved them both, he told himself. He was safe here, safe from casting caution to the wind and confessing his own love, sparing both of them inevitable misery when they discovered that love didn't conquer all, and that being together would turn their lives upside down—and very likely not for the better.

He'd done the right thing. The noble thing. That's what he told himself, as the grey sea became white-tipped with crested waves, but the more he repeated it, the less he believed it. He didn't feel noble, he felt stupid. He'd become so accustomed to his vow never to let his heart be broken, so accustomed to believing Jessica's avowal that she loved first and only her career, that even though he'd heard her heartfelt words, he had not listened. He had made a decision, and he had been intent on forcing that decision on her, because it kept them both safe. He'd been trying to protect her, to spare her the pain of his continued presence. To give her what she wanted more than anything, Taravay, and with it her precious career, without her feeling guilty. He hadn't been running away, he'd been doing what was best for them both, and one day she'd thank him for it.

Why then, when it was too late, was he feeling he'd got it all catastrophically wrong? Because his heart was already breaking? Would it be more painful to try and fail? Rather than acting nobly, was he a coward, as she had implied, for not taking the risk? But any future they had together would be a compromise, and compromise wouldn't make her happy. More than anything, he wanted her to be happy.

Yes, he'd definitely done the right thing. It was better she didn't know how much he loved her. Murdo dropped his head onto his hands. He loved her so much, and it hurt so much, sitting here, knowing that he'd likely never see her again. The future beckoned, a dark, endless tunnel that he didn't want to travel through. Jessica made every day an adventure. She made him laugh. She riled him and she roused him. She made him see the world differently. When he was with Jessica, he was alive. Looking back on the bleak times on Taravay before she came, what he saw now was a shell of himself, alive but not living. Was it his fate to become that man again?

If she loved him half as much as he loved her, if she was feeling even half as bereft as he was right now— no, no, no, he couldn't bear it. If she loved him as he loved her, as she'd told him, so bravely, at such risk to herself, was she too looking at the future and thinking it bleak? It must have taken her every ounce of courage to speak as she did, and to hold to what she said in the face of his horrible, misguided silence.

Regret made him feel physically sick. He loved her so much, and she loved him. His heart, which he'd been so determined would never again be given the chance to break, was already in pieces. Was hers in the same state? What had he done? What the hell was he doing here?

He *was* afraid. He was afraid that they wouldn't be able to find a way to be happy together. He was afraid of compromising all that he loved and admired in Jessica. He was afraid of the future, because he had no idea what it looked like, but when he looked, and saw a future that was without Jessica in it, that's when he became really terrified. That's when he knew for certain he was wrong. That's when he decided to match her courage, and to place his life and his heart in her hands.

The weather was closing in. Murdo got up, gazing out at the sea, trying to gauge just how bad it was likely to get. The safest thing would be to stay here and wait it out. But he was done with playing safe. He thought of Jessica, alone on Taravay thinking he didn't love her, and he wasn't prepared to wait a minute more than necessary before he told her that he did. He would take his chances on the open sea before taking his chances with Jessica.

The storm raged all night, the wind howling through the rafters of her croft, gusting under the door, making the fire billow smoke. Jessica lay awake listening to the crashing of the waves, the battering of the rain, nursing her impotent fury at the stubborn, principled man she loved, telling herself that at some point, having bared her own heart and soul would bring her solace. By morning she felt empty. The prospect of any future seemed bleak. Simply dragging herself out of bed took what little energy she had left.

Outside, the landscape looked like a watercolour painting that had run. A pale yellow sun bled into the pale blue sky that was bleeding into the silver sea. A grey seal was basking on a rock near the jetty, and in the distance, a speck that must be one of the Ness *sgoths* out at sea fishing. She stood clutching her mug of tea, watching as the boat neared, telling herself that it was Finlay or Grahame, even though it was sailing from the wrong direction.

She knew it was him. Her hands shook so much she dropped her mug. He was returning to pack his belongings, or to inform her of the terms of his precious trust for the island, or to collect his post or some such thing. She must not get her hopes up. She had accepted he would not love her. She really had.

Her legs were already taking her down to the jetty. She watched, sick with anticipation, bracing herself, as he approached, his clothes soaking wet, his eyes darkly shadowed. She would not feel sorry for him. She too had had a sleepless night. She too must look a haunted spectre. She crossed her arms and rooted her feet to the jetty. She would not speak first. She had nothing left to say.

'Jessica.' He tied up the boat quickly and jumped ashore. 'You're furious with me, and rightly so.' He ran a hand through his hair, sending water droplets cascading. 'I had a speech ready, but I can't remember it now.'

'I don't want to hear a speech. You made your feelings perfectly clear yesterday.'

'I didn't.' Murdo grabbed her hands. 'That's what I've come back to say. I got everything wrong, and I'm so sorry.'

She would not let herself hope, but it was there all the same, a fluttering in her belly. She *would* not speak, for fear of betraying herself.

'I love you, Jessica,' Murdo said. 'I fell in love with you—not from the moment I met you, that's daft, but it feels like that now. Only I didn't want to call it love, because you're right, I was scared.'

She wouldn't speak, but she let her fingers curl around his.

'I'm scared I won't be able to make you happy. I'm not a man that deals easily with compromise.'

'That, I know to my cost.'

'You do.' He smiled shakily. 'You know me better than I know myself, at times. It's one of the things that I love about you, and one of the things I find hard to deal with. I don't know how we can work this, Jessica, but I want to try, because…' He bit his lip, swallowing hard. 'Because,' he continued roughly, 'when I thought of life without you, it wasn't a life I wanted. It wasn't a life at all, a shadow existence. I love you. I'm so sorry it took me so long to say it, but I'm begging you, will you give me another chance?'

It was raining, mizzling rain in a grey sky, but Jessica could have sworn the sun had come out. 'You love me? You truly love me?'

'With all my heart and soul,' Murdo said fervently. 'And I'm ready and willing to take a leap of faith on that.'

She struggled to speak, for her heart felt as if it might burst out of her chest. She cleared her throat, managing a smile. 'A leap of faith. That's what brought me here in the first place.'

'It won't be easy, mind. There will be many obstacles to confront.'

'One of the many things we have in common, my darling Murdo, is that we both relish a challenge. A challenge we will meet head-on and overcome.'

He laughed. 'Indeed, and if we can make an entire island fit for the Nineteenth Century, why not make a marriage fit for it too?'

'Marriage?'

'Not because I want to take care of you, I know you're perfectly capable of taking care of yourself, but because I want us to be husband and wife. Two halves of one entity. And I want the world to witness that. Will you marry me, Jessica, *mo ghràdh*.'

'Moh chry?'

'My love.'

'*Mo ghràdh*,' she repeated softly. 'My darling, Murdo, the answer is yes.'

'Oh, Jessica.' He pulled her into his arms, pressing his face to her neck, saying her name over and over. 'I thought I'd lost you.'

'Never.'

'I love you so much.'

She touched his cheek, making him lift his head to meet her eyes. 'Show me,' she said.

A slow smile dawned on his face. 'Now? I'm half-drowned…'

She wrapped her arms around his neck. 'No more words.'

She kissed him. He tasted of rain and salt. She kissed him, telling him what was in her heart, and his kisses too spoke of love, and for long moments on the quay they clung together, the sheer relief of holding each other enough. Then, suddenly, it wasn't enough, and they walked quickly, hand in hand, up the steep path, stopping to kiss, passionate kisses, muttering desperately of love, until they reached Jessica's croft, and the door slammed closed behind them as they kissed, tearing at each other's clothes, kisses that became wilder and wilder as their hands roamed over flesh they thought forever denied them, as they redis-covered each other, roused each other to new heights, and then reclaimed each other. Lying beneath him beside the smouldering peat fire, Jessica trembled with love and desire, watching him watching her as he entered her, telling him she loved him as they quickly found a rhythm, as her body melded around his, and as the waves of her climax made him cry out seconds later, their bodies as one, their hearts joined together.

'*Mo ghràdh*,' Murdo said, 'whatever happens, I will love you always.'

Chapter Thirty

Taravay, August 1879

Jessica woke wrapped in Murdo's arms, as she had awoken every morning for the last three months, in the tiny bedroom of the croft on Taravay Beag that had been Murdo's and which was now theirs. And as they did almost every morning, they smiled into each other's eyes, and they made love. Slow, tender love it was this morning, because it was their wedding day.

'Starting as we mean to go on,' Murdo murmured into her ear afterwards. 'Doing things the wrong way round, defying convention.'

Jessica trailed her fingers across his chest, splaying her hand over his heart. 'We can do this again in traditional fashion, after we've said our vows.'

'Now that is a promise I will hold you to, *mo ghràdh*. For now though, I'm going to make good on my other promise, and that's to prepare you a bath, and I'd better get a move on if we're not to commit another cardinal sin, and be late for our own wedding.'

Jessica watched with lazy pleasure as he got out of bed, admiring the curve of his buttocks, the dark tan of his forearms giving way to the paler skin of his shoulders. She knew every inch of him, had kissed her way over every part of him, and she planned to do so again tonight, their first night together as husband and wife.

Their sharing a croft had caused a minor scandal at first, but it had, surprisingly, been the Reverend Muirhead who put an end to most of the gossip, by publishing their bans not only in Taravay church where he had read them three weeks in a row, but by reading them out again in the church in Ness.

It was the minister, who had become not only a staunch ally to Murdo but a good friend to Jessica, who led them on the short walk, later that morning, from the croft to the church. Murdo was dressed in the Macleod plaid, while Jessica wore a turquoise silk gown which happened to be the colour of the sea that day, as it rippled over the silver sands. She carried a bouquet made of her favourite wildflowers—thistles, campion, and orchids. Together, hand in hand, she and Murdo walked down the aisle of the packed church, where Niseachs shared the pews with an odd assortment of engineers, builders, stonemasons, and three of the new crofting families who had settled in the village. More wildflowers were arranged in vases on the altar, meadow buttercup, marram grass and bell heather bringing the machair into the church.

Hands clasped, she and Murdo said their vows in

Gaelic first and then in English, and as he placed the ring on her finger, and leaned over to whisper in her ear, *I love you,* the congregation burst into spontaneous applause. Jessica thought her heart might burst with joy and happiness.

'I love you, Mrs Macleod,' Murdo said as the sun began to sink.

'I love you, Mr Macleod,' she said, reaching up to kiss him. 'It's been a wonderful day.'

'It has,' he agreed, smiling. 'The perfect time to lay the past to rest once and for all. Are you ready?'

She handed him the box containing the bible and the letters. Murdo set the box in the deep hole they had dug at the base of the standing stone, before quickly covering it over with earth and stones. Together, they stood on the edge of the cliff, and he hurled the key out into the sea, before turning towards her. 'New beginnings, Jessica?'

'I'm ready, whatever form that might take.'

He wrapped his arms around her. 'As long as we have each other, we can achieve anything.'

Glasgow Herald
August, 1880

Yesterday a historic event took place in the Outer Hebrides. The island of Taravay, which had been owned by the Macleod family for many genera-

tions, was formally handed in trust over to the islanders. In a unique ceremony held at Taravay Castle, Mr and Mrs Macleod gave the deeds to the newly appointed factor Mr Finlay Murray.

Taravay, formerly a typical Hebridean island inhabited by crofters but Cleared some years ago, has undergone a transformation under the guidance of Mr Macleod, a successful businessman, and his wife, a landscape gardener of some renown. A rebirth, in the words of the former owners, which would allow traditional ways of life to flourish, while at the same time opening up new markets for highly skilled crafts such as spinning and weaving, while opening the island itself to visitors. To this end, Taravay Castle, which was once the ancestral home of the Macleods, has been extensively renovated and is now a luxury hotel boasting an astounding ten water closets, also offering the latest hydropathic treatments for guests. A new jetty can accommodate a steamer berthing there, though there are also on offer pleasure sailings and fishing trips on smaller vessels.

'Taravay is now fit for the Nineteenth Century and beyond,' Mr Macleod informed us. 'My wife and I hope that it provides others with inspiration regarding what could be achieved on other islands, whose beauty and potential has been un-

der-utilised. *We are delighted to announce that, having secured investment funds, we are beginning work on the island of Eilean Vas using the same approach.' Mrs Macleod added, 'We have demonstrated that green shoots can flourish in even the stoniest and most unlikely of places. As a gardener, that gives me enormous satisfaction. In my experience, all it takes is a lot of love and a little perseverance.'*

* * * * *

If you enjoyed this story, be sure to read Marguerite Kaye's previous historical romances

Uncovering the Governess's Secrets
His Runaway Marchioness Returns
"The Lady's Yuletide Wish" in Under the Mistletoe
Lady Armstrong's Scandalous Awakening
The Earl Who Sees Her Beauty

Historical Note

Though I've almost convinced myself that it's real, and have even looked on Google Maps for it, Taravay is a figment of my imagination. The geography is loosely based on the island of Taransay, just off Harris in the Outer Hebrides, but I've moved it north so that it's off Port of Ness in Lewis. As you may have gathered reading this book, Ness is a place very dear to my heart, being home to my mum's maternal family. I've tried to capture some of my own enchantment with Ness (weather and all) in my descriptions, but I owe much to the history, *Am Port*, published by Comunn Eachdraidh Nis, and to the many stories my mum and her cousin Joan have told me. The lighthouse keeper on the Butt of Lewis was one of my mum's cousins. The names of several other relatives are etched into the stone of the inner harbour, which they helped to build. I've named the captain of the steamer after yet another cousin, and *sgoths*, the Ness fishing boats, were built in a yard by yet another. Henrietta (usually Etta) was a name I was surprised to discover several times in the graveyard at Ness just last year, and determined to use it. I'm sure I've got things wrong, and if I have its all my own fault. And I confess to at least one abuse of history—there was no Post Office in Port of Ness until 1880, and it wasn't connected to the telegraph until 1888.

The custom of burying men and women on opposite sides of the graveyard is one that I read about in the book, *Harris in History and Legend* by Bill Lawson. There's also a poignant chapter in this book about assisted immigration from Harris and Lewis. Sadly, many islanders were forced to immigrate as a result of Clearances. *The Celt* took passengers from Harris to Campbeltown to join the immigrant sailing ship, *Hercules*, which also picked up passengers from Skye, and it was reading this that gave me the idea for Laird Macleod's Clearance of Taravay.

Before 1855, there was no formal registration of births, deaths and marriages, nor any standard format when they were documented. Church records were kept, but were far from all-inclusive. If a burial was not paid for, it was often not recorded. Sadly, children who died in infancy were often excluded completely from any records, their births and deaths unmarked.

I love making connections with other books and places I've visited. Taravay Castle was inspired by the ruin of MacLellan's Castle in Kirkcudbright, which

I saw on a day out with my mum and two of my sisters. Drumlanrig and its gardens play a pivotal role in *A Lady of Intrigue*, one of the books I co-wrote with Sarah Ferguson. Jessica's idea for gardens like rooms was inspired by my visits to the wonderful garden at Sissinghurst designed by Vita Sackville-West and Harold Nicholson.

Jessica's gardening ethos owes a lot to Gertrude Jekyll, a real landscape gardener and almost her contemporary. I first read about Gertrude Jekyll in Olivia Laing's wonderful book, *The Garden Against Time*, and in one of those research coincidences, came across her again in Jane Robinson's *Trailblazer: The First Feminist to Change the World*, when she designed the garden for Girton College. As to the succulent garden that Jessica makes for Murdo, I stole that idea from a dry stone garden my friend Peter has just finished constructing.

Doubtless I'll be told at some point that Murdo's language is anachronistic. It is indeed, I've littered his speech with current colloquialisms to make him sound Scottish, not Victorian. Sorry, but not sorry!

MILLS & BOON ®

Coming next month

THE DANGERS OF DECEIVING A DUKE
Louise Allen

Celebrating Louise's 75th Book!

The kiss was not gentle, but hungry, as though both were famished.

She was not an innocent. She had been married. But this was not right. Not there, not now. Not ever.

That was his conscience, shouting at him against the thrum of his blood, the aching need and desire for her, the answering desire Cat's body was signalling. Her mouth was open under his, the heat, the dart of her tongue and the nip of her teeth acting like a shot of brandy in his blood.

They were as one in passion and, it seemed, in tune in more ways than that, because, in a split second it was over. She drew back, even as he lowered her carefully to the floor and straightened, stepped away.

'That was a very bad idea,' Quinn said, controlling his voice with an effort. 'I apologise.'

'That realisation appeared to strike us both at the same time. No apology is needed.' Cat sounded equally breathless.

She moved away a little, but not, he thought with relief, out of wariness, but to brush the dust from her skirts.

'We agreed that a cat may be friends with a duke, did we not? But friendship is as far as it can go.' Her clothes apparently ordered to her satisfaction, she looked up and met his gaze squarely. 'I am not in the market for a *carte blanche*, Quinn. And no other offer is conceivable, is it?'

Continue reading

THE DANGERS OF DECEIVING A DUKE
Louise Allen

Available next month
millsandboon.co.uk

COMING SOON!

We really hope you enjoyed reading this book.
If you're looking for more romance
be sure to head to the shops when
new books are available on

Thursday 26th February

To see which titles are coming soon, please visit

millsandboon.co.uk/nextmonth

MILLS & BOON

LET'S TALK
Romance

For exclusive extracts, competitions and special offers, find us online:

- **f** MillsandBoon
- **X** @MillsandBoon
- **O** @MillsandBoonUK
- **♪** @MillsandBoonUK

Get in touch on 01413 063 232